MACHINE GODS

GODS

MICHAEL G. THOMAS

First published in the United Kingdom in 2012
by Swordworks Books.

ISBN 978-1-909149-09-0

Typeset by Swordworks Books
Printed and bound in the UK & US
A catalogue record of this book is available
from the British Library

Cover design by Swordworks Books
www.swordworks.co.uk

MACHINE GODS

MICHAEL G. THOMAS

PROLOGUE

It was nineteen years since the last battles of the Great Uprising had been won in 340CC. That terrible war had started as a decade-long series of violent terrorist actions that exploded into open revolt on a number of worlds. The Confederacy was almost totally destroyed, with entire planets turning to join the rebels and their violent pseudo-religious faction. From the violence of that war, emerged the creation of the Centauri Alliance, an artificial political and social structure that absorbed billions of war-weary citizens. The worlds that once fought on opposite sides joined together into this new Alliance, and much to the surprise of its many critics, the Alliance survived. As years move to decades of relative peace, a new golden age for mankind seemed just on the horizon. Scores of well-established colonies now existed in worlds of

Alpha Centauri as well as Sol, the ancient solar system that housed the original eight planets of humanity. Out on the fringes, a whole array of new colonies was founded as far away as Epsilon Eridani, Gliese 876 and Procyon. These new colonies were only a few months or years old, but already great fleets of industrial ships and corporations plowed their way through space to exploit them in every conceivable way. The vast populations from the overpopulated worlds like Carthago, Prime and Terra Nova flocked to the new opportunities offered outside of their old systems.

In the middle of the Great Uprising, an Anomaly was found that connected Proxima and Alpha Centauri together. This technology was quickly reverse engineered, and the construction of the Network began. By creating a series of artificial Spacebridges, it became possible to connect stars and worlds several light years away. In a matter of months whole chains of these Rifts, as they became known as, were constructed, and the Alliance expanded at an exponential rate. Whole industrial, commercial, and civilian corporations were founded to take advantage of every new world and resource that was located and made available.

It was not just the children of Earth that now lived in this new age of mankind. A new race now shared their worlds; one created as terrible weapons in the war during the Uprising. Large numbers of these monstrous beings were saved from the thrall of the enemy, and they soon became the most dependable soldiers in the last years of the War. Now that the fighting was over, these Jötnar, as they were named as, had found peace on their prized planet. This almost inhospitable jungle world was called Hyperion; a planet seeded with vegetation back when the first colonists had arrived in Alpha Centauri so many hundreds of years earlier. It was this world that had been the scene of the last battle of the War. A terrible and savage battle that stopped the violence but also gave Alliance scientists clues to create a new kind of Spacebridge; one that when built in the appropriate place, could take them further than just a few light years, and one that after years of hard work would send humanity out to the Orion Nebula and their encounter with destiny.

It was in this new part of the galaxy that the greatest discoveries were yet to be made. Alliance ships soon moved into the area of space around the first star system to be explored, New Charon, and in less than a year, a dozen primitive colonies were under construction. Tens of thousands of citizens uprooted and moved in to explore and harvest the riches that were there. Alliance scientists sent their top people to study the newly discovered technologies that were smashed and abandoned on many of the planets and moons. This was also the first confirmation that sentient life had been found outside of the human worlds.

All of these discoveries paled into insignificance when compared to the first contact between humanity and their brothers in the stars; a race of people know only as the T'Kari. A people of knowledge and technology, they numbered in just the tens of thousands after having been almost completely annihilated by the same enemy that clawed at the worlds of the Alliance. With offers of peace and equality, the T'Kari requested and was granted status as citizens of the Alliance, and the first stage of the multi-species Alliance began.

The Alliance appeared strong, with its scores of worlds, billions of citizens, thousands of marines, and fleets of military ships. The hidden enemy, one that had plotted and connived to bring down the Confederacy appeared to have vanished, perhaps forever. All that remained were its violent children that included T'Kari Raiders, a small group of corsairs and bandits that flocked like carrion to the weak worlds of their kin whenever the situation favored them. If only the Raiders had given as much thought to the Jötnar as they had to raiding civilian outposts. It was the only way the Black Rift would have avoided discovery by the Alliance.

CHAPTER ONE

Trade and industry were the prime drivers behind the first Terran colonies that spread out from Earth and the other planets of the Solar System. As people settled on new and fragile colonies, so did their need for supplies and materials increase. Moving ahead to the new worlds of the Alliance that were spread over many light years, and it is easy to see how so many major trade corporations were able to thrive. As each new moon or planet was opened up for exploitation, a gold rush of civilian companies would rush in to snap up the mineral, settling, and trade rights. Without this successful and competitive industry, it might have taken centuries to make progress in the Orion Nebula, as opposed to the much shorter reality of just a few years.

Origins of Private Space Travel

Teresa Morato checked the scanner one last time as the heavily modified six-wheeled Bulldog moved down from the ridge. The large, bulbous tires stuck out underneath to fill the flanks of the V-shaped hull. Originally intended for use in asymmetric warfare, they were one of the few survivable vehicles in the Alliance inventory for use against both mines and missile systems. Two more identical vehicles bumped along the trail behind them, leaving a long dust trial that followed them like a cloud of flies. The road on the moon of Zatha Seven was in a poor state of repair, much like all the facilities on the inhabited moon. This didn't make it unique though, as it was the same through the rest of the T'Kari colonies that had survived the ravages of the genocide committed against them over the last hundred years. None of the thriving cities on the planets remained, just the shattered remnants of a few dozen moons where they had lived in hiding for so long.

"Drone is in range, feed coming up now," said one of the technical operatives who sat behind the driver, facing a number of video screens.

On cue, the three cameras on board the aircraft appeared on one of the flat panel displays. Like all the equipment in the vehicle, it was heavily reinforced and embedded into the internal bulkheads of the Bulldog. The video feeds included detailed data on height and target identification. Teresa examined all three, her eyes darting between the many shapes. From the air, the compound looked quite small, but Teresa recalled the briefing she'd had via videoconference less than an hour earlier. More importantly though, she knew how big the colony was that lay beneath it.

"Any idea why they hit this one?" asked the technician.

Teresa ignored him and pointed at the shapes on the display.

"Are these all the landers that we detected during our descent?"

The man nodded.

"Yes, that's also backed up by the distress data sent to us before the civilians went dark."

"Show it to me."

The man seemed a little irritated at being ordered about, yet Teresa Morato ignored it. She was thinking of the mission now and nothing else. The man could think about whatever he liked, providing it didn't interrupt her operation. The last video transmission from the colony appeared on the screen closest to her; the voice of the T'Kari male speaking automatically translated by his suit's translators.

Are they ever out of those damned suits? she thought, skipping to the part she was most interested in.

"...thirty-two minutes ago. Our surveillance masts detect three Raider vessels. Our defenses have destroyed one..."

Teresa moved her hand across the display to jump ahead fifteen seconds.

"...landed. Forty, no fifty Raiders and a machine.

Retreating underground."

The face of the T'Kari male moved closer to the screen; his face looked pained and sweat ran down his face. Even though he wore a visor, it was clear, and so every hair was visible on the high-definition video. Gunshots were now audible in the distance, as well as the crump of explosions. To Teresa's trained ear, it seemed to be specifically grenades and there were the unmistakable cracks of L42 rifles.

That has to be what was left of our security unit, she thought angrily.

The moon was a low priority mining outpost for the T'Kari, and APS had been contracted to bolster the security with just a single six-man team, including communications gear and a single air defense unit.

"Please hurry, we cannot hold out much..."

He then staggered backward and lurched to the side as if being struck by a heavy object. Dark armored shapes rushed past before the video feed finally cut. Teresa wiped her brow and looked back to the aerial feed. She counted the shapes with her hand, mentally comparing what she saw with the video from the T'Kari and the other signals from inside the compound.

"Okay, we're in the right place. Those must be the landers. Look at the outline. They are the same specification as the light transports the T'Kari use as heavy loaders or shuttles."

The ex-military vehicles made quick progress over

the uneven surface as their semi-active suspension made minute adjustments with each revolution of the wheels. The high-speed shook the passengers about, and it was only the semi-stabilized mounting used on the seating that allowed Teresa to continue to watch the screen with any kind of accuracy.

"Look!" said the technician.

He pointed at the landers, and a column of figures moving off to the right on the third display unit. The first of the group reached what looked like a wall or perhaps an entry point to the compound. One of the shapes staggered and then dropped to the ground. A white flash sent dust out from the wall before the attackers unleashed a fusillade of gunfire. They then continued into the breach as more and more figures rushed out from the landers. Teresa slammed her fist down onto the flat metal mounting near the display.

"Damn it, they are inside already. We're going to be too late," she muttered bitterly.

Teresa wiped her long black hair away from her face and focused her efforts on the task at hand. She had a lot to worry about these days and not just this operation. Being ex-military though, she knew when it was time to switch off and to concentrate. For the next few minutes, or however long this took, the operation would be the only thing to occupy her mind. The screen to her left showed four video feeds from the civilian compound that was home to almost a thousand T'Kari. The ancient masonry was being blasted to powder, as several teams of lightly colored Raiders rushed through the complex. She tapped the driver on the shoulder.

"How much longer?"

"Less than a minute. When we hit the next bend, we'll be at the breached perimeter."

"Good," she replied calmly.

Teresa Morato then turned her attention to the forward facing screen. Unlike most civilian vehicles, the Bulldog had no windows or vision slits. Instead, the entire front was a large display that showed camera feeds in all directions from the vehicle. Teresa tapped the left screen to bring up the layout of all three Bulldogs. They had been heavily modified to carry her unique cargo, three teams of Jötnar warriors. These three-meter tall synthetic creatures had been the final generation of Biomechs created in the Uprising, but they had become some of the most stalwart and courageous fighters in the Alliance.

"Okay, this is it. Now remember, the compound is twenty meters underground. We breach the perimeter and then take the two entry points so that none of them can get out. One team per breach and Gun's hunting party."

Gruff acknowledgements came back from the other two vehicles. She glanced over her shoulder and to the massive armored form of Gun. He was the leader by rights of seniority of his people, yet these last few months had been spending time filtering groups of Jötnar to the APS private security firm. Officially, this was just a way for them to earn money, but Teresa knew better than that. He was using APS as a way of keeping his youngest warriors experienced and ready. Not that Teresa minded; the two were close friends with a long history. She smiled at him, and he returned it with a slow nod.

Typical Gun, she thought.

"Ten seconds!" shouted the driver.

Teresa took a last calm breath before giving the command.

"All teams, weapons free!"

The three armored vehicles slid around the final bend and crashed through what remained of the damaged perimeter fencing. It was a new addition to the site, as were all the buildings on the surface. A dozen corporations were already busy with their deals on these moons, and she could see their motley collection of equipment, machines, and vehicles all over the complex. But more importantly, they were already burning. Teresa glimpsed the scanner built into the display, noting that over thirty bodies had already been identified in just a few seconds.

That's not why we're here. We need to get to the T'Kari, and fast!

The small armored column pushed onward and through the outer section of the compound. This was the least developed part of the site, and mainly consisted of a rough road and stacks of raw materials, many of which had now toppled over. In the distance were a number of thick, black smoke columns. They drifted upward in lazy spirals, disappearing into the ink blackness of the sky. The effect was mesmerizing, but Teresa was alert. She found the first target before the computers could even differentiate them from the ground clutter. Two Raider ships of T'Kari design were waiting out in the open. Each was twice the size of an Alliance shuttle, and she quickly estimated they could carry about fifty people, perhaps more. Shapes moved about them, armored forms in lightly colored plates of ballistic armor.

"Raiders," she said under her breath.

Each Bulldog was had a robotic turret mount fitted to the topside of the vehicle. It was equipped with a pair of chain-fed L48 cannons that fired the large 12.7mm caliber rounds previously used in the Marine Corps. These projectiles were variable mode charges that detonated on contact or proximity, depending on the setting chosen. All three of them opened fire at the same time, and the effect was devastating. Those Raiders caught out in the open were shredded by the overwhelming firepower. A few returned fire; but their rounds bounced harmlessly off the double layered plating on the Bulldogs. They crashed through the Raiders and moved on and toward the two entrances that led into the main compound. One Bulldog continued firing at the Raiders foolish enough to not hide, while the other two tore chunks of the two spacecraft sitting impotently on the open landing pad. The ammunition did terrible work at this range, and the two were quickly rendered useless by the attack.

"Good work, prepare to dismount!" Teresa said, doing her best stay calm. Her pulse was now pounding with nerves and excitement. She'd experienced battle many times before, but the thrill it gave her had never left, not even since leaving the Corps so many years before.

Do I miss it? Hell I do!

Her Bulldog screeched to a halt, and the large armored door on the right dropped down to form a sturdy ramp to the surface.

"Go!" roared Gun.

Gun was first out of the Bulldog and running for the dark octagonal doorway that was cut into the rock. It had already been badly damaged, presumably by the Raiders. Teresa watched him from the camera feed in the vehicle. He was inside the structure as the last of his team jumped down from the ramp. She spotted the darkened doorway flash several times, and then the other three were inside and following him in. Teresa looked back to her bank of video screens; each showing multiple feeds from the modified military armor all the operatives wore. As private contractors, they made use of surplus military gear and this was no exception. With the disbanding of the Jötnar Battalion, a great deal of military equipment for their oversized bodies had been sold off cheaply. Gun had been able to purchase large amounts of it while the rest was melted down for scrap or bought by companies like APS. Jötnar smiths on Prometheus and Hyperion had produced aftermarket ballistic plates that were now fitted at key points along the shoulder, chests, and elbows.

"Bravo and Charlie teams hold your positions. Alpha, keep moving."

Teresa moved her eyes slightly to check on the status of the other two groups of operatives. The second vehicle had deployed its four Jötnar unit to the doorway recently entered by Gun. Two moved inside a few meters while the other two took up their posts on the outside. Teresa nodded in satisfaction and then looked over to Charlie Team. They were at the second entrance but had stopped and were looking around it.

"Charlie One, what's the problem?"

"The door, it's been sealed from the inside," came back the gruff sound of the team's leader.

Teresa scratched her forehead as she rechecked the overhead plan of the compound. According to the data supplied by the T'Kari, these were the only two surface entrances on this side of the mountainside. There were other shafts, but the next was six kilometers away.

"Understood."

Dull yellow flashes danced about her screens around the broken and burning equipment.

"Ambush!" growled Alpha One, and the video feeds

from each of his squad blurred. At first Teresa almost panicked, but it was nothing more than the Jötnar moving quickly. They spread out and returned fire with their modified coilguns. Bright blasts of energy slammed into dark shapes that looked out among the compound.

"Omega, it's an ambush!"

It was her codename and one chosen for a number of reasons, not least because of her stern attitude that she'd adopted in the company, and the fact she was the last link in the chain of command. There was nobody higher than her in APS when on operations. She'd only returned to combat operation in the last six months as their finances suffered in the drought of work. Even so, Omega was the designation she often used in these operations, and she was starting to like it.

"Bulldogs, keep them busy!" she said in a calm and controlled voice.

The two crews in each of the small vehicles altered their positions slightly to ensure the lighter armored rears of their Bulldogs were places away from the gunfire. Even as they moved, the turrets on each tracked around and opened fire with a devastating roar. Any of the Raiders arrogant enough to move out of cover was instantly shredded.

"Thanks, Omega," said the Jötnar leader of Team Charlie.

"Secure the site, Bulldog Three will follow you for

support. We don't need any more surprises."

Just ten meters inside the underground compound, and Gun was already feeling in his element. He moved quickly but not too quickly. Gun and his people had spent many years hunting the stray creatures on their jungle world of Hyperion. They were fast and smart, frequently outwitting their hunters. He'd seen a good number fall to ambushes or traps laid out by the smarts ones. Of the Jötnar that survived such ordeals, each would become wiser, stronger, and more useful to him. As he rushed down the tunnel, he continually panned from side to side, looking for signs of traps, hidden enemies, or concealed weapons; another fifteen meters further inside, and he was rewarded by a small shape on the left. He stopped, and the other three Jötnar halted and took up defensive positions. They took aim with their military issue coilguns, and one turned around to cover their rear.

"Alpha One here, I have a defense mine. They must have left it on the way down."

"Show me," Teresa replied from the Bulldog on the surface.

Gun shook his head and leaned in closer to the object. He made sure not to move too close though, just enough to get a clear view to show those topside.

"Yeah, that's okay. Our data show that as a T'Kari shredder. You know what to do."

Gun nodded, reaching down to his right thigh. Fitted

to his armor with Velcro tabs were a number of circular plates surrounded by ceramic teeth. He grabbed one and pulled it from his leg. Gun then reached out and fitted it onto the end of his coilgun and twisted to clip it to the muzzle. The weapon instantly recognized the fitment of the device and changed to a blank blast projectile. He took aim at the device on the wall.

"Clear!"

With a firm pull on the trigger, the coilgun sent a low power magnetic block to the muzzle, striking the back of the plate with a thump. The plate in turn discharged a sticky filament web that enveloped the device and instantly froze solid. Immediately after firing, the plate detached from the barrel and fell to the ground. The weapon flashed on the readout and changed back to conventional projectiles.

"Pacified," he said under his breath and then moved on.

The tunnel continued for a short distance further before reaching a large open hallway. The walls were smooth and metallic, and overhead a number of yellow lights cast a sinister glow over the whole area. At the far end was an arched entrance leading out into what appeared to be a large open space.

Teresa continued, "Alpha Team, that's good progress. The archway leads to the plaza. Our data from the T'Kari says that it is about the size of a freighter hangar, with buildings and paths around the internal structure. The habitation areas are interspersed with the commercial zones. Be careful."

Gun moved ahead until he reached the archway. He peered through the opening and into the plaza. It was lighter than he'd expected. Bodies littered the ground, and the sound of gunfire was much louder. About twenty meters away stood a large bipedal machine. Near to it were a dozen of the Raiders in their dark, battle scarred armor. Another group of Raiders appeared in the far distance, and between them they dragged a dozen T'Kari civilians, some of who were not even in the suits Gun had always seen them wear.

Interesting, he thought with wry amusement.

"Dead T'Kari and Raiders here," his nearest comrade said.

Gun threw him a quick glance. The Jötnar was about to lift one of the bodies to check.

"No!" he snapped back in reply.

Gun was no ordinary Jötnar. He was the first of his people to fight against his creators. Now he was their leader and the most revered of all the Jötnar. When he spoke, his people listened. The Jötnar operative instantly removed his hand from the body and bowed down gently.

Gun looked at him intently but kept his voice low, "Good. Mines under bodies are a classic. Waken learned that the hard way Terra Nova."

He looked back to the arched entrance to the plaza.

"So I hear."

"Omega, we're going in!" he said in a calm voice over the intercom.

"Affirmative."

Gun leapt out from the entrance and into the plaza. Now that his vision was cleared of obstructions, he could see the damage wrought by the Raiders. Small numbers of bodies lay scattered, and although most were armored, he suspected they were thorough attackers. The great machine in the middle somehow spotted him and turned around. It roared something in an unrecognizable tongue, and in a flash the Raiders were rushing to Gun. He didn't hesitate and killed two with his coilgun before they could even reach him. Then he was in the middle of the group and swinging his rifle like a club. His three comrades followed in a wide line. They went to work like a farmer moving across a field.

A shredder grenade exploded in the middle of the melee, killing one Raider and tearing a leg from one of the Jötnar. He fell down but continued to fight.

The great machine settled down on its haunches and lifted its clattering arms to defend itself. Gun was unable to shoot before it swung at him. He ducked to the left and grabbed the massive metal appendage as it moved near his face. Even three meters in height, Gun was dwarfed by the machine that towered another meter above him. He was thrown off to his side, and the great beast strode in, kicking one of the Raiders out of the way to reach the wounded Jötnar. Gun shook his head and pulled himself up, but he was too far away to help his wounded comrade. The machine lifted one of its heavy metal feet ready to bring it down on its head.

"Hey you!" came an amplified voice from the tunnel entrance.

A volley of high-power coilgun rounds tore at the machine's head. It staggered back, losing its footing. Gun wasted no time, pulled a thermite charge from his left leg, and leapt onto the flailing machine. Both arms waved at him, but incredibly, he was able to fasten it to the waist and then rolled off to the side. A bright white flash filled the plaza, followed by a massive heat surge, setting one of the Jötnar on fire. All of them watched in silence as the machine burned and melted from the intense heat of the charge while the reinforcements helped extinguish the fire on the wounded Jötnar. Teresa Morato emerged from the darkened entrance, her coilgun held up to her armor shoulder. Her visor lifted up to reveal her smiling face as the Jötnar rounded up the dozen Raider survivors.

Gun staggered over to her with an equally please look on his face. At the same time, the T'Kari civilians started to emerge from the safety of their homes and businesses. They all wore the traditional protective suits that looked like lightweight armor, but only a few wore helmets or head protection.

Two of the Jötnar dragged one of the surviving Raiders over to Teresa. His clothing was more ornate than the others, and embellished with details on the shoulders and chest. Teresa noticed the shape of Echidna, the great, coiled beast, on his right breast. He snarled at her and shouted. She raised an eyebrow at the noise before his translators unit kicked in.

"The T'Kari are not your friends. They hide Helios from you, and you will suffer for it!"

Teresa looked to Gun and exchanged a bemused look before turning her attention back to the Raider. She was surprised that the T'Kari turncoat was able to communicate so easily with her. It had taken the T'Kari much longer. It was as though he'd already had significant exposure to her people already.

"You tell me then."

The Raider lifted the side of his mouth up with a cruel smile.

"The devourer of worlds is coming. It will start with Helios. The T'Kari will be next, then you!"

He started to laugh, a high-pitched laugh that did nothing to engender sympathy from Teresa. Gun seemed even less impressed and stepped closer still before tapping him on the shoulder.

"Raider," he said calmly.

His fist followed and struck firmly into the Raider's open visor. It struck his nose with a sickening crunch. He pulled back his hand to reveal gushing blood and a bitter-looking Raider.

"Take him!" Teresa ordered a newly arrived team of APS operatives.

"The rest reform your teams. We have a compound to clear out, and according to my scans, there are a few of them left waiting for us."

Gun laughed as APS operatives flooded the place, checked the wounded or secured the prisoners.

"Pah! Cowering in fear more like!"

Teresa looked back at him and realized for the first time in what seemed like decades, how much Gun enjoyed this kind of violence. It instantly brought back thoughts of Spartan. She shook her head at the idea.

Those two are much too alike!

CHAPTER TWO

The world of Private Military Contractors was shaken apart by the Terra Nova incident of 358CC. A PMC team from Alpha Company assaulted an Alliance Special Operations Group in the middle of a major operation. The blue-on-blue incident resulted in thirteen military deaths and the crash of a civilian aircraft, with the loss over more than two hundred citizens. Cuts in military spending, and reliance upon faceless security companies, started a purge of unprecedented proportions. This took place just a year after organizations, including Alpha Company and APS Corp, took over low intensity security operations throughout the Alliance. The incident brought about a public outcry that saw dozens of contracts torn up and the stocks in these companies plummet. The gold rush years were gone and of the thirty-two security companies, just seven remained a year later, each fighting for the meager work that remained.

Private Security Directory

The Alliance Marine Corps squad of four moved slowly through the main access corridor. Leading them was gruff-looking Sergeant Maria Belgard, who moved with speed and aggression in her step. The other four marines carried their L52 Mark II carbines across their bodies as they marched down the left-hand side of the Prometheus Seven Space Station. Navy crew stepped aside to let the security team pass by. From the way they moved, it was clear this was no simple security detail. They were going somewhere in particular, and the fact that they had their weapons at the ready indicated they expected potential trouble. They reached the end of the corridor and split to cover both sides of the thick glass doorway. To the side was a metal plaque that read simply APS Corp. The Sergeant looked to the other marines, and each nodded they were ready.

"Do it!" she snapped.

The first marine placed an electronic device over the control unit for the door. It flashed once, and the door hissed open to reveal a small foyer area leading to three rooms and what looked like an eating area. Directly in front of them stood just one man, a three meter tall Jötnar, with thick, muscular arms and a scarred upper body. His head and neck were almost double the size of a normal man, yet obviously still just a man. He was stripped to the waist and evidently not expecting to see the marines. As the five entered the APS Corporation space, he turned and glared at them.

"What?"

"Under Title 72 of the Centauri Alliance Constitution, passed through the Alliance Senate seven hours ago, all Private Security contracts, operations, and establishments aboard Alliance military installations are revoked. You will hand over all PMC personnel and equipment to our authority for repatriation back to your civilian headquarters. The Jötnar took in a long, deep breath and then moved a step closer to the marines.

"Stand down, civilian. I am authorized to..."

He swung his right arm, knocking the carbine from the first marine's hand, and then delivered a heavy punch with his oversized paw of a hand. The man was unconscious before he hit the ground, much to the shock of the others. He took advantage of their confusion and grabbed the next nearest marine, lifting him up by his neck. The other two marines jumped forward to help their comrade and to take up his weight to prevent him from being hanged.

"Do you know who I am?" growled the Jötnar.

Sergeant Maria Belgard shook her head and simultaneously drew her sidearm from her waist. She lifted the pistol and pointed it directly at his forehead.

"I don't care if you're the President of the Centauri Alliance. I have the authority to arrest any unauthorized civilian on board this station. Now, drop the private and put your hands behind your head, or I'll shoot you where you stand.

The side door opened and in walked a middle-aged Hispanic woman. She was short, lightly built, and wearing cargo pants and a white t-shirt. Her face was red from exertion, and both of her hands covered in cloth wraps for sparring. She looked at the scene and then directly to the Jötnar.

"Commander Gun, drop the marine."

Without even a glimmer of hesitation, the massive Jötnar dropped the marine. He hit the ground gasping for breath, and the two marines that had been trying to help their comrade bent down to help him to his feet.

"I'm Teresa Morato, and this is Commander Gun. If you lay a finger on him, you can expect two things to happen. One, you'll be dead within the minute. Two, every single Jötnar from Prometheus to Hyperion will turn on the Alliance like the Biomechs did back in the Uprising. We've only just got back from an operation, and I have zero tolerance from assholes with ego issues. Are you that stupid, Sergeant?"

The female marine looked at Teresa carefully. She was aware the senior executive had been a marine in the past. In fact, the exploits of Spartan and Teresa Morato in the Uprising and the years afterwards had become infamous. Though neither had achieved a major rank in the military, they had both been instrumental in ending the War. She had no idea, however, that the woman would be present.

The Sergeant replaced her pistol in her holster and indicated for the four marines to leave the room.

"I apologize, Mrs. Morato. I have to..."

"No," replied Teresa in an irritated tone. "My name is Ms. Morato, and you will take me to see Admiral Anderson immediately. I'm sure you are aware that to carry out orders such as these requires the full authority of the senior officer on this station."

She paused and watched the Sergeant, looking carefully at her body and face for signs of the strength of her position. The Sergeant said nothing.

"Well, do you have it?"

Sergeant Belgard looked confused, if only for a second. She was clearly angered at being spoken to by a civilian, but she was also well aware of Teresa's reputation as both a warrior and a businesswoman.

"The paperwork has been signed by my Captain, and he is the senior Marine Corps member on board."

Teresa turned away a fraction and smiled inwardly. It was a minor victory but a face saving one at that. She'd already seen the news and had sent her data off-site and away from the station. Even so, she'd expected to be contacted privately by the Admiral, not by the rough hand of some jarhead. Teresa noticed the look the Sergeant had when looking at Gun who was standing nearby. The figure of the Jötnar commander was certainly impressive to one unfamiliar with his people, especially as he had become something of a legend in the Alliance. The synthetic giant was famous for creating a sanctuary on the hostile jungle world of Hyperion, much to the consternation of Alliance citizens. Any Biomechs that were captured alive were sent there to be integrated with the Jötnar. With the creation of the Spacebridge to New Charon, the Jötnar had spread to moons and worlds. Even so, even Sergeant Belgard knew that Gun, their most famous leader and warrior, was sacred to them.

"I see. In that case, I would be happy to come with you to see the Admiral."

The young Sergeant seemed to relax and moved to the door before realizing that Ms. Morato still hadn't moved. She looked at the older woman's body and couldn't fail to be impressed at her fitness and muscular build. Teresa spotted her looking at her and was forced to hide a grin.

"When I'm changed, of course. I'm getting enough attention dressed like this as it is."

She then turned and walked back to her room. The Sergeant watched her go with a deflated look on her face. Gun grinned at her discomfort before his face tightened up. For a second, Sergeant Belgard feared he might attack her. Instead, he spoke in a low, gravelly voice.

"Teresa Morato is a hero of the Marine Corps. We've spent the last three days getting back from an operation against T'Kari Raiders. You should show respect."

He then also turned to disappear off into one of the

three rooms, presumably to get changed into something more suitable. The Sergeant wished, for the first time since she was transferred from Terra Nova, that she were somewhere else.

* * *

The crippled Alliance light cruiser ANS Imperator drifted slowly through the debris field. Her engines had been out of commission for more than a full day while fires continued to burn in her forward sections. Coolant sprayed from the ruptures along her port flank and into space, along with quantities of escaping fluid and gas from the other impacts. This damage had combined over the hours to produce enough lateral thrust to start moving the ship in a lazy circle towards the rest of the debris in the asteroid field. A hint of noise caught Spartan's attention, and he turned his head to see his old friend, Khan grinning at him.

"What?" he asked, always suspicious of that expression.

Khan chuckled to himself at the view from the assault shuttle. Unlike the other humans on board, Khan was one of the Jötnar; a people prized for their great strength, power, and ability to inflict damage. His people had been artificially created and indoctrinated by the enemy back in the Great Uprising over two decades ago and had almost turned the tide of the War. He was twice the size of any man in the shuttle with his massive three-meter tall frame, thick muscles, and armored suit that gave him the look of some ogre or monster of old.

"Well?" continued Spartan, "What's so damned funny?"

Khan nodded to the crippled ship that drifted slowly and silently through space. Contrary to what most people expected, there was no sound in space and even the blasts that had occurred when they'd originally damaged the ship had not even registered inside their shuttle.

"Only you would destroy your ship to catch your enemy."

Spartan looked as his friend smirked. Two of the other APS operatives sitting nearby were forced to hide their faces from their commander. Spartan wasn't just in charge of the team, he was their boss, and also one of the most highly respected former marines in the Alliance military. His exploits and his somewhat direct approach toward people had become almost legendary. The operatives had been stuck inside their shutdown and deactivated shuttle for seven hours now and anything, no matter how banal, was more interesting than watching and waiting.

"Hey, that was the plan, remember? For this kind of prey we need the right kind of bait."

Khan raised an eyebrow at the explanation. Spartan exhaled in an annoyed fashion.

"Look, I've been working on this one with Alliance Intelligence and the T'Kari for seven months now. We have to catch them before they move on to the next system."

Khan simply raised his eyebrow again and settled back down to watch the ship.

"Catching T'Kari Raiders, is that all we're needed for now?"

Spartan tried to relax, but it was difficult. In the last two years a lot had changed, both for him and his wife Teresa, as well as their company. APS Corporation had been their baby, something they'd invested themselves in fully, both in terms of time and money. Yet since the Alliance had made contact with the T'Kari in the New Charon Star System, things had turned for the worse for people like Spartan. The exploitation of New Charon had begun in earnest with new colonies appearing, like the old gold rush towns on Earth, in a matter of months. At the same time, the amount of competition from new, aggressive corporations had grown massively, as had the number of lavish contracts. It didn't take long for somebody to make a mistake though, and the entire industry had imploded. While the Alliance funding had almost completely dried up, more and more money was being fed directly to the Navy, and Spartan had been forced to seek contracts with whoever could afford APS' fees. He tried to shake the thoughts of his crippled company behind him and instead looked back at the ship.

ANS Imperator was anything but an Alliance warship. She was a hulk, salvaged from the fighting decades earlier when the Uprising had begun back at the Titan Naval Station. Imperator had been one of the first casualties and had been used ever since as a storage hulk for ammunition, and unstable or dangerous supplies. Burn marks on her outer hull were not from any kind of recent incident. As far as Spartan was aware, every piece of damage on the ship had occurred many years before he'd even laid his eyes on her rotting hulk. He looked back at the small group of specialists inside the shuttle. The cramped interior was barely big enough to contain the eight of them and their equipment and weapons. Just weeks from his fiftieth birthday, he was already starting to feel aches in his joints. Luckily, he was stronger, healthier, and fitter than most men in their twenties. Advances in biotech, food, and bioengineering meant a man could serve as a marine grunt for decades longer than had been possible in the past. Lovett noticed the look on Spartan's face and knew his friend was hurting. He tried to lighten the mood.

"Hey, it could be a lot worse. At least the T'Kari know the value of military assets, even if our own citizens don't. If this mission works, we might get security contracts for the T'Kari fleet."

Spartan nodded but said nothing. Lovett was correct, of course. The T'Kari, though very much like humans, had a number of differences that still astounded him. Their complete lack or even belief in physical violence had left them vulnerable, and he was not surprised the enemy that had so very nearly destroyed humanity had so successfully torn T'Kari society apart. Luckily, the violence exhibited by Spartan and his corporation, directly in front of them, had proven his worth and gained them a prized contract to provide specialist security work for the alien race. Though the Alliance patrolled the system, they refused to operate under any kind of T'Kari command. APS Corporation was different, and it was for that reason alone that Spartan suspected his company even still existed. The other six operatives were all men and women he trusted implicitly, though James Lovett was the only one of them, other than Khan, that he'd served with back in the Marine Corps.

"Spartan, I've got a question," said Isamu Takeda from Kerberos, the newest member of his team. His tightly sculpted face and jet-black hair made him stand out from the rest of those still working for APS Corporation. Spartan nodded.

"Who the hell are these guys? I heard that when you, Khan, Gun, and the others first met the T'Kari on Hades, the enemy attacked you. Didn't they also have T'Kari warriors fighting with them?"

Spartan nodded again, looking to Lovett who was doing his best to try not to laugh. The politics of the New Charon Star System were complicated, and most of the operatives now working at APS had been employed for their technical or military skills. Only the more senior members had much of an idea what was actually happening in the System.

"Isamu, what happened out here seems pretty clear to me. Hundreds of years ago, the enemy that we've been fighting started a civil war with the citizens of the T'Kari. It went on a lot longer than our Uprising, and this is the result. Their worlds are devastated, and their population reduced to almost nothing. Ayndir, their leader, explained to me that whenever the T'Kari reached a stage where they might recover, the machines would return."

Isamu looked a little confused at the response, and Spartan was already wishing he had some of his old crew back. With the shortage in resources, he'd been forced to recruit whoever he could find.

"Like Pontus and Typhon then, back home?"

Spartan breathed out with some satisfaction.

"Yes, the enemy, whoever they are, seem adept at several things. They are masters of biomechanical engineering, space travel, Rift construction and most of all, at sending or indoctrinating agents to start wars in their name. Based on the advanced technology of the T'Kari, I would suggest they hit races once they reach a certain level. We've only just spread out from our own worlds, and that might be just the signal they needed to start their operations in Alpha Centauri."

Lovett listened with interest as Spartan tried to explain what was happening as best he could. He often had difficulty trying to get his head around what had happened, and meeting the T'Kari had made it even more complicated to him. He leaned forward and interrupted the conversation.

"What I want to know is, who the hell this enemy is? Where are they, and how are they getting technology and these agents through to people like us and the T'Kari?"

"Yeah," Khan added.

He had been keeping quiet while the others talked. His race of synthetic creatures had the unfortunate background of having been bred and trained to fight against humanity in the Uprising. Though their programming had been removed, there were still many that distrusted, or even hated those that were left, still referring to them as Biomechs.

"I'll tell you something else. When we find where they live, you won't be able to hold the Jötnar back. We have a score to settle."

Spartan placed a hand on his friend's shoulder. He knew it wasn't just the fact that Khan and his people had been built and abused by the enemy that had used the mythology and iconography of the beast Echidna. It was the losses and the continuous discrimination and abuse his people suffered every day. No matter how many battles they fought in, or how many died on behalf of the Alliance, there were still thousands, perhaps millions of citizens that considered them as no more than barbarous dogs that needed to be put down.

"Khan, we all have scores to settle with them."

A light blinked inside the craft, and it instantly drew his attention.

They are here!

Spartan directed his gaze back to the crippled ship and quickly identified a dark shape moving slowly toward the hulk. It was shaped much like the other T'Kari ships they had come across over the last month, but this one was equipped with large metal ribs along its flanks. Spartan pulled his electronic secpad from the pouch on his armor and brought up the known schematic for T'Kari Raider ships.

"Okay, it's the one. Wait for my signal, and then we go in. Ready?"

Each of those waiting patiently in the shuttle nodded in agreement. Even though they'd been waiting for hours, now that the mission was about to go ahead, they moved as though rushed. Khan watched the ship and nodded to Spartan while pointing to its flank.

"Look, they are sending in a salvage team."

Spartan watched as the ribs opened up, and like fleas on a dog, the suited T'Kari exited the ship and used their EVA thrusters to move around the damaged vessel. Spartan checked his L52 Mark II Assault Carbine one last time. It wasn't necessary; it was more a ritual, and one he always carried out at the start of a dangerous operation like this one.

"You think their commander is on the ship?" asked Khan with some suspicion.

Spartan shrugged.

"You saw the reports. The small groups of enslaved T'Kari have been hunting down their brothers for generations. This ship has raided throughout New Charon with impunity for seven months now. If the commander isn't here, then where will he be?"

Khan looked as though he agreed, but he declined to comment. Spartan released his grav-lock, moving closer to his old friend as he made his way to the airlock seal.

"Anyway, we get paid by the T'Kari whether he's there or not. Now we find if the price they paid for the information was worth it."

"They're inside," Lovett added in his calm voice.

Spartan took a deep breath and prepared himself for what was to come.

"Good. All units converge on the target."

He pulled the triple levers that released both stages of the airlock. There was no mass ejection of air as the craft had already vented its surplus atmosphere in the last hour. As the hatches opened, the eight elite operatives of the APS Corporation left the shuttle. They each latched themselves onto a ZeroDrone and then moved away with slow, gently acceleration. The extra-vehicular movement drones were a recent development of the gear used by shipyard workers to move equipment and tooling about in zero-g environments. Spartan and Khan took the first and were pulled through space and toward the waiting ship. As they moved, Spartan watched another three teams, each using the same gear and equipment as they moved from their own hiding places in the debris field.

Twenty-four operatives for one corsair. It had better be enough, Spartan thought.

He was now starting to wonder if perhaps he had been just a little bit too optimistic during the planning stages. They continued forward like a swarm of flies toward their target. All four teams targeted different access areas of the ship, with Spartan's team taking the main loading bay. The briefing with the T'Kari had implied that the loading bay on this class of ship would give them the quickest route through to the bridge of the vessel.

"Take it easy and keep movement to a minimum. We need to get to the door before they know we're there."

Spartan and Khan approached the bay and watched its ribbed hull with interest. It was heavily scored and marked, unlike anything either had seen before on ships. There were markings though none were fully intact, but they did betray the origins of the craft as one of the T'Kari fleet. They made it to the underside of the ship and clamped the ZeroDrone to the hull. Both ensured their magboots were firmly in place on the ship and proceeded to walk the short distance around the overhang and onto the actual landing bay. Technically, they were upside down, but those distinctions were somewhat irrelevant in space. The exterior of the bay was a large open space, with a number of magnetically shielded sliding doors fitted on one side to allow spacecraft or people to exit the ship.

"Get in position and wait for the signal," he said calmly.

They all moved down onto the landing platform and toward the sliding doors. All wore the modified PDS armored suits that were usually worn by Alliance Marines. Even Khan wore a custom suit, one of many that were being manufactured back on the fiery world of Prometheus. His was cruder in comparison but still fully sealed and included many of the features originally used in the massive Marine Corp Vanguard assault suits. He took up position to the right of Spartan and lifted his right arm to point it at the doors. Unlike the others, his carbine was actually built into his armor. It meant the ammunition feed could be fed from ammunition boxes on belts.

"Red Team is in position," announced their leader.

The other three teams were in position and were now waiting at their pre-determined zones. Spartan acknowledged the message and double-checked on the others. They needed just a few more seconds, and he would have twenty-four well-trained operatives, all armored, and heavily armed for the mission.

Isamu finished placing the series of six small modules on the metal plating in a wide circle. Each was connected to the next with a small wire, and as he placed them, the rest of the team watched nervously. It was a standard issue breaching charge, based upon a shaped charge unit. Spartan watched him carefully; aware that any mistake here would leave them all trapped outside. Isamu knew his trade, and in a matter of seconds, the unit was installed. The rest of the team backed off to the required safe distance of four meters. Finally, the signal came from the other teams; they were all ready.

Here we go again.

"Now!" barked Spartan.

The charges flashed, and the metal plating disintegrated, blasting into the vessel. The air pressure inside must have been the same as the outside, or else Spartan would have expected the debris to blast out into space. Either way, he didn't have the time to consider it; he had a job to do.

"Everybody inside, secure the vessel, and locate the commander."

Spartan was in first, with one hand on the metal structure so he could pull himself along in the zero-g environment. His right hand, however, grasped his L52 carbine. He'd already set it to the lower power mode. It gave him a high rate of fire, without the excessive armor penetration issues that could prove problematic in an environment such as this. Once through the breached door, he was inside the landing bay itself. There was no light, and he was forced to activate the shoulder-mounted lamps on his PDS suit. The room was large and contained two small craft, presumably shuttles or light transports of some kind. The configuration wasn't too different to the small cobra craft used in the Alliance. He lowered his lamps and checked to see how they were secured. Much like their own ships, the craft was held down with a form of magnetic clamp.

So, they have power. Where is everybody?

He kept moving, the other seven close behind. The computer systems were all off in this part of the ship, but as he approached the main access door into the rest of the vessel, his suit picked up readings.

"You getting this?" he asked.

"Yeah, there are heat blooms on the other side of this door. I'd say our friends are preparing a welcoming committee for us."

Khan pulled himself closer and pointed his weapon at the doorway.

"I say we breach and introduce ourselves."

Chatter from the other teams showed a very different situation. The status indicators on Spartan's suit allowed him to monitor each of them in terms of heart rate, blood pressure, and even their suit's supplies. Two of the other teams had run directly into crew, and it looked like they were in the middle of a firefight.

"Spartan, aft section is secure, one hostile down and seven prisoners."

He nodded to himself.

"Good work, keep moving. We need the commander."

He recalled the dossiers he'd read that had been compiled by the best people in Alliance Intelligence. Apparently, the data had come directly from the T'Kari, but Spartan doubted some of that. The information was sparse and had mainly consisted of lists of previous targets, along with some of the combat procedures used. Spartan could have obtained better information himself, but with the changes in procedure, he was finding access to people becoming more and more difficult. What he did know was that the leader of this vessel was apparently responsible for raiding T'Kari colonies for the best part of last decade. He was one of the former commanders of the T'Kari Scouts, an elite team that patrolled throughout the New Charon Star System to watch for signs of their enemies. Lovett watched him thinking and was forced to tilt his head toward the door and potential hostiles on the other side.

Get your mind on the job, you fool!

He almost kicked himself for letting his mind drift at such an important point. He looked back to those around him and checked they were ready. They waited for his signal. Isamu had already placed charges on the inner door.

"Assault pattern alpha," he stated firmly and moved off to the left.

Isamu triggered the charge, and this time the metal blew out toward them. It instantly told them that this part of the ship was pressurized. Spartan was already through, and as he stepped in, he triggered his suit's built-in entry-assault module. It was specially designed by the APS Corporation for such operations. A dozen small charges were launched from units fitted to his shoulders. They exploded just three meters away with a roar and a bright flash. Spartan's visor automatically blackened for a brief moment and then returned to normal. It was a large rectangular room with racks on the walls for equipment and weapons. A number of computer displays covered the left wall. A raised platform to the right was topped off with a smashed helmet. The ceiling and walls were deeply ribbed, much like the exterior of the ship.

"Spartan, watch out!" cried Lovett.

He lifted his weapon and counted the enemy quickly before taking aim. There were six T'Kari Raiders in dark armor, with their bug-like helmets and close fitting metal plates. The shock charges had scattered them, yet they were already bringing their weapons to bear.

"Now!"

Spartan took aim, but Khan opened fire first. The burst of mag rounds from the Jötnar's L52 carbine hit the nearest two and sent then spinning into the corridor behind them. Spartan took aim at the third, but its hands were already raised, and the rest seemed to give up in seconds.

What's going on in here?

Spartan moved ahead, and the team secured their

prisoners. He looked at the corridor behind the room and took a few steps before stopping. The reports on his helmet showed no casualties with his team, but there was something else inside. It showed up as a large target, approximately five rooms from their current position. He looked back to his team.

"Three of you stay with Lovett. Don't let them leave!"

He then looked to Khan.

"The rest of you with me, quickly!"

He placed one foot in front of the other and let the automatic mag seals do their work as he stomped out of the room and into the innards of the ship. The other operatives were covering similar ground, and all making their way to the same objective. Isamu and Porter watched the flanks; Spartan and Khan took the middle ground. They moved through to the next batch of darkened rooms, finding nothing but empty space. There were no computers, storage containers, or even people; and that made each of them nervous. Of them all, Spartan was starting to feel the coldness of his nerves.

Where is everybody? This ship can't just be full of empty space.

Spartan paused for a moment, his suspicions now raised. The ship was large, easily bigger than a frigate and should contain a crew of at least a hundred, possibly more.

Surely they aren't all on the crippled vessel.

Khan stopped next to him and looked confused.

"Problem?"

Spartan shrugged.

"I don't know. I've got a feeling. Something isn't right."

Khan moved his head very slowly in agreement.

"I agree. Where are the guards?"

The radio exploded into noise as the leaders of two of the teams cried out for help.

"Spartan, there's something in here. We need to..."

His voice changed to screams of pain, and the occasional gunshot rattled out in the background. Spartan listened to the sounds and voices as carefully as he could. It was messy, but he could just about make out the sound of people and weapons. Khan listened to the same in his suit before looking directly into Spartan's eyes.

"Biomechs!" he said with nothing but venom in his voice.

CHAPTER THREE

The Helios Rebellion would test the strength of the smaller, but more powerful Alliance Navy in ways that had never been expected. In the past, the mixture of vessels had left them limited in ability to respond to crisis. Now her fleets of warships, escorts, and fighters would once again be responsible for shipping marines to the frontline. This time, however, it would not be to help secure Alliance territory. The Helios Rebellion would be the first time humankind put military forces onto an alien world. It would not be the last.

Naval Cadet's Handbook

The Biomechs were first encountered in large numbers during the fighting on Prime. They had surged from the infamous Bone Mill and became the catalyst that turned the insurgency into a full-blown war. Until that moment, the fighting had consisted of just the mysterious movement known only as the Zealots. Once the Biomechs were revealed, the war turned around into a full-scale uprising, with entire worlds turning to one side or the other. The horrifying creature that stood in front of Spartan looked like the first generation of warrior that had crawled from out of the Bone Mill. He lifted his L52 Mark II carbine, and the memories of those first encounters flashed before his eyes as if they were only the day before. He remembered the smell and the sound of them as he fought them across spacecraft and colonies throughout the old Confederacy. These creatures were the size of a pack animal, had four legs, and mutilated bodies. The ones at the start of the War had been constructed from donor organs, tissue, and brain; this one looked no different.

"Protect him!" shouted Khan.

The small group of armored fighters pulled ahead to help defend Spartan. Even so, the creature moved quickly like a gruesome spider. With no discernible gravity aboard the ship, the speed of the operatives was greatly reduced. The Biomech creatures, on the other hand, were able to use the ceilings and walls with ease, grasping with their four limbs and grabbing and pulling at any uneven objects to give them mobility.

"Forget me, just open fire!" barked Spartan.

He opened fire with his carbine, sending each of the mag rounds deeply into the center of the monstrous thing. The coilgun was the standard issue weapon in the Marine

Corps, and used magnetism to super accelerate projectiles without the need for propellant. It was triple-barreled and capable of a rapid-fire mode, whereby it used each of the barrels one at a time to launch the rounds. When needed, it could also use ultra high power single shots. By default, Spartan retained the rapid-fire setting that could cut a man in half at short to medium distances. The other operatives opened fire just in time for two more of the creatures to appear. Both pushed off from the wall, drifting at speed toward the ground, and although rounds slammed into them, their momentum kept them going. They crashed directly into Spartan and Khan and sent the four as a spinning mass of guns, limbs, and blood. Emergency seals clamped down behind them to contain the atmosphere that was quickly escaping from the damage to the ship.

"What the hell is going on?" shouted Spartan, more to himself than the others.

He spun about wildly and crashed into the back wall. The weight of the Biomech was immense, and if it hadn't been for the reinforced torso of his PDS suit, he would have been crushed to death by the impact. One of the Biomech's arms flailed out and knocked his carbine from his hands.

Bastard!

Spartan was used to this kind of messy close-up combat and so tugged the M11 tactical bayonet from its sheath. The precision-made high carbon steel weapon was perfectly built for the Marine Corps. It was one of the few pieces of equipment he'd been allowed to keep after leaving. Though simple in its design, it was constructed to be capable of functioning without breakage in operating temperatures of -25 to 135 degrees Fahrenheit. With the skills he'd learnt back well before being a marine, he stabbed the weapon repeatedly into the Biomech's neck. Most amateurs would have used the edge of the blade, but he knew the power of this weapon lay in precise and powerful strikes with the tip. Each stab embedded the blade deep into the thing and sent spurts and blobs of blood pumping from its flesh.

"Spartan, there are more!" shouted Khan.

At the same time, Khan snapped the creature's neck that lay just a few centimeters in front of his face and threw his spare carbine from his armored suit to Spartan. It drifted and almost missed, but a last minute grab by one of his other operatives caught it and spun it back around to Spartan. He pulled back the slide and took careful aim. It was only a low-powered sidearm but did carry a substantial twenty-round magazine with reinforced tip 'castles' ammunition. The final creature pulled itself toward them, but this time they were all ready. The volley of gunfire tore holes out of the enemy as it moved lifelessly toward them. They moved off to the sides where they could be certain of keeping their flanks protected, and then pushed on.

"All units secure your positions. This ship is infested with Biomechs, I repeat; this ship is infested with Biomech creatures. They are hostile and will attack you on sight. Stand your ground and prepare for assault. You have full clearance to use your weapons."

The confirmations from the two other squads still in contact quickly acknowledged his order. Spartan knew full well that wandering about in such an infestation could quickly result in the loss of every single one of his operatives. He'd seen it so many times before where teams of soldiers or marines had been trapped or surrounded by the creatures. In a confined space, they had a massive advantage where their strength, speed, and ability to sustain terrible wounds were more useful than long-range firepower. Of all the men and women in the Alliance, Spartan was probably the single most experienced and successful fighter of the Biomechs.

"Spartan, we're getting readings from deeper inside the ship. I'd say the Biomechs are here to protect something. I also have three signals falling back to this part of the ship."

Spartan looked to Khan. The Biomechs falling back was something unfamiliar to him. In previous battles, the Biomechs had simply pushed on repeatedly until they had achieved total victory. By withdrawing, they were allowing a level of tactical skill and awareness that hadn't been seen before.

"Maybe there is something a little more interesting than these bastardized creatures on this ship?"

He stamped his heavy magnetized boot onto the skull of the nearest dead Biomech, as if to emphasize his anger. It crunched through the creature, leaving broken flesh and bone on the bulkhead. Even though he wore a fully sealed suit, his face was easy to see, and he was angry, very angry. As he looked down, he seemed to pause, fascinated by the grisly destruction on the ground.

"Khan, do these look familiar?" he asked bitterly.

Khan was already picking through the remains before casting them aside. He nodded at Spartan.

"Yeah, they are similar to the beasts we still hunt on Hyperion, same bone structure and muscle placement; no way are these synthetics. They've been butchered, just like our creatures."

Spartan looked as if he was waiting for something different. Khan looked back at the skull and spotted something. He moved his head slightly to get a better look.

"You're right, they aren't exactly the same. These creatures are closer to the T'Kari than us. Look at them."

He held up the shattered head of the nearest dead creature. Though badly crushed, it still retained most of the shape. Spartan looked at it carefully, paying particular attention on the muscular jaws and forehead. He'd actually met similar ones on board a transport trying to flee the fighting at the Siege of Titan. Just thinking about that fight sent trembles through his body. They were fast, strong, and deadly in close combat. He looked down and examined the broken arms of the thing.

"Yeah, they are far less developed than the ones we fought back home. I think you're right. They've been harvesting T'Kari and using them as raw materials for these creatures. I bet that's how they beat them in the end. The two things we know about them is that they are highly advanced but also completely useless in physical violence. These creatures will have been the perfect weapon to use against them."

Khan shook his head.

"They aren't as strong as our enemies though, and we still beat them," replied Khan with unashamed pride; the fact that his people still hunted the mutated creatures, once more confirming his feeling of superiority.

"Alpha, the Raiders are about to leave the wrecked ship. You've got eight minutes, tops." It was a dull voice from the well-hidden transport they'd all arrived on.

Spartan nodded to himself at the news. It forced his hand but made his job much easier. He had no interest in staying aboard this ship a second longer than was absolutely necessary.

"Affirmative, prep yourselves for immediate extraction."

He then looked back to his small team.

"Let's finish this."

He pushed away from the walls and drifted further

inside the ship. Khan was right behind, followed by another two of the operatives. They moved quickly through the vessel but came across no signs of the T'Kari or their mutated creatures. It took a full minute to cover the distance to the main corridor directly in the center. A number of large doorways ran off in different directions; the largest surrounded by glyphs. Spartan recognized them immediately as T'Kari writing.

"This is it. Ayndir explained to me at the intelligence briefing that this is the marker for the command section of the ship."

"Let's get in there then," said Khan.

He pulled himself through the doorway and inside what should have been the command section. The lighting was low, but the sensors on all the operatives' suits were flashing with warnings. There was life in this part of the ship, more so than anywhere else. They moved even deeper until coming to a bank of machines surrounded with clear tubes filled with fluid. The pipes ran out into the walls and bulkheads. Spartan looked at it all with a mixture of surprise and repulsion.

"Above!" cried Khan, simultaneously lifting his right arm.

The bright flashes from his arm-mounted weapon slammed into the creature's soft flesh, and just as before, each one was cut to pieces and chunks of flesh scattered around the weightless interior of the ship. Three more of the creatures emerged from the shadows before the assault finally stopped. Each of the APS operatives moved closer to the machine and the pipes. Spartan examined the structure but noticed the engineering was definitely not the same as the equipment he'd seen on human ships. The principles were the same, but this looked unique to the T'Kari. The head was the most obvious part of the creature that shared some of the important facial features of the T'Kari.

Why the hell are there Biomechs on a T'Kari Raiding ship?

As the four looked on, a dark shape appeared from the blackness. They all lifted their weapons, expecting another onslaught from the foul things. Instead, it was a man wearing a respirator and odd clothing. He staggered and flailed about as if he'd never moved in a weightless environment before. Khan lowered his arm slightly as he looked at the figure, a glimmer of recognition showing on his face. Spartan knew him immediately.

"Pontus?"

The man looked as if he was nodding but then twisted his head about. He lifted his hands and drifted up to the ceiling before crashing and spinning out of control. He then dragged and clawed at the floor, trying to move toward the APS operatives. Unlike the biomechanical creatures, he was having a hard time making any sort of progress in the zero gravity of the ship.

"What the hell is wrong with him?" asked one of the

two operatives, waiting at the flanks of Khan and Spartan, but neither looked at them, as both seemed awestruck by the sight of the man. One of them lifted his carbine, but Spartan reached out and blocked him.

"No, not yet!"

Instead, he moved out in front and grabbed hold of the man. He pulled him straight and pushed his weightless body up against the wall. His clothes were different, more like those worn by the T'Kari civilians, and there were bruises and cuts on his face. He yanked and tugged at the mask on his face, gasping in the thin, barely breathable atmosphere.

"Who...who are you?" he demanded with great effort.

Spartan pulled him close so that the man was directly in front of him. He'd wanted this man for so long, and it took every measure of self-control not to shoot him where he stood.

"You know me, I'm Spartan," he said through clenched teeth.

Pontus looked back at him without even a glimmer of recognition on his face. It was then he spotted the smashed remains of the Biomechs and recoiled in terror. It was this reaction more than any other that surprised Spartan. The last time Spartan had seen Pontus; he'd been with the machines and Biomechs of the enemy as one of their trusted commanders. Spartan gripped tighter and pulled the man close once more.

"Don't play games with me. Your name is Pontus, and you are the most wanted man in the galaxy."

Khan moved to Spartan and gazed upon his sworn enemy. The man seemed just as terrified at the sight of Khan as he was at the other non-human creatures on the ship.

"You worked with the machines," he stated, his voice dripping with venom. "You helped them and the Biomechs to wage war against your own people. Millions died because of you."

Khan, normally stoic in these situations, clenched his right fist, desperate to exact some revenge for the massed suffering of his own comrades at the hands of Pontus and his friends.

"Pontus?" cried out the man, "No...no, that's not me."

Spartan lifted his armored fist in a threatening manner and looked into the eyes of his enemy. He could see genuine horror and fear staring right back, and it worried him.

"I don't know who...my name?"

He reached for his face as though expecting to find somebody else.

"Who am I? Where am I? Are we in space?"

Khan shook his head angrily.

"Tell us what are you doing here?"

Pontus started spluttering, his voice confused and scared. Spartan was forced to lower his hand to try and calm the man. After a few more confused words, his voice started to make some sense.

"I woke up on the bed in there, with the others. The pod opened, and I fell out, and moved toward the door... and here."

He then turned to Spartan and grabbed him, pleading desperately and pathetically.

"Please...you have to help me. There are things in there, terrible things."

The other two operatives pulled themselves around the pipes and machinery in the center of the ship. They moved with great skill in the weightless environment, better in fact than most marines could have managed. One disappeared behind the large pieces of metal before quickly reappearing.

"It's like the AI hubs they used on our ships."

"Hubs? Are you sure?" asked Spartan.

The man nodded back without even checking.

"Yeah, I saw the vids. This is definitely the same tech."

Spartan had expected to find exactly that. He recalled the incidents years ago where the Zealots, a religious terrorist organization, had made use of biomechanical creatures to wage war on the colonies. These half-machine and half-biological systems had been miniaturized and sneaked aboard military ships so that they could be turned on the fleet. He suspected this ship had been configured to operate in much the same way.

"So this warship is controlled by that thing?" asked Porter, pointing at the pipes. Spartan heard him and was struck by how little some of the people of his age actually knew about what had happened in the past. The stories of the artificial brains controlling ships in the War had been a great scandal at the time. Now it appeared, it was nothing much more than old and irrelevant history.

"Yeah," Khan muttered. "They install the gear, and the pipes feed the brain."

Khan turned his attention back to Pontus.

"What about him?"

Spartan looked a little confused. He tapped a button and the visor of his suit hissed open to reveal his face in clear detail.

"I don't know."

He looked at Pontus and recalled the last time he'd seen the man. It had been in the last days of the War. Hundreds of Alliance marines had been sent to rescue the survivors of destroyed warships in the area. In reality, the planet had been the site of the enemy's main Spacebridge that led directly into Alliance space. Pontus and his comrades had been there, as well as machines of war, Biomechs, and legions of troops. Victory at Hyperion had ended the War but also given them the information needed to travel far into space, information that conveniently linked them directly to the shattered worlds of the T'Kari.

"Pontus, you and your comrades tried to control our

people through your facility on Terra Nova. Remember?"

He saw nothing, not even a basic glimmer of recognition from one of the enemy's masterminds. Spartan decided to take a slightly different, and potentially more dangerous, route.

"Your brother, Typhon, you must remember him? I killed him with my bare hands two decades ago."

Again there was absolutely nothing from the man's face. The ship started to shake, and both Khan and Spartan realized it was commencing an engine burst. If it accelerated away while they were on board, they would become trapped on the ship. Spartan didn't even hesitate. He swung his arm around and blasted the control system, pipes, and machinery. Chunk of plastic, metal, and finally blood, sprayed out in globs of free-floating mess. The rumble from the ship died at just the same time. An indicator light flashed on his suit; it was from the Alliance frigate ANS Serenity.

What the hell are they doing here?

Another message, this time a priority message from their transport came through over the sound system. Though he was an Alliance citizen, this operation had been fully funded through trade agreements between his teetering APS Corporation and the T'Kari on Hades.

"Alpha, we have an Alliance frigate on intercept course; they'll be here within forty minutes."

Spartan looked to Khan who showed no sign of

emotion on his face.

"If we tell them, then they'll seize the ship, and we lose the contract," he said plainly.

Spartan sighed. APS Corp really needed this business, and the security contracts on several of the key T'Kari mining installations in New Charon would keep them going for another five years. He also knew what the threat of the Biomechs had been, and could be again. Khan looked at his changing expression and knew right away what his old friend was thinking. Spartan connected directly to the communications officer on board the warship.

"This is Security Manager Spartan of APS Corporation. We've discovered potential Biomech activity on this vessel. Advise an exclusion zone until the situation is under control."

There was no immediate reply before a surprised sounding woman's voice came back.

"Spartan, I know who you are. This is Alliance controlled space, and I am preparing a boarding party of marines to search all ships in this area. Stand down and prepare to be boarded."

He hit the disconnect option and looked back to his team.

"We need to secure any prisoners and get out of here. Alliance can mop up, but we have work to do. Let's go."

He moved in the direction where Pontus had first appeared, while the other three followed with Pontus in tow. It meant he was forced to pass directly alongside the machinery and equipment in the center of the ship.

No guards other than a few substandard Biomechs. Why is that?

They found the open doorway where Pontus had come from. The room on the other side was filled with pods laid out in a massive lattice. In the center a cluster of them were all open, but there were no signs of people or anything else nearby. Spartan pushed on to reach the left-hand cluster. The pods were dark, but as he approached, the hardened glass flickered and the pod lit up. He looked at the figure inside with horror.

"Gods, have you seen this!" he cried out.

Khan stopped at his side, looking at three pods before he spoke.

"Each one if different, and there are creatures I've never seen. Some look like T'Kari. There are two more humans to the right."

Spartan moved over to one of the pods in question and looked inside. He stared intently at the face. He looked on in fascination as though gazing at some great miracle before shaking his head and pulling himself back. It contained a man, but a man he was all too familiar with.

"What is it?" asked Khan suspiciously.

"Typhon, he's in that pod and still breathing."

Khan moved along the ceiling and lowered himself down to look.

"No, it's not possible. I saw you kill him on Terra Nova."

Spartan pushed up to the ceiling so that he could pull his bodyweight behind while looking down at the pods. He counted over a hundred, of which only two more contained humans. He noticed at least five T'Kari figures, but none looked familiar to him. The others contained creatures or people he couldn't even imagine to have seen before. He finally stopped and turned back to join the others near the entrance.

"There are different types of pods in this place."

Khan looked back in the direction they'd come from as if expecting danger. Spartan pulled himself down to the floor, and his boots clumped as they made contact with the metal floor.

"The ones running around the outside all contain Biomechs of one type or another. Some of them are open, probably contained the creatures that attacked us. The others in the center are a mixture of different creatures, including people like us...and him." He finished by pointing at Pontus. Several dozen of the outer pods lit up, and light flashed down the sides of the units. Hisses and a gas or mist gushed from the seals. Then one by one each one started to unlock.

"This isn't a Raider ship. No way is it just cruising through New Charon and initiating attacks. We've found something else, something unexpected," Spartan said.

"Like a Spec Ops ship?" asked the youngest operative.

Spartan looked surprised, but also a little impressed

at the suggestion. A Spec Ops ship would make sense, at least based on the information they already had. He seriously doubted it would be of any used as a Raiding ship with its interior filled with pods and their unusual cargo. In the past, he had worked on all manner of covert operations, and this ship would certainly be ideal for the insertion of indoctrinated figures into different societies.

Maybe this is designed to train and drop off agents into different worlds?

He then remembered the number of Raiders currently making their way back from the crippled ship. The scans had shown they were T'Kari, or at the very least, they were wearing the armor and spacesuits of the T'Kari. The problem was why were they on board the Alliance ship if their sole purpose was to insert operatives into different societies? Then it dawned on him.

Of course, they must be looking for intelligence or supplies. Maybe even body parts for use in their Biomech creatures. He turned and looked at the pods. *This could be a factory ship just as much as it a Spec Ops vessel.*

He sighed, now becoming more than a little annoyed at what he'd found. Back in the War, he'd spent time aboard one of the enemy's transports and discovered similar pods where Biomechs were being constructed. The similarities were obvious between the craft, but the discovery of Pontus and Typhon was completely unexpected. If nothing else, this had changed things from a simple piracy issue to one of Alliance-wide security. That meant he was now obliged to inform the Alliance authorities, but he was stalling, knowing full well it would end up as a major loss for him personally and for his company.

"We should move, those things are opening," Porter Reade, the younger of operatives suggested as he pointed to the nearest pod.

Khan looked at the movement and lifted him arm, ready for any sign of danger to either himself or the rest of the unit. Spartan nodded firmly in agreement.

"Yes, we need to get off this ship, but I want answers as well. Can you get that pod open?" asked Spartan, pointing to the unit containing Typhon.

Porter was also the most highly rated when it came to advanced electronics and programming. It was the key reason Spartan had pushed for him to join the dwindling company. It was just this kind of job for which his talents were hopefully ideally suited. The young man nodded and jumped up, kicking at the wall. He moved effortlessly through the open space and grabbed at the pod. At the same time, the first two pods on the outer side of the ship opened to reveal the sinister shapes of Biomechs.

"Keep them busy!" shouted Spartan.

The first was riddled with holes before it could even climb out, but the second was much quicker. Even the way its legs moved suggested stronger limbs and a greater intelligence. Spartan took careful aim and struck one leg before it vanished behind the other pods. Khan started to move forward, but Spartan lifted his fist and signaled for him to stay.

"No, we need to be ready to leave. Stand your ground and cover him."

Khan took aim with his own weapon and waited for the creature to show its face. At the same time more of the pods opened, and the long limbs and vicious skulls of the creatures appeared. Spartan knew they were now in trouble, but he had to get the body of Typhon. If they could obtain intelligence from him, it could be worth more than any discovery they'd made so far. It might even save his company. He tapped the connection to ANS Serenity once again.

"This is Security Manager Spartan. We have discovered large numbers of prisoners and Biomechs on board the target ship. Please dispatch boarding parties as soon as possible. We have Pontus and Typhon in custody."

The reply was almost instantaneous.

"Spartan. Is this a joke?"

He looked directly at Pontus, still being held to avoid him escaping, and sent a still image from his suit's cameras directly to the warship.

"See for yourself. We have about a hundred prisoners, and they are all related to the uprisings."

This time there was a much longer pause.

"Spartan, there are standing orders for the capture and

execution of any remaining commanders of Echidna, the Zealots, or their allies. Can you stop her from powering up?"

Spartan took aim and fired at another two of the creatures but like the previous one, these had gone to ground. He glanced about but could find none of them. He turned to his left and back to his team.

"Porter, how much longer?"

The young man lifted a hand but continued to work.

"Just a few more seconds!"

The suit's intercom came to life with chatter from the other squads.

"Alpha, the T'Kari are back, and they're on their way to you. We held them back as long as we could, but they have machines with them. You need to get out of there!"

Spartan looked to Khan who had received the same information.

"Machines?" he asked incredulously.

"Yeah," replied Spartan slowly. "I don't want to find out. We are out of here, now!"

Luckily the pod hissed open, and Porter quickly dragged the unconscious body of Typhon and moved back toward them. A shape at the doorway caught their attention, but it was Lovett and two of his squad.

"The rest are heading back to the transport. We have the T'Kari prisoners but you need to move it! They've taken control of the engine room, and I can promise you..."

He was cut short by a massive vibration through the ship.

"Spartan, a Spacebridge has just opened in the center of the debris field. Are you off the ship yet?"

The small group moved as quickly, all trying to move the prisoners as best they could. As they rushed away from the hideous interior, the creatures scuttled about, maneuvering to find the best position to attack from. Spartan pushed past the mashed machinery in the center of what was the command part of the ship and noticed three T'Kari warriors connecting up cables. One spotted him and aimed a rifle.

"Cover!" he cried

With great effort, they dragged themselves to safety as quickly as they could. A burst of fire struck about them, rupturing the leg armor of Porter's suit. He cried out in pain as blobs of blood squirted out from the damage.

"Spartan!" called out the Captain of the Alliance vessel, "The T'Kari ship is making for the Spacebridge. Get out now or disable her engines. You have ninety seconds before you reach the point of no return."

Khan emptied a long burst of gunfire toward the T'Kari, but unlike the Biomechs, they were agile and pulled themselves behind the machinery to avoid the weapons fire. One also lifted up and shot back at Spartan. The dull rumble inside the ship increased, as did the gunfire from the T'Kari. Then one of the creatures appeared and pushed away from the wall. To Spartan and his comrades' surprise, the T'Kari Raiders opened fire on it and managed to kill it before it crashed nearby. More creatures appeared, but one of the T'Kari grabbed a control unit and pushed hard. The creature landed on top of him, tearing off his right arm with brutality that shocked them all. At the same time, they were all thrown back against the back walls. Spartan was pinned to the wall before realizing it had now become the floor. He picked himself up and looked to the others lying prostrate or crumpled along the wall before looking to the T'Kari. They stared right back but didn't fire.

Great, we're going through a Spacebridge on a ship filled with pods, Biomechs, machines, and whatever these T'Kari Raiders are.

* * *

Captain Alyani Tinychai watched the shape of the T'Kari warship on the mainscreen, deep inside the armored hull of ANS Serenity. No sooner had the T'Kari ship entered the breach before the Spacebridge shuddered and deactivated, leaving nothing but empty space around it.

"Get me Admiral Anderson on the horn. Something is going on out here, and I don't like it!"

Her communications officer replied smartly and went about getting a connection to the main command center in the System. Captain Tinychai, in the meantime, turned her attention back to the area of space where the Spacebridge had been. The remains of the crippled Alliance ship were still out there, as well as a hidden civilian transport and shuttles. She sighed before turning to her XO.

"This isn't good. I need drones out there to check the ship."

She turned and pointed to the transport.

"As for her, get a boarding party on board. I want her Captain brought aboard for questioning."

Her XO saluted and turned to his console.

"Captain, Admiral Anderson is on the line," her communications officer called out.

She nodded and pressed the button, activating the audio and video connection at her end. The face of the aged but experienced Admiral appeared.

"What is it Captain?" he asked, almost in a bored tone.

"Admiral, we've just located the remains of a derelict ship, as well as a T'Kari Raiding ship. We assume it is one of those that have been attacking T'Kari colonies in the area."

"And?"

"Well, Sir, Spartan from the APS Corporation was also here. He was on board the Raider vessel when they entered an uncharted Spacebridge. It has now closed, and there is no sign of the ship, or of Spartan and his operatives."

This news seemed to get the Admiral's attention. He paused as he considered the news he'd just received.

"Secure the area and lay out surveillance probes. I will

be in touch shortly."

The screen went blank, and she was left to consider her options. She was a young Captain, perhaps the youngest in the fleet, but she was also known for playing by the rules and taking no chances. If what Spartan had said was true, then something suspicious was going on, right under their noses.

Whatever is happening out here, I'm going to figure it out, she thought seriously before turning to her navigator.

"Bring up all the charts for this region of space and overlay functioning, collapsed, and potential Spacebridge sites. Things are not as they seem."

CHAPTER FOUR

New Charon was the first Star System to be colonized in the rich cluster known as the Orion Nebula. Just months after the arrival of ANS Beagle, great fleets of military and civilian ships spread through its moons and planets. New Spacebridges would eventually be constructed and the great Network expanded to include dozens and finally hundreds of stars. Few realized how New Charon would become the Nexus of a myriad of peoples, our own included.

A Concise Guide to Interstellar Travel

Teresa entered the conference room aboard ANS Beagle with some feeling of trepidation in her heart. Alongside her walked the great bulk of Gun, the leader of the Jötnar, and right now, the only person she could honestly trust. As she moved inside, she thought back to the message she'd just received from the APS Corporation's head office. A number of the senior executives had sold off their stock, and she half expected a hostile move to occur at any moment. Teresa really wished for it to just be over so she could get out of the business. Inside the room, she spotted the figure of Admiral Anderson, as well as several Alliance and T'Kari officials, and her attention immediately turned to them. The door shut behind them and Gun looked to her, a suspicious look on his face.

Okay, what the hell has Spartan done now?

The Admiral beckoned for her to sit down, and she calmly complied. If it had been anybody else, she would have remained upright, but Anderson was a man with which both she and Spartan had a long history. They'd met during the operation to rescue Spartan at Prometheus and had worked together ever since on a great variety of operations. Admiral Anderson had been the commander of the Prometheus Research facility on the other side of the bridge, but in recent months had transferred permanently to this new sector of space where he was responsible for all Alliance activities. She made herself comfortable and then looked directly across the table toward the seated Admiral.

"Ms Morato, thank you for coming to see me," he started.

It was formal, and in her experience that wasn't a good thing.

"Gun, you are always welcome here."

Gun nodded but said nothing. Words meant little to him, only action, and he had yet to hear anything from the assembled group. Unlike the others, he remained standing, mainly because none of the chairs were suitable for his great bulk.

"You've heard the news with regards to the bill that has just been pushed through by the Senate? All private security companies have been blocked from working on board Alliance funded facilities. This includes stations, ships, and bases such as this one. I know this is a blow to you and Spartan. You built this company up with hard graft after leaving the Corps. I understand that investors from the Carthago Trade Consortium are in the process of initiating a hostile takeover of APS Corp. That's got to be hard for you?"

Teresa inhaled and did her best to suppress feelings of anger. She'd only just heard the news herself and was livid. The Consortium was an entity built from a number of traders, mining companies, and speculators. They'd become rich in the last year, while APS had been hit as public support faded for the private security companies. But what worried her most was the anti-Biomech language being used by their executives.

"Yes, Spartan would be furious if he was here. If they succeed, their first order of business is to cancel all contracts with Biomech operatives. We have over three hundred on our books, half being Jötnar."

"Your people are the finest warriors we have met. You will always find work alongside out people," said one of the T'Kari while gazing upon Gun.

The alien's voice was synthesized, as with all of their species, due to their reliance upon their suits' inbuilt translator system. Gun's great size and strength had been a source of great wonder to the T'Kari. His people had been treated as honored guests ever since, much to the surprise of Alliance High Command. Admiral Anderson looked taken back by the announcement from the aliens.

"Ms Morato." He was formal for the benefit of the others present. "Things are changing fast in this sector. We are having a hard time keeping up with what is happening."

He nodded to the three T'Kari representatives who waited patiently.

"Since meeting our friends here, we have started to learn a great deal about the many worlds outside of our own systems. There are stars, planets, and races we never knew existed before. The T'Kari are the first, and we hope to meet others, if any of them still exist. There are many questions coming from our politicians, generals, and the public at large. Who are we? Where do we come from, and are we related in some way to the T'Kari?"

The three aliens sat motionless in their civilian body armor, listening patiently as the suit translators altered the sounds into their own tongue. The suits were very much like those worm by their warriors but missing most of the armored plates and extra equipment. Their resulting figures were similar but far more slender than that of humans and their skin pale like glossy alabaster.

"Nonetheless, this isn't important right now. As of today, we have some rather more important issues to contend with. As you know the Alliance has established a number of bases through T'Karan, at the invitation of the T'Kari."

Teresa nodded but still found it odd that the region of space so recently called New Charon had changed name. She recalled hearing something about the T'Kari calling the star T'Karan, and that their name derived from the star itself. It had been a political decision, but she suspected many in the Alliance would continue to use its given name. The Admiral continued explaining, this time in a slightly quieter voice.

"Many T'Kari have visited our own worlds to share knowledge, technology, and resources. In many ways this is our Golden Era, and our citizens have embraced them with surprising courtesy."

He stood up and walked around the room to Teresa.

"Plans have been in motion for over a year now to send an expedition with T'Kari guides to visit ancient worlds that we have never even heard of. The opportunities in the worlds of science and economics are staggering. All of this has been accelerated because of a new development that involves your husband."

He looked at Teresa. She could see his expression already changing.

"As you might expect, Spartan has managed to get himself into another situation, and one that has now altered the direction and timeframe of this operation. He's got himself into trouble," he then looked over to Gun, "and so has Khan."

This part grabbed the attention of the weary looking Gun. As the unelected leader of his own people, he was well used to responsibility, but Khan was something else. They were like brothers, and the group of four had witnessed some of the greatest and most violent events in the history of the Alliance together.

"He's managed to get himself into major trouble again, this time with a group of T'Kari Raiders in the asteroid belt. It's about two astronomical units from the red subgiant star here in T'Karan."

Gun looked down to Teresa, who was by now looking very worried.

"What exactly was he doing there that caused this situation?" asked the Admiral.

Before Teresa could answer, one of the T'Kari lifted her hand. She started to speak; there was a short delay before the suit converted the voice to something more familiar.

"Spartan and the APS Corp were carrying out security work on behalf of our mining outposts in the asteroid belt. Raiders have been appearing and attacking our transports. We arranged a contract with APS to assist us with the capture of them."

Teresa looked at the T'Kari and wondered why they were unconcerned at giving up private information so freely, and for no obvious benefit to themselves. She looked to Anderson and noticed he didn't seem suspicious of the information; it looked more like he was worried about something.

"Admiral Anderson," she started, "the T'Kari Raiders are a small group of perhaps five or six ships and several hundred exiled T'Kari that have been preying on their brethren for years. If you recall, last year when the T'Kari co-signed the Hades Accord, they provided us with a detailed history of their people, and we did the same for them."

Admiral Anderson nodded in agreement.

"Yes, I am well aware of the information the T'Kari shared, as well as the information that is only now coming to light since your last little, well, assignment?"

Teresa looked at him and then to the T'Kari who looked on with nonplused expressions on their faces. Admiral Anderson continued speaking before she could say any more.

"The Raiders started attacking at roughly the same time as our victory at Hyperion. It would appear that our victory also weakened the enemy's outposts in T'Karan. We've found the remains of the Rift entrance, as well as factories and equipment on Hades. Something remained in this part of space though, and the T'Kari are now telling us that it might be to do with a number of their recent exiles."

Teresa was surprised at the tone used by Anderson. She knew him well enough to recognize that he was angry, and perhaps a little disappointed at the information he'd received from the T'Kari. It didn't come as much of a shock to Teresa, however she was surprised they had given them so much information to start with. The slightly taller of the aliens nodded and then spoke with hushed tones. The translator built into the armored suit worn by the alien altered her voice. It was machinelike but perfectly serviceable English.

"We brought this matter up with your Senate, and they assured us that your ships had T'Karan secure. We were still the victims of three Raider attacks."

Anderson scratched his temple with frustration.

"Yes, and we stationed five Alliance vessels around your moons for protection. The last attack was forced back, and we destroyed the ship before it could escape."

The T'Kari representative nodded in agreement.

"Yes, and for that we are thankful. Even so, we arranged an additional contract for extra security to assist with the protection of our people, especially after the losses we sustained after the attack on Hades. APS has provided us with large numbers of excellent operatives. Without them, the Raiders would have taken even more slaves."

Teresa tilted her head to Gun.

"The Jötnar are the most requested of our personnel for this kind of work. Any time Raiders arrive, they always give ground. It is like they have a genetic fear of them."

Admiral Anderson sighed as though becoming bored with the discussion.

"Look, I know where Spartan was and what happened. What I don't know is why he was there. How did he find it?"

"It?" asked Gun, now intrigued.

He said no more and waited for Teresa to explain. She paused for a moment, knowing full well that there were a number of implied levels of secrecy involved with her contract. The T'Kari nodded to her in a gesture she could only assume meant it was acceptable for her to speak.

"Very well." She looked at them before turning back to the Admiral. "Khan's people found a lead, and Spartan was leading four of our best teams to investigate. The plan was not just to stop the Raiders. This time we were supposed to capture them, and if possible, return them to Hades for trial."

The Admiral turned to the T'Kari.

"Your capital? When were you going to tell us that you were paying Alliance citizens to conduct private operations in this Sector?"

The senior of the three remained motionless, with just

her mouth moving.

"T'Karan may be under the jurisdiction and protection of the Alliance, but we will continue to exercise our right to self defense, as well as to operate under our own laws on our colonies."

The other two nodded politely in agreement. Now Teresa was beginning to worry. The Admiral seemed to be avoiding the one subject she was most interested in; that of her husband, Spartan.

"What has happened?" she blurted out, unable to keep quiet any longer.

The Admiral leaned on the table, trying to look as compassionate as a man in his position could be. The T'Kari listened in, but it appeared they were already familiar with what came next.

"It seems that whatever Spartan found has become more than just of interest to the T'Kari. He found a ship alright, but it didn't just have T'Kari Raiders, It was also infested with harvested Biomechs."

This caught Gun's interest. Like all the Jötnar, he had made it his duty to find and rehabilitate all and any Biomechs. The harvested creatures were something else though. Like Frankenstein's monster, they were actually constructed from the material of the dead or dying. Whereas Gun and his fellow Jötnar were actually synthetically manufactured, but some would argue that their raw material was still originally sourced from the same place, but perhaps not directly to their faces. The Admiral stood up and moved back to his previous position on the other side of the table. He then beckoned to one of the naval officers, an old, white-haired Captain she was unfamiliar with. The man tapped something on his secpad, and a three-dimensional model instantly projected over the table. The Admiral then continued.

"Now, you can see the main asteroid belt that lies between the second and third planets of T'Karan. We've received contact from one of our patrol ships, ANS Serenity out on patrol in this sector. They found Spartan and several others on board a T'Kari Raider and embroiled in some kind of major gunfight."

Gun laughed to himself.

"Yeah, sounds like Spartan."

Teresa looked less amused by the story, however. She had no doubt he would be involved in such a scenario, but she was also well aware that Admirals didn't request to meet with you to discuss it.

There's more to this, she thought.

"A Spacebridge opened up right in the middle of the asteroid field, and the Raider escaped."

Teresa jumped up at the mention of the ship vanishing.

"What do you mean, just opened up? Where is he? Don't you know?"

Admiral Anderson shook his head.

"No, we do not. The ship and the rest of his team

vanished with her."

Teresa looked panicked, but the Admiral lifted his hand to calm her.

"I have spoken with our T'Kari friends, and they tell me that the whole of T'Karan is filled with potential Spacebridge sites. They thought all were either sealed or being monitored. This one suggested there could be others, and if true, who knows what else is out there. They've already told us of the ones they know about, and we have drones and equipment monitoring each one. It would seem there are many more that we don't know about."

Gun seemed intrigued at this information.

"Yes, I saw the information on Hyperion about this. There was a map of different stars. It was like a network of tunnels."

"Exactly, though our information until now has been, well, somewhat scant," replied the Admiral.

He then nodded to the Captain nearby, and he changed the model of the asteroid belt to a number of images from the ruins of Hyperion. Teresa and Gun instantly recognized some of the designs.

"This design only shows the access points to the Network in Alpha Centauri, as well as the key nodes in other star systems and galaxies. What it doesn't show is the detailed maps of other areas. T'Karan, for instance, all it shows is one connection in and a dozen more heading back out. Each of these is being guarded by drones and T'Kari and Alliance patrols."

Teresa tried to absorb the information, but the thought that Spartan, the person she cared about the most other than her children, simply overrode her other thoughts. With every extra word they spoke, she imagined the horrors he might be facing with creatures, machines, and alien worlds, all of them light years away. The Admiral continued speaking, but his words started to fade into background noise. Eventually, it lowered, and she looked back at the Admiral to see him staring at her, waiting for a response.

"Well? What do you think? Are you up for this operation?"

She looked over to Gun who actually looked quite excited at the prospect. She considered asking for confirmation, but the idea of explaining that she hadn't been listening was far from ideal. Instead, she nodded politely before asking one last question.

"What about Spartan?"

The Admiral looked to the T'Kari and spoke quietly before moving back to her. His face was serious, and it was clear that whatever had been discussed was significant to both the Alliance and the T'Kari.

"If this mission succeeds, it will give us our only chance of finding him. More importantly, I think this is the only way we will be able to bring him back home. We need to understand the rest of this Network, and the only way to get the information is by performing a full reconnaissance of Helios and all Spacebridges from it."

Gun snorted at the comments.

"Spartan is no fool. He has Khan with him, and I have no doubts about those two. Spartan and I used to cause heads to roll, but with Khan, pah!" He turned to Teresa.

"I wouldn't be surprised to see them in control of that Raider ship and enjoying the sights of Terra Nova in the next few days."

He did his best to reassure Teresa, but even Gun found it impossible. Teresa tried to smile, but she couldn't manage it. Spartan had gone missing in the past, but this time it was different. By entering one of the Spacebridges, he had travelled to a destination that could be anything from a light year to thousands of light years away. There simply wasn't a way to track him down other than visiting every star for thousands of light years, a task that would take centuries and resources that simply didn't exist. The whole idea was in fact an almost impossible task. The door opened behind her, and in walked two marine guards. They stepped to the side and waited in silence. Gun nodded to the Admiral and then moved out and through the door. Teresa started to follow him but paused, and then turned back. Admiral Anderson had a concerned, serious expression on his face.

"I know you must have doubts, but the knowledge this expedition could obtain will help secure Spartan's life, and guarantee the safety of the Alliance. The T'Kari are willing to share critical data with our leadership, in exchange for our military support in leading this expedition to Helios. The Taskforce will assemble at Hades in three days. I will pass on the details to you."

Teresa nodded, still having no idea what she had just agreed to.

"There's just one thing," she finally said, now desperate to learn anything.

"What are we expecting to find there, and how will it help us or Spartan?"

The Admiral moved around the table, placing his hand on her shoulder. To most it would be something too familiar, but their history was complex, and the trust between them could only be earned through struggle and combat.

"Helios is apparently the center of something important. The T'Kari have not been there for a long time, but they say it will give us all the information we need to map and protect the Network once and for all."

Teresa was unconvinced. This was the first she'd heard about Helios, and the idea they would arrive to find a map detailing the arteries of space sounded like a fallacy to her. The Admiral could see her confusion, so he hardened his tone slightly.

"Teresa, this operation is critical, and for it to work it will require a combined effort that includes people from both our societies, T'Kari and the Alliance. Now you and Spartan have a colorful past, which is true. But one thing nobody can argue with is your ability to get the job done, and the T'Kari have already seen this. They want you on this operation...and so do I."

The room was quiet for a moment as he let his words sink in.

"Extraordinary times call for extraordinary measures, and we need every man, woman, and child, even Jötnar to be ready. You weren't there for the meeting of the Joint Chiefs when we briefed the President. There are concerns, serious concerns that Pontus and his cronies could show up at any time. We have the intel on Helios, but how is it going to affect us? The Alliance can't afford any more schisms. We need strength, and we need unity. More importantly though, we need a full and complete picture of what the hell is going on out there."

Teresa looked up at him and thought of Spartan, and the people that worked for their company. What he said sounded interesting, but she had other commitments now. The Admiral could see her hesitation and sensed the moment was now. He reached into his jacket pocket and handed her his secpad. She held it up, noticing it was the front page of her own military dossier. She looked back at him in confusion.

"We need you back. As of thirty minutes ago, your corporation's contracts in T'Karan were terminated, as were all those in the remaining PMC Corporations. I understand that in the next hour your senior executives will be forced to ask for emergency financial aid, or have your assets liquidated."

Teresa twisted around in surprise. Her face contorted in anger. The conversation had moved on from Spartan and this operation, to one concerned with the destruction of his company and her livelihood. She wanted to shout, but the Admiral lifted his hand to stop her from saying anything else. Gun walked back into the room with his hand on a guard's throat. He must have heard Teresa and had returned to help her.

"Gun, it's okay, stand down," she spat out, looking back at Admiral Anderson.

"Due to the launch of the operation, our resources in New Charon will be spread thin. I've been given the authority to appropriate any assets I deem necessary to secure this region. APS Corporation has resources, people, and skills that are needed. It will remain as a shell corporation, with your employees signing new contracts with Alliance departments, if they so wish. If you agree to this, it is my firm intention to look after your people and what is left of your company's finances. All executives will be offered posts in the Alliance bureaucracy already being established out here."

Teresa knew Anderson was a loyal friend, and there was little, if any chance he would try to take advantage of her or of Spartan. She could only assume this was a plan he had been working on to ensure that APS Corporation continued to function, even after being officially shut down.

"What if I say no?" she asked.

Anderson smiled.

"Well, actually, I heard a rumor that the hostile takeover is imminent. You can wait it out, but do you really want to be part of a failing Corporation as it is stripped apart by its new owners? This way your people keep their jobs, and you retain at least some of your assets."

Teresa had half expected something like this to happen. APS was on its knees, and she was surprised they'd staggered on this far. Only the T'Kari contracts had kept them in the black. The more she listened to Anderson, the clearer it was becoming he'd planned this little rescue for some time.

"What about our operatives and combat teams? What about us?" she asked, pointing to herself and to Gun.

Admiral Anderson seemed to positively glow at this question.

"My friends, I would like you all to reconsider your re-enlistment into the Corps. The Chairman of the Joint Chiefs has given me the authority to reinstate former personnel, and I have a position for both of you and any of your crew, if you're interested. I cannot assign you to my command staff. That would raise many questions. But

I do have a unit that is in a shambles. It needs people with experience to whip it into shape, and you two are definitely in that bracket."

Teresa looked to Gun who appeared equally surprised.

"I could do with your leadership as well, Gun. A Jötnar commander is just what this unit needs, and it will mean you will both be very close, if and when I need people I can trust," the Admiral added mysteriously.

The hostility towards Gun's people was well known in the Alliance. It had led to them being removed from the Marine Corps itself, and was one of the main reasons Gun and the others had turned to mercenary work or operating with the private contractors. The chance to return to the Corps rather than stagger on with the ailing business was tempting. Anderson beckoned to them both.

"I suggest you get packed for your trip. You need to get going, and fast!"

She looked a little confused, but he added just a few more words.

"I've forwarded data on the fleet and those commanders present, Major. You might check the force disposition of your new battalion. Your clearance levels have been restored, as has your payment account with the Alliance."

With that he beckoned to the door where Gun waited patiently. Teresa was now even more confused than before. Gun, on the other hand, looked even happier at whatever they had just signed up for. She shook the Admiral's hand

and finally left the room. The door shut and left the two of them out in the corridor. Two marine guards watched but said nothing, instead acting like statues or sentinels. Teresa started to walk to the right side of the corridor, and once Gun caught up started to speak.

"Did you get any of that?"

Gun burst out laughing, and the loud roar of his powerful voice echoed down the corridor like a mechanical hammer. His frame was massive, and next to the slight body of Teresa he looked more like a giant. They passed by more marines, and each of them glanced at him before turning their eyes away. The Jötnar had been an important part of the Alliance for years now, but the sight of one in the flesh was always a cause for conversation. Gun had been the first of his kind to turn on his makers and had a reputation for violence but also fairness. He was also the leader of his entire race, and that was something of great interest to all those aboard ANS Beagle. The fact that the leader of the most powerful race in the Alliance chose to work with APS Corporation was one of their greatest assets, and a reason behind their success. They moved on further down the corridor before he finally answered her.

"Teresa, you managed to miss that? You just agreed to assist with the combined Alliance-T'Kari Helios Expedition."

She stopped and looked hard at him.

"The combined Helios what?"

Again the leader of the Jötnar laughed and shook with pleasure. Like all of his people, he had little time for politics or discussion. He liked to explore, fight, and eat. Though sometimes even the most bizarre topics seemed to amuse him, in this case it was Teresa. Everything else to the Jötnar was a chore.

"It is a mission to another part of space, a place we have never seen or heard of before. Anderson said the T'Kari call Helios the holy place that links the seven peoples together at a single point. They suspect there will also be a link back to our own system. They have been cut off from there for a century because of the wars with the enemy and his followers, and it control access to hundreds of worlds."

Teresa stood in disbelief at what he'd just said.

"Wait. We're sending an expedition to this place? Where is it?"

Gun actually seemed to genuinely smile at this news.

"We don't know yet. It is a secret. The T'Kari say they guard it, but no ship has traveled there for a century. That is why we will go together, one big happy family."

He then leaned closely as if sharing a great secret.

"Somehow I think this peaceful expedition will include a lot of warships and marines, don't you?"

Teresa felt so stupid that she had managed to miss the most important part of the briefing. By her estimate, she must have drifted in and out through twenty minutes of talking and discussion. Spartan had managed to get into trouble before, but this time it was different. Her children were away, and all but her most distant relatives were light years away on Carthago. Even though her old friend Gun was there, she could feel coldness in her body; the coldness you felt when everybody else had gone and just you were left. Not even her company remained to offer much in the way of solace.

How the hell did I miss all the detail? Is this dementia?

She started to worry. In theory, it was possible with her in her forties, yet medical knowledge and genetic manipulation had progressed so far that she had the body and fitness of a woman twenty years younger. There were marines in service now that were still passing the combat fitness tests in their sixties. These weren't generals either, these were low and middle-level officers that moved and fought in the frontline with their troops.

No, it has to be something else. It must be the stress catching up with me.

They continued along the corridor with a cheery looking Gun and a mortified looking Teresa. The more she thought, the less she could believe the words from Gun's mouth. She started to worry that either her memory or mind was starting to fail her. This part of the ship was slightly different and consisted of a much narrower corridor, but with a long run of narrow windows running down one side. It provided a perfect view of the Rift that would take any ship in this system directly back to Alpha Centauri and the many worlds of the Alliance. Sitting just in front of the Rift was the menacing shape of the jewel of the Alliance Navy, a Crusader Class warship. These mighty vessels were of a similar size to the older designs of cruisers but required less crew. They were fitted out with more advanced weapons, artificial gravity, and enough space to carry a powerful contingent of marines. They were truly the first universal ship design. Teresa looked at the vessel for a moment before turning her attention back to their operation.

"Gun, how much did I miss?"

He looked to her and smiled gently.

"Couple of minutes, Anderson said he'd go over the details with the leaders of the expedition on Hades. We need to leave quickly. The ship is on her way to Hades and leaves within the hour."

"Ship?"

Gun nodded slowly.

"Yes, we're getting a ride on the most powerful ship in the entire fleet, her."

Teresa looked back at the grey warship as a number of fighters moved past her flanks. Another ship came through the Rift and moved slightly above the first ship.

"Which ship is that?" she asked, though more to herself.

"Anderson said we were getting ANS Crusader, and he wants us as part of this big adventure."

Crusader, huh? The flagship of the entire Navy.

She looked at the vessel for a moment and back at her friend, suddenly remembering the words from Admiral Anderson.

"Major?" she exclaimed.

Gun simply beamed back at her.

"Don't you remember? We're both back in the Corps."

She looked at him with nothing but bewilderment on her face.

Gun roared with laughter and banged his fist against the window, much to the horror of a group of passing marines. Teresa noticed he seemed more alive and more excited than he had in years. She tilted her head slightly, and he looked back.

"My people are finally managing to govern themselves. I need a break, and some time back in the Corps is exactly what my muscles need! Hell, if this works out maybe we'll get more of my brothers into the Corps. Wictred and Hunn managed it; maybe we can get some more in?"

With that, he tensed his arms and clenched his fists, feeling the blood pumping through his massive body. Teresa couldn't but be in awe at the sight of him, yet seeing him becoming excited at the prospect of action returned her mind to their many battles in the past. Like him, she'd enjoyed her service, but she never had the bloodlust or pleasure in battle that he seemed to have.

Still. I need to do something to help Spartan, and taking part in this expedition is better than sitting around and waiting for APS to die, she thought, while the great bulk of Gun continued to writhe about in excitement at his prospects.

"Gun, you are one crazy bastard!" she laughed.

CHAPTER FIVE

The T'Kari were as unexpected as the results of the Helios Expedition. With different races to compete with, and new trade routes opening up almost daily, the prospects for humanity were simply to rise to the challenge or to fall aside. Luckily for all of those in the Orion Nebula, humanity chose the former.

Orion – The future?

Spartan opened his eyes and looked about the interior of the ship. As before, the lighting was poor, and it took a few seconds for his eyes to adjust. His suit's heads-up display indicated that only a small number of his operatives remained on the vessel. The connection to the transport had gone, as had the connection to the shuttles.

Great, that's a good start.

He lifted himself up and instantly felt the pull of gravity.

Either the artificial gravity was functioning on the ship, or more likely, the engines were still on full burn and creating a single gee of gravity as a side effect. He spotted the shapes of his comrades nearby. They appeared to be unconscious though none appeared dead; at least the information in his armored suit told him otherwise. According to the suit's sensors, he was now almost completely out of oxygen and power.

Dammit, what's it like out there?

A quick glance inside the armor showed both gravity and a safe, breathable atmosphere. He didn't hesitate and immediately activated the seal on his helmet. The visor hissed open, and the odd, damp smell of the ship's interior wafted inside. Khan was started to stir nearby, and he walked over to check on his friend. There were bullet holes nearby but no signs of an enemy. As he moved to Khan's side, he tried hard to remember what had happened. He recalled the creatures, and then finally the images of the pods in the room returned to him. It was the sight of the unconscious Pontus and Typhon that shocked him to his core. He almost tripped over at seeing the face of the most hated men in the Alliance.

"What happened?" asked Khan.

Spartan looked around the corridor and started to recall the gunfight and their failed attempt to escape. They'd been staggering and falling as the engines powered up before all had been thrown down. He could still feel the gravitational pull as they had accelerated to wherever they were going. Each of his operatives finally stood up, apart from Porter who remained on the ground, grasping at his leg wound.

"Well, I think you can assume they managed to get the engines going. What we need to know is, where the hell are we?"

He checked once more that his team was intact. Lovett and two of his own operatives were all off to the right and getting up. Upon seeing his commander, the former marine called out.

"Spartan, we've got a problem."

"Really?" replied Khan in a deeply sarcastic tone.

He walked over and at seeing the Porter, indicated for his own people to tend to the wounded man. He then quickly checked his carbine before reaching Spartan and Khan. Like Spartan, he wore his rugged complexion well for a man in his forties. Years of Marine Corps training had indoctrinated him with a firm interest in keeping both mind and body fit. He'd opened his own visor, and his face was visible to all of them.

"The last signal from ANS Serenity warned of a Spacebridge activating."

"You think we went through?" asked Spartan.

Lovett shrugged.

"Maybe, it would explain why we're picking up no signals of any kind on this ship."

"Yeah, I wondered about that. Where's the rest of the crew? Before the engines powered up we were attacked by those creatures as well as the T'Kari Raiders."

"No," Kahn said in a firm voice, "the T'Kari Raiders only fired on us when we shot at them. They killed one of the creatures that was heading for us."

The other two marines paused for a moment as they considered this piece of information. Spartan was especially surprised as he could only remember trying to shoot them, but he had no doubt in his mind of what Kahn had seen.

"Maybe they were aiming for us instead?"

Lovett moved his head back a few inches in surprise.

"T'Kari making targeting errors, are you serious?"

They were interrupted by the sound of gunfire somewhere off in the distance. Shouting followed it, but the words were unintelligible. Spartan looked at the ground, desperately looking for his weapon.

"Everyone, arm yourselves. This doesn't sound good!"

They spread out, examining the damaged equipment and broken bodies of the Biomech creatures to find their missing equipment. All but one of the rifles were quickly uncovered, leaving just Porter unarmed. Spartan unbuckled his pistol and tossed it to the injured man.

He caught the gun in his left hand and pulled out the magazine, checked the ammunition, and then readied the weapon. It made use of the same technology as the coilgun carbines used by the rest of the team but slimmed down into a pistol-sized weapon. He'd heard of the weapon, but as far as he was aware, they were only just out of the testing phase and not even ready for Alliance special forces.

"Nice piece," he said quietly, while wondering how Spartan had obtained it.

The sound from inside the ship continued but maintained a similar level of volume. Spartan looked to both Khan and Lovett. They looked equally confused at the level of noise.

"Well, what do you think?" asked Spartan.

Khan stepped away from the wreckage of their previous fight and looked further down the corridor in the direction of the gunfight. He turned his head around and threw back a smug grin.

"There's only one way to find out."

Spartan agreed and bent down next to Porter, indicating for Lovett to move closer. The man was evidently drugged and slightly confused. Spartan tapped the panels on his left arm, and a hatch opened to reveal a status indicator. It was designed for medical diagnosis and confirmed the suit had pumped in the correct levels of painkillers.

"Hey, Porter, it doesn't look so bad. I want you, Lovett, and the other three to secure this area. Wait until we get back, understood?"

Porter nodded weakly to his commander, his eyelids fluttering as he did his very best to stay awake. Lovett, on the other hand, looked frustrated at what he had just heard.

"You want us to stay back and wait? What if you run into trouble?"

Spartan smiled grimly.

"If Khan and I can't handle it, then we have seriously big problems. I'll take Isamu as well. He'll be handy if things need blowing up."

The young operative grinned at the comment but not sure if it was actually intended as a complement. Spartan leaned in closer to Lovett so that only he could hear his next words.

"If something happens to us, it will fall to you to get the rest out alive. I'm counting on you."

James Lovett, the APS operative, friend, and former marine saluted back in style to which the two of them were most familiar with. Spartan straightened up and returned the salute. It was a simple gesture, but to the other operatives it marked the distinction between those that worked together and those that had served together in the past. Only Khan, Lovett and Spartan could claim that bond at this time. Spartan looked to the others and moved off into the corridor. Khan stomped alongside him, his massive feet crunching on the ground, and his weapon at his waist but ready for action. Isamu almost had to jog to keep up. The corridor appeared to run the length of the ship and included narrow doorways at fixed intervals on both sides that led to a variety of different rooms. Isamu moved off to examine the first pair of doors. There was a surgery on one side, and on the right lay a small medical bay with a dozen beds. They were both empty of either people or equipment. He looked over to Spartan and Khan.

"Empty, nothing in either of them."

They pushed on and past a set of security rooms. These were of more interest and while Isamu and Khan guarded the corridor, Spartan slipped inside one of them. It was shaped almost like an upturned mushroom, with lockers and cases fitted to the curved walls. There were empty weapon racks and an observation station that appeared to be nonfunctional. One light flickered on a console, but as he reached out to touch it, the light flashed three times and went out.

Weird, he thought, surprised.

Spartan moved back into the corridor and was immediately taken aback by the sounds coming from no more than fifty meters away. It was the unmistakable howl of Biomechs as they stabbed and thrashed at an unseen foe. Lovett and Isamu were already tucked behind the nearest bulkhead, with their carbines trained in the direction of the sound. Spartan kept low, checked his weapon, and then looked in the same direction. About three more doors along the lights were all out, but there were black shapes moving.

Your visor, you fool!

He activated the setting, and the visor dropped back down, along with its plethora of readings from the suit's inbuilt sensors. Just a quick selection with the retina-based scanner tool allowed him to select the different imaging modes. Thermal quickly picked up body shapes, but when he overlaid infrared, he could see a confused but terrifying image. A group of the Biomech creatures was busy thrashing away at the shapes of four humanoid warriors.

"Uh, Spartan, are you seeing this?" Lovett asked.

He must have been using the same vision modes as he quickly spotted the shapes out into the distance. He pointed with one hand, and Spartan concentrated his vision on the four humanoids. At first he had as hard time identifying them, due to their thermal signature being effectively camouflaged, presumably with technology of some kind.

Who the hell has that kind of equipment?

As soon as he thought it, he knew the answer.

"It's got to be the T'Kari, maybe the ones we saw earlier?"

Khan took aim with his weapon but didn't fire. Spartan watched for only a few more seconds before satisfying him that the T'Kari were truly in combat and that it wasn't some sort of ruse.

"Okay, we move in fast and clear the area. Do not engage the T'Kari unless fired upon. Understood?"

The two nodded in agreement and as one, the three of them covered the short distance toward the battle. As they moved nearer, it became obvious that the humanoids were fighting a losing battle. One was either dead or badly wounded; the others were falling back and firing short bursts to keep the creatures back. They moved so fast that by the time Spartan had opened fire, they were almost back to where he was standing. The gunfire from Spartan and Isamu took chunks out of the first Biomech and sent it crashing to the ground just as it was lunging for one of the alien humanoids. The other three jumped to the sides and accelerated toward Spartan.

"I have this!" shouted Khan.

He emerged from the cover and with his right arm lifted, aimed directly for the creatures. Unlike the carbines used by the other operatives, his was attached directly to him armor and benefitted from both the stability the suit offered, as well as the larger capacity magazine that fed from inside the armor. With a bright flash, he filled the corridor with mag rounds, aiming directly for the creatures' torsos. Although the others carried on shooting, it was the continuous and accurate fire from his gun that brought down two of the beasts. The third managed to get close enough to leap at them.

"Get down!" cried Spartan, and both he and Isamu rolled to the side to avoid the monstrous thing. It lashed out but only Khan remained, and he refused to give ground. It landed directly on top of him and twisted his arm to the side to avoid the gunfire. He staggered back but incredibly managed to stay upright.

"Burn, you bastard!" he called out, dropping down on his left leg to move his center of gravity. The two pushed against each other, but Khan was by far the most skilled. He finally managed to upright the creature so that it lost its balance and collapsed onto its side. Khan ripped out a savage weapon that looked more like a medieval mace than anything more complex and brought it down hard against the thing. With a splatter of blood and gore, he killed it but continued striking; making absolutely certain it was dead. He stood up to check on his comrades.

"Spartan, you alive?" he called out, with barely a breath out of place.

The other two APS operatives emerged from the dark sides of the corridor, both covered in blood from Khan's savage and violent assault. They kept their weapons raised though, aiming them directly at the three standing T'Kari Raiders. Spartan moved in front of them and lowered his weapon, lifting his left hand in a submissive gesture. The Raiders looked at each other and spoke several words before also lowering their firearms.

"Well, this is interesting, don't you think?" he asked sarcastically.

The six stood in silence, each looking at their opposite numbers and probably thinking exactly the same thing.

Isamu had never seen their kind up close before, but both Khan and Spartan had on several occasions, not least when they'd fought alongside them on Hades nearly two years earlier. Though identical in build to their kinsmen throughout New Charon, there was something very different about them. It took a few seconds before Spartan realized their armor was scored and marked from attacks. At first, he assumed it had been from the battle, but the more he looked, it was clear the damage had been caused over time. Their armor was dark grey or black, and none of them carried T'Kari issue weapons.

"What do we do?" asked Isamu.

Khan stood out in the open, his mace in his hand still dripping blood onto the floor. The Raiders looked at each other once more. One lifted his hand and beckoned for them to follow. He turned and walked away with the other two directly behind him.

"Well?" asked Isamu.

Khan looked to Spartan with bemusement.

"Follow them, but don't get too close. They may not be great in hand-to-hand, but they are damned fast, and they might have friends down there."

They followed at a safe distance, keeping their weapons low but doing their best to not look too threatening. They moved past a number of doorways until finally reaching a set of three wide airlock seals. The leader of the group said something to Spartan, and then did something with his hand on the door. It hissed and all three hatches unscrewed to reveal the lavish interior of a starship. Dozens of screens, computers, and equipment filled the interior but appeared to be completely empty of people. The Raiders moved inside and made directly to the front where the curved black wall showed line after line of green text. Spartan stopped and examined it carefully. He'd seen the T'Kari writing before, but none of this made much sense to him.

"Where are we?" he asked.

Spartan forgot for a moment that these particular aliens seemed to lack the knowledge of their kin with regards to conversation with other races. Again the leader said something and moved its hands over the computer units. A number of sounds flickered through this part of the ship and other displays powered up.

"Spartan, do we want to be here?" asked Isamu with trepidation.

With a flash, the dark, curved wall changed to the ink blackness of space. At first it was as if the wall had vanished, but Spartan had seen this technology plenty of times before.

"Don't worry. It's either a projected display or the outer skin can make itself transparent."

He tried to sound confident, but with every sound his hand kept moving toward his carbine that hung loosely on its sling. As he watched, his eyes adjusted to the light, and he could see hundreds, then thousands of dots from the stars that surrounded them. A haze like the gas of a nebula filled the lower half, and a group of gray shapes to the right resembled a shoal of fish. It took a few more seconds to realize that it was in fact a formation of ships.

* * *

Teresa waited inside the CIC of ANS Crusader with a look of disbelief on her face. The rest of the crew went about their duties as normal, but there was nothing normal about the fleet assembled in front of her. In her decades of military service, she'd witnessed many war fleets; most of the time when being shipped to another battlefield on board a Marine Transport, such as the venerable ANS Santa Cruz. Teresa Morato was present during the epic space battle around Prime back at the start of the War. Her body still winced at the memories of the injuries she sustained while landing under fire on the Titan Naval Station. Even so, the sight of such an armada of Alliance warships, civilian transports, and a small group of T'Kari ships was something she'd never before seen.

"This is supposed to be a peaceful expedition?" asked Gun with amusement.

Teresa turned an eye to him, noting the self-satisfied expression on his face.

"Gun, you don't have to come," she suggested

mischievously.

"Why not? Hyperion is running just fine with the chiefs in charge. I could do with a little action."

"What makes you think there will be action?"

Gun nodded to the assembled ships.

"You think they are all there because we are expecting an easy ride. Trust me on this one. Helios is not going to be as simple as they say it is."

He then pointed to the Crusader class warships.

"If you ask me, the Alliance has a plan, and they aren't keeping us in the loop. You've heard the rumors of Biomech ships like that Guardian ship the T'Kari destroyed in the Rift."

He leaned towards Teresa.

"I've heard that others ships have been spotted moving in and out of this part of space."

Teresa exhaled slowly, almost sighing at his words.

"Come on Gun, you know better than to listen to the gossip on this ship."

Gun raised his eyebrows in amusement.

"If you say so."

Teresa was still surprised at how his use of language had altered over the years. She remembered him back when they'd first met as enemies on Prometheus. He and a small group of his kin had turned on the Zealots and their masters and helped them to escape. He'd only known a few words back then and had carried a massive Gatling gun strapped to his arm. It had earned him the moniker Gun and it had stuck ever afterwards.

"We're meeting on Hades within the hour for a full briefing with the General and the main T'Kari and Alliance commanders. Maybe we'll learn a little more then?"

Gun shrugged at her, evidently unconvinced at her suggestion. She looked back at the assembled fleet and gazed at the powerful lines of the many Crusader class warships. They were large and filled with weapons and marines. It sent a shudder through her body as she recalled her own experiences when forces of this size were assembled. Then she thought of Spartan and tried to imagine what he could possibly be up to. That directed her thoughts to their venture since leaving the Marine Corps, the APS Corporation. As they were leaving, she'd had a short but angry conversation with the remaining board members. Almost all of them were looking to dump their shares. It had been painful, but their actions had made it much easier for her to cut her links with the company. She'd handed over control of the major assets still technically belonging to the company to the Alliance before relinquishing control. Those still working would be given the option of leaving with a modest financial package, tempting offers of work as contractors for the military, or enlistment with a bounty. She suspected the older generation would take the money.

I wonder what Spartan would think.

Based on those she knew, she was convinced the majority of the combat operatives would choose direct NCO entry to the Corps after a short retraining interval. It wasn't ideal, but she kept telling herself that any other decision would have left them in a much worse position. Gun looked at her and knew she was thinking about the recent events prior to leaving ANS Beagle. The XO of the ship approached them both.

"Commander," he said while nodding to Gun and then looked to Teresa.

"Major Morato, it's good to see you back in the Corps, and your promotion is well deserved. You have served the military and the Alliance with honor and dignity," he said firmly and then tried his best to give a friendly smile. "Back where you belong."

Teresa recognized the honesty in his voice; there was genuine warmth. For a woman in her forties, it was quite a feat to be back in the Corps. It wasn't unique, of course. Many former marines had re-enlisted, but she was returning with a promotion from her final rank as Captain nineteen years earlier. Spartan had left as a full Colonel, but neither was ever likely to get much further. Teresa realizing her mind was elsewhere, returned her glance to the XO, and saluted him.

"Thank you, Sir. Has there been any news of where I am to be posted?"

The XO shook his head.

"No, sorry, Major, you will need to speak with the General on Hades. He is making a few changes. There are rumors the Jötnar Battalion may be reinstated. A concession I think to keeping the peace and also finding your mercenaries official work. Something tells me they are worried your people may get bored with the PMCs being culled."

Gun nodded happily.

"Yeah, would you rather have us on your side or waiting about for somebody with a cause?"

The XO couldn't tell whether he was joking. The Jötnar leader had grown in intelligence and wit over the years, to the level that the XO actually felt he might be a better officer than some he had met on his own ship; such was the Commander's military skills and knowledge. He decided to treat it as a joke.

"Very true, I've seen your people in action many times before. I thought it was insanity to disband the Battalion to start with. Still, there will be plenty of unhappy people when they hear the news."

Gun clenched his fists in irritation.

"They can always fight their own battles, if they have the stomach for it."

The XO grinned at this.

"Quite."

He turned and walked back to the small group of officers to speak with Captain Harris, the commander of the mighty warship. He glanced at the two new arrivals and nodded.

"How does it feel to be back?" asked Gun.

Teresa smiled at him.

"Feels like I never left. Spartan would feel just the same."

* * *

The T'Kari Assembly was an unusual building. It had been carved directly into the rock of the moon, and its doors were built from the same stone. The primitive looking exterior betrayed the exquisite interior that was filled with statues of T'Kari from eons past. Teresa and Gun waited patiently inside the structure, soaking in the lavish detail. The colors had faded and there was some damage, yet the vast room retained its greatness, even after being abandoned for so long. Gun nodded toward the entrance. As Teresa turned, she spotted a procession of the alien warriors; their helmets removed and carrying their rifles up on the shoulder like a human soldier.

"They even look a bit like soldiers now, don't they?" chortled Gun.

He was less than inspired by what he'd seen of the T'Kari in combat. They were fast on their feet and agile, but their tactics were primitive. They had no idea of how to fight in close range combat. In short, they were the exact opposite of the Jötnar.

Maybe that's why they treat us like Gods? Gun wondered.

The procession continued inside with Ayndir, the T'Kari leader at the front, along with several senior figures of their people. Teresa looked around the rest of the Assembly Hall, noting there were about fifty in total, and this figure included a substantial marine contingent; as well as a Jötnar squad wearing the armor manufactured in the factories of Prometheus. She looked at each of their faces, trying to recognize as many as she could. All the company commanders for the three battalions of marines were there, as well as their commanding officers from the ships in the small fleet.

Ah, there he is.

Teresa had spotted Admiral Anderson was present. Though he now had to report directly to the new office of the Joint Chiefs, he was still the highest military authority in New Charon. She moved to the next man before noticing the movement from Gun. She could see a look of genuine pleasure on his face. There were only two people that did that, and she turned, half expecting to see Spartan, but instead it was the aged form of General Rivers, now Chairman of the Joint Chiefs of Staff. He saw her and smiled briefly before turning his attention back to the T'Kari. Standing directly behind him was the younger Brigadier General Daniels, a man with whom Teresa and Gun had fought alongside just as much as General Rivers.

"If Rivers and Daniels are here, then we can expect a fight," Gun said gleefully.

A few of the naval officers nearby snarled at him, and Gun laughed, immediately drawing the attention of those in the hall. Ayndir noticed him and bowed gently. It was a measure of the importance they placed on the Jötnar that the other T'Kari soon did the same. Normally, Gun would have simply laughed, but even he realized the solemnity of the occasion and of their response. He lowered his head in respect to them, and Teresa watched in amusement. The procession continued once more, and Teresa leaned into towards Gun.

"Bowing to the T'Kari, are you? Very nice."

He scowled at her enjoyment of his action.

"It's hard to find friends of the Jötnar. These T'Kari are the closest thing we have."

Teresa looked taken aback at his comment. He could see she was hurt, and he lifted his hand to rub his face.

"With a few obvious exceptions, of course," he said, trying to make up for it.

They turned their gaze back to the group of high-ranking people and watched them move around to the front. Teresa recalled when a more formalized command structure had been proposed. There been a lot of fuss, but she could appreciate the importance of creating a military High Command that could report back directly with the civilian command structure. It was a new system and based upon the similar system still being used by countries on Earth back in the twenty-first century. The General was now the leader of the Joint Chiefs, while active representatives from the Navy, Marine Corps, and the brand new Colonial Guard made up the rest of the body. The Guard was a territorial unit to provide disaster relief and short-term emergency forces. It lacked heavy equipment and weapons or the ability to leave their home colonies, something that was outlawed by the Senate. General Rivers had been voted in over the last year and advised the President directly on military matters. The others stood near him were unfamiliar to her.

I don't know any of you, though, she thought.

Teresa turned her attention to Ayndir who had now reached the front and turned to face the audience.

"Greetings, my friends, it is a pleasure to see you once more as we embark upon this great adventure," she said in a high-pitched voice.

It was the first time Teresa had heard her speak in English without the use of her suit's translator. By the look of the other people assembled, it was also quite clear that nobody else had either.

"Strange," Gun said quietly.

Teresa looked disapprovingly at him, but his only response was a wide grin. She looked back as Admiral Anderson and the Defense Secretary moved up to the raised area near the front, between two beautifully carved stone sculptures. They showed ancient T'Kari in primitive armor and carrying weapons that looked similar to spears. Like much of the art Teresa had seen, these two images were designed to show their physical forms off to perfection. The T'Kari leader looked to her two comrades and nodded gently. This was the first time Teresa had seen her old commander, the General, in this position. He'd rescued them during the fighting on Hades when a force had come through a Spacebridge and attempted to wrest control of New Charon. Ayndir placed her hands together, and a beautifully detailed model of a star system appeared. She started to speak, but this time it was in her native tongue, and it took a brief moment before the suit translators kicked in.

"Our two peoples have come together as friends and allies in these last two years. We have provided you with technical assistance, and you have provided manpower and security. Even so, recent events show us that our shared enemy is near. In the past, we would have hidden, but with our combined strength, we have the confidence to allow you into our circle."

The senior officers and officials nodded at these words. All of them, including Teresa and Gun, knew the basics of their operation. They were on a fact-finding mission to obtain intelligence on the Spacebridges and the enemy. It was the details that Teresa really wanted to understand however.

Okay, so you are our friend, and now you think we're tough enough to do something. Why do I think this means we will get our hands bloody on their behalf?

She looked at the alien, specifically at her mouth as she struggled with the English words.

"We have experienced much the same strife and struggle on our worlds as you have. Agents sent by the enemy also forced us into wars amongst our neighbors and ourselves for centuries. We are now all that is left of the T'Kari Empire. We are but a fraction of our former selves, but we will rebuild with our skills and your help. Today is a day that will be remembered by future generations. It is the day that our two peoples united forces against the darkness that turns us against our own people."

Ayndir nodded and seven T'Kari entered the open space. They held up seven icons on staffs. Teresa recognized one immediately as the scythe type marking that was present on the clothing and armor of the T'Kari. The others were completely new to her. She thought what they might represent, and it quickly occurred to her that they must be something to do with the other T'Kari, perhaps lost worlds or colonies. Ayndir interrupted her thinking and confounded her with her next words.

"Even though our many worlds and billions of people thrived, we were never alone. A few of our great empires were connected via Spacebridges that we built, much like the one you constructed to reach here. Over time, we located a great Anomaly in space that allowed multiple Spacebridges from different sources to coalesce in one star system. We worked together to create this system over a hundred years to create the great Network. When completed, it allowed travel to the center and then back to any of the connected empires."

The model transformed to show a convoy of ships entering a Spacebridge, only to appear outside of a massive planet surrounded by further Spacebridge entrances.

"This construction allowed travel and trade between scores of great empires in much the way we are connected to the rest of your worlds. For many star systems, it was the only way to retain contact with others, while a small number maintained additional links to each other dependent upon distances and technology."

The image changed to show a living, thriving model of hundreds of star systems with thousands of ships plying trade routes. It was an image of a system that could only be dreamt of in the far less developed Alliance. Teresa looked at it with fascination, trying to imagine what it would be like to live in a place filled with so many people and species. The map was spherical in shape with groups of stars around the outside of the ring connected by green dotted lines. Different colors then moved from each of them to the central yellow point. The image quickly changed to show badly damaged images from the surface of ravaged worlds. Great cities burned and the skies of each one were black with smoke.

"As you have already learned from our conferences on your capital world of Terra Nova, our history is just as complex as your own. For the purposes of this expedition, it is important to understand the significance of Helios. To do this we must return to the Great Enemy and his place in the downfall of the T'Kari."

Gun shook his head, and Teresa was convinced she could hear him complaining. Like him, she had heard the stories of the T'Kari and the struggles they'd been involved in. There were few in the Alliance that hadn't lapped up the stories of battle and defeat. Even now the T'Kari were something new and foreign, and that always caught the attention of the masses. As Ayndir continued, it was obvious she intended on providing far more detail than ever before.

"We are just one race of the many hundreds that we know of. Most vanished long ago, either through disease, war, loss of resources, or simply migrating to new and better places."

Teresa smelled the air in the place. It felt damp and alien. Even so, the low-level lightning and subtle mist coming in from the vast open doors gave the place an almost mystical feel.

"Each of our peoples was connected, just like the spokes of a wheel, to this central point that we call Helios. This star system is rich with worlds, people, and resources.

It is the focal point for all of us, due to the collection of Spacebridges that we built. None of us controlled this region; it was free for us all, and people from a hundred different races lived there in peace. As I explained, a small number of these systems were also connected directly to each other as well as to Helios. We suspect that your own worlds also share a hidden connection with Helios."

The Alliance leaders at the front seemed unfazed, but the audience of Navy and Marine personnel was surprised by the information. Teresa looked at their faces and to the front where Daniels was looking directly at her. He nodded as though he'd just shared important knowledge with her.

"One of the lesser races was a planet of biomechanical engineers who perfected the grafting of machine and the living. For a long time, they were one of the many people with Spacebridge connections to Helios. This was until the day they decided Helios should be theirs."

Again the imagery changed to show paintings and artworks of an ancient war, with millions of warriors locked into a never-ending struggle. Vast fleets of ships clashed with great armies of machines, and entire planets appeared to be engulfed in flames. Even Gun seemed moved by the imagery.

"The war was terrible, and for a thousand years the enemy controlled Helios. He used this time to seed planets and worlds with machines and technology that we suspect was placed in case it was needed in the future. We do not speak of their true name outside of our own people; instead, we call them simply the Great Enemy, or sometimes the Great Devourer."

She waited for a moment and looked out to her audience. They were captivated by the information, especially the details of the enemy. She looked to her own comrades before continuing.

"It was this race of people that sent agents to light the fires of insurrection, the fires that started civil wars that raged for hundreds of years. This continued until only seven of the old empires remained, and of course, the eighth, the Great Enemy."

The T'Kari lifted up their icons at this point. Those present looked at them, but without specifics, they were just faceless objects.

"What happened to the others we will never know because of what occurred next. Perhaps they managed to break the Rifts and isolate themselves. Many were destroyed, and now nothing remains of them other than their sterile worlds and ruins."

The image changed once more to show a dark gray world with nothing but rocks and debris on it. Teresa could only assume this was one of the sterilized worlds.

Doesn't look much different to this moon, she thought, deciding to keep her thoughts to herself.

"To preserve what was left, we grouped our last

forces together and forced the Enemy back into his domain before collapsing his Rift to Helios. We used the technology of the Helions to do this. With the Enemy contained, we all agreed to seal our Rifts to Helios. This was drastic and left each of us weaker, but is also denied access to the Network and our worlds. The Great Enemy was quicker, however, and in the time it took for us to leave Helios and shut down the Rifts, he left spies, equipment, and soldiers behind. It didn't take long before we turned against ourselves and tore our own worlds apart, ready for his arrival. Even without the Rifts, the Enemy retained a number of its commanders in our territories, one of which oversaw our destruction. Only by keeping the knowledge of the sealed Rift hidden, did we stop him escaping and doing the same to the others."

Ayndir lifted her hands outwards as if to encompass everything.

"All that remains of our people from that final war can be seen here."

She paused while the Alliance guests drank in her words. Only a few, including Teresa and Gun, were unfamiliar with this last piece of information. Even so, it was of monumental significance. Teresa's first thoughts were the questions so many Alliance citizens had been asking since ANS Beagle had travelled through to New Charon, deep inside the Orion Nebula.

Where is the Enemy, and why is he not attacking?

"With us beaten, the Enemy left a handful of us in hiding, though for what purpose we do not know. We wondered for many years why we had been saved, but none ever discovered the truth."

Ayndir beckoned for one of her commanders to approach. He wore scarred armor and had the look of an experienced leader about him. He stopped in front of the Alliance leaders, shook their hands, and turned to the small audience.

He spoke through the translators of his suit, "I am T'Kron, commander of the Exiles. We are the sworn defenders of the sealed Rifts. We are now just six ships and two hundred T'Kari."

Gun grinned at the sight of a T'Kari warrior, "So, have you heard of these Exiles before?"

She nodded and whispered to him, "Spartan spoke with Ayndir about them. They patrol the Rifts and watch for signs of the Enemy. They have the weapon that can disrupt and collapse Rifts. The ship that helped us was one of theirs."

Gun nodded with interest. T'Kron used his hands to change the shape of the image being shown, and this time it moved back to the rocky world of Hades, the inhabited moon on which they all currently stood upon.

"A Guardian ship was left here along with their commander, a number of agents from different worlds, and a garrison, based on this very moon."

He pointed to the ground.

"They appeared periodically and attacked us if we tried to move out from our remaining settlements, while they continued to stockpile equipment and machines. It is our belief that this force identified your worlds generations ago and established these stockpiles ready to be used to break your people, just as they did with us. They were in the process of leaving to attack you when our moon's Rift was destroyed with atomic weapons. Your work I believe?"

He paused as those in the audience familiar with the Hyperion incident considered his comments.

"With all our space-based Rifts sealed, we were finally safe, but dared not raise our heads too quickly in case it was a trick. Seventeen years later, your people arrived in our system, and that is when we found the Enemy had a secret. They had kept a back door into New Charon, a way to bring in ships and warriors when the time was right."

This news caught the attention of most of those present with surprise. Evidently, the General and the other commanders already knew of the information. Teresa could see the fear in the eyes of the Alliance officers standing alongside her. It was a fear she could understand.

Gun looked less concerned at the news, and she leaned in to speak, but a sudden hush silenced the room. The T'Kari commander hadn't finished.

"Together we held back their forces before more ships could arrive and destroy the Guardian vessel. Your arrival, and the arrival of the Enemy from this unmapped Rift, has caused us great concern. We understood that only Helios and the great wheel of Rifts could connect our empires together. Now we find there are other bridges through space. We had assumed this meant this part of space was secure. With the news from the asteroid field now public, it would seem not. There are other Rift entrances here that we are unfamiliar with. If there are unmapped points, then it is safe to assume the same is true for your own worlds, if the Enemy has any more forces in your part of space. The Enemy could potentially appear and strike any world at will, and before ships can be mobilized for defense."

This piece of information sent a shudder down Teresa' spine; the very idea of a hidden network reminded her of places like Hyperion back home. Places where Rifts had been kept hidden and allowed the movement of people, equipment, and even ships into weakly defended areas. Gun moved and pushed to the front. He completely ignored the protocols of a briefing and interrupted the commander. Two marine officers moved hesitantly to apprehend him, but he glared at them and clenched his fists; he meant business.

"I'm getting tired of secrets, hidden enemies, and agents."

He turned and looked to those watching and listening.

"Who the hell is behind all of this, and what do they want?"

The hall fell silent. It was a question so many of them had wanted to know, some for years, others for decades. Teresa felt uncomfortable, but then the mood seemed to change. At first it was the Marine Corps officers, then almost to a man they started asking the same questions.

General Rivers nodded at their words and moved to a position directly next to the T'Kari leaders. The aliens, who until now had seemed calm and confident, were starting to move about. Flustered looking T'Kari guards fidgeted at the walls as if expecting trouble.

"Quiet, please!" he called out with great authority in his voice. He then looked over to Gun.

"Commander Gun, leader of the Jötnar, and a great friend to the Alliance. I know you have questions, but this expedition must get moving and quickly. Please, let them finish their briefing."

Gun considered stepping back but then shook his head.

"No, General. Who is this Enemy? Who was on Hades, and what do they want? Where do they live, and when are we going to end this?"

The room was deadly silent, with just the deep breaths of Gun punctuating the silence. Ayndir lifted her hands and beckoned to one of her assistants. He approached, and they spoke in agitated tones for a few seconds before indicating for the General to approach. He spoke for almost a minute and then moved off to the side to make contact with somebody on his secpad. The T'Kari leaders stood silently, waiting while the General spoke in hushed tones to an unseen figure. This went on for several minutes before he moved back and simply nodded to Ayndir. The leader of the T'Kari pressed a button. The image changed to show a dark outline of what appeared to be some kind of bipedal monster. It was tall, thin, and its multiple limbs hung down low from its close fitting armor. There were only a handful of people in that open space that recognized the figure for what it was.

"Echidna," Gun hissed, surprised and angry.

"These are the foot soldiers of the Enemy, and you discovered the remains of one of them on Hades itself," Ayndir explained.

CHAPTER SIX

Echidna had started off as a simple religious symbol that had been adopted during the Uprising. Only in the last days of the War did it become clear that the demon was something more. Rumors from the marines that fought on Hyperion, suggested the demon herself had led monsters and mechanical beasts in a violent last stand. Only those that fought there ever truly knew, and no video or still imagery of the event existed in the public domain in the following months. Some of those veterans were driven mad by the things they saw in that last battle, but as always, it was the demon Echidna they spoke of.

Holy Icons

"It was the image of Echidna, the half snake, half woman that had been found in iconography for decades now. The sight of the demonic looking monster kept everybody at the summit enthralled. Khan and Spartan had seen the creature first hand through the Rift on Hyperion. Teresa had seen the shape only briefly, as it had entered the human worlds, just as it had been destroyed by the implosion. At the sight of the beast, Gun became almost excited. Teresa, on the other hand, felt very different emotions while Gun's blood pumped with excitement at the opportunity to face a mighty foe. Teresa felt nothing but worry. The creature she'd seen so briefly nearly two decades earlier sent old memories stirring through her body.

"Foot soldiers?" she said, without thinking.

Gun looked over to her with a grin. His initial surprise at being shown the image had quickly changed to excitement at the sight of something so strong and powerful. She hadn't seen him that excited in a long time.

"Yeah, now that is an enemy worth fighting!"

The audience became aroused as a dozen T'Kari entered the room and formed up around a cloth-covered column. Teresa hadn't even noticed it before, due to the low-level lighting in this part of the hall. Ayndir looked to them and nodded. Her people pulled on cords, and the fabric fell away like silk. Beneath the covers lurked the dark, twisted shape of some horrific monster. Many of those present recoiled at the sight of the thing. It was nearly twice the height of the Jötnar, standing almost six meters, and its torso was a sickening fusion of woman and mechanical beast. It was bipedal but a long serpentine tale coiled around it and along the ground. It had the limbs of the machines they had fought on Hyperion, but the body was closer to Gun and his Biomechs followers.

"This is the beast you discovered, and we suspect it was this very machine that controlled this sector before your people destroyed the Rift," explained the T'Kari.

All eyes were on the great demon.

"We recovered the body a year after and placed it here. Look at it; this is the face of the Enemy, one of their trueborn soldiers. In the past, it was rare to see one. They are masters of deceit and manipulation and use others to fight their battles for them. There are none better at biological manipulation and fusion with machines."

General Rivers looked at the monster for some time before taking over the briefing. He was one of the few there that had not been taken by surprise, and Teresa could only assume that was because this had all been preplanned days, perhaps weeks earlier.

"This is all very interesting, and you can read the full details upon your return. The President already has this data, and it is the reason we are all here."

He took in a deep breath.

"Most of you have already seen the reports from High Command, and you've already been briefed on the basics on this mission. The Alliance is stabilizing, and our new colonies out here in New Charion, but also back in Alpha Centauri, are thriving. We have a few minor problems, like the troubles on Carthago, but in general, we are doing better than ever. We've made contact with the T'Kari and even our battle-brothers, the Jötnar, are creating successful colonies with or without our help. This is a golden age for all of us and our citizens, and our politicians want it to stay that way."

He waited, watching them all carefully.

"But…there is an evil out here, an evil that turns brother against brother, and as we have seen from the images of the T'Kari, they will stop at nothing until entire societies are reduced to ash."

His face altered slightly as he spoke and described the devastation wrought by their enemies; he almost seemed to snarl.

"Our policy until now has been one of enlightened self-interest. We will get involved when, and if, it is to our mutual advantage."

He continued speaking while Teresa whispered quietly to Gun.

"Mutual advantage?"

Gun sniggered and then spotted a marine officer glare at him. He looked directly back at the short man and raised a questioning eyebrow. The man looked away. Gun turned back to see Teresa shaking her head at him and indicating at the General who continued to speak.

"The discovery of these new Spacebridges in the Orion Nebula, change the strategic situation drastically. This means the enemy could have the capacity to strike at any point, and that leaves us vulnerable and at a disadvantage. Ayndir assures me this secondary level of short-range Rifts would take months, perhaps even years for ships to navigate. She also says they would not allow a ship to reach Helios or any of the old empires. Only the long-range Rifts they, and the other races, built have the power and positioning to allow that kind of travel."

He looked out to the group of assembled officers, recognizing some of their faces, some by reputation and others personally.

"Even so, what if any of the enemy's ships from this sector were able to appear outside of Kerberos, or Terra Nova? The T'Kari assure us this could not happen, but can we take that chance? In hours they could be landing legions of troops, dropping bombs, or destroying shipyards. We have neither the manpower nor the technology to repel attacks like these."

A marine officer approached his side, spoke briefly, and walked away. The General continued.

"Some want us to withdraw from this part of space, to leave the Orion Nebula, and concentrate on our old colonies. The referendum taken last month says otherwise. Our citizens want our new territories to be protected and more importantly, they want this enemy that has started so many wars to be hunted down and destroyed. Based on this information, the President, with the full approval of the Senate, has issued orders for the military to secure our colonies, at any price!"

This news sent a chill through the room as each of the military officers digested his words. Already it was starting to sound like a call to war.

"Both I and Admiral Anderson have advised the President that we need information, and we need it as quickly as possible. We fought the last war blind and with few friends. This time we need to know as much as possible, and perhaps pick up a few allies on the way. We have been given an important mission, no, a critical mission to the survival of our species, and together with the T'Kari, we will succeed."

He looked back to the creature.

"We encountered this thing two decades ago. I was there and witnessed the fanaticism of their warriors. If these beasts are merely the foot soldiers of this enemy, then we definitely need to know more. Just one of them is a horrific opponent. An entire army could lay waste to cities. As Commander Gun has already asked, where do they come from? Who are they, and what do they want? Helios is the first-stage in answering these questions, and with that knowledge, we can put a plan into action to safeguard the Alliance. Helios is the central hub in this collection of ancient races. Even more important though, it is how the enemy can send troops to us, or to any of the other six empires, assuming they even still exist."

Ayndir nodded calmly and then started to speak in her

high-pitched voice. As before, there was a momentary delay before the translator kicked in. Teresa looked to Gun who was now mesmerized by the demon.

"What do you think?" she asked quietly.

"I think we're going to be heading somewhere dangerous. The creatures are massive!" he replied happily.

They both turned to listen to the T'Kari leader.

"We have kept the T'Kari Rift, as you call them, secret. This strategically critical region of space is our greatest secret and known to our people as the Helios Gateway. It will take us directly to Helios. The capital world is much like Terra Nova and controls Rifts that connect to dozens of star systems. Helios is at the center of this great web. From this one key point, every one of the empires can be reached. Even the lands of the Enemy can be accessed from Helios through the Dead Rift. Whoever controls Helios, will control the Network and access to the Dead Rift."

These few words captivated the audience, especially the menacing Dead Rift.

"The Helions are directly related to my own people. There are some that say they are our brothers, but we are different as we are similar. They are obsessed with science and technology, to a level that greatly surpassed our own, and use this power to control access to most of the Rifts. If they still live, they could prove a powerful ally. We will travel with your expedition to act as an intermediary, and also to take you through the Helios Gateway. I will now leave you in the capable hands of your military commanders. I will make our facilities available to you, if any require them."

She then turned and walked away from the hall along with the rest of the T'Kari. General Rivers and the others waited until every single one of them had left before banging his hands together.

"Right. Officially, we are on an intelligence-gathering mission, but I think you can all see where this is going. New Charon is our beachhead into this part of space, and it now looks like the whole area is about to get much more complicated. I've looked at the data, and it is clear that this Network of Rifts is both a major weakness and a strategic asset that we have to control. Helios maintains the Network, as well as access to each of these old empires. Once we have take over of the Network, we can monitor traffic to all of these worlds. Ayndir suspects there will be a Rift entrance back to Alpha Centauri. We can't take the chance that the enemy could get hold of this strategic backdoor. If we control this region, it means ships could travel from Terra Nova directly to Helios, and then on to any of these old empires, assuming any remain."

Several of the naval commanders started speaking in excited tones to each other.

"That's right," announced General Rivers. "That means an Alliance ship at any planet within three days! If we cannot do this, then we will have to deny it to the enemy, because he sure as hell will be doing it to us. Assuming, he doesn't already run the whole show."

Teresa looked to Gun and nodded in agreement.

"Makes sense, the quicker we have control of this thing, the quicker we can find Spartan and the others."

Gun said nothing.

"There is a good chance we will run into either these Helions, or possibly forces loyal to the Echidna if for any reason these aliens have already folded. Space is about to get very complicated, and I don't need to tell any of you how serious this is. I want every Marine unit and Navy ship ready for combat operations in the next twelve hours, even the recruits waiting for their unit replacements and new commanders. We are sending twelve warships, including six Crusader class vessels and three Marine battalions. We are also bringing science vessels, transports, and heavy equipment. Former private security units from APS Corporation have been transferred to us, and they will travel aboard the civilian ships to provide unit security."

The officers present seemed unsurprised at the news. Teresa quickly realized they must have been briefed well in advance, and she started to wonder what else had been decided without her knowledge.

"Admiral Anderson will be leading this operation, and your specific orders await you aboard your ships. If all goes well, in just under a month, we will make contact with a second civilization, expand our frontiers, and obtain knowledge to protect our worlds."

Most of those present assumed the briefing was over, but before they could leave, he nodded toward Teresa and Gun. They both shifted suspiciously.

"There is just one last thing I want to say before you leave, and it concerns Commander Gun."

All eyes were now on the Jötnar leader.

"I consider the disbanding of the Jötnar Battalion to be nothing short of a crime. I saw firsthand what they were prepared to do and still do for our citizens. When we return from Helios, it is my intention to push for its reinstatement in the Alliance. I know it is a long time in coming, but we could do with the support and strength of the Jötnar, and I am getting sick of the racism and bitterness still prevalent."

This sent a surge of interest through the group. Gun looked to Teresa with a confused expression on his face. She looked equally surprised at the news.

"In the meantime, we have access to the skills and experience of two of our most experienced leaders, Major Morato, formally of the Confederate Marine Corps and of course, Commander Gun, leader of the Jötnar and of the illustrious Jötnar Battalion. Both played a vital role in the War, and both have been reinstated to Alliance service with full Marine Corps ranks and privileges. They are joining the headquarters of the brand new and under strength 17th Marine Battalion aboard the new ships ANS Savage and ANS Sentry, where their skills will whip them into shape prior to arriving at Helios."

The other officers looked both amused and surprised at the postings. Teresa had no idea what to say with regards to the unit. She'd not heard of them, but then things had changed substantially since she'd been in the Corps. The General then turned his gaze from the audience and directly to Gun and Teresa.

"The 17th is out here for training. I need the manpower though, and you know what I need and how to get it. I expect the 17th to be a unit even Colonel Spartan would be proud of, and before we enter the Helios Gateway!"

To their surprise the assembled officers started to clap. Teresa was at a loss as to whether it was spontaneous or planned that way, but it was still a pleasant surprise for a change. The two looked at each other, but Teresa was speechless. The mention of Spartan had stunned her, especially the reaction from the Navy and Marine Corps officers present. She felt transported back to her days in the Corps, and a feeling of wellbeing pushed up through her body. Gun, on the other hand, had no problem in expressing himself and lifted both of his massive arms up into the air.

"Yes!" he roared.

* * *

Jack Morato entered the lush jungle themed training arena. It was his final test as the Alliance military assessed his performance and suitability for promotion in the Marine Corps at the end of the first year. He was dressed in a gray cadet uniform and carried an L48 training rifle. At his flanks moved two similarly equipped cadets. The only difference between them was that they were both women, and they were quickly tiring of his attempts to get their interest. Over the last year, Jack had built up quite a reputation, to the level that the female cadets either sought him out, or made a special effort to avoid him.

"I can hear them," whispered the shorter of the two women, a young oriental woman with a deep scar running along her forehead. Her name was Thai Qiu-Li, and Jack was still finding it hard to match her shooting skills out on the range. Jack moved closer to them but kept his head low. She indicated with her hand to the right, and Jack moved in that direction before lying low behind a tree. As he peered around its trunk, he marveled at the realism of its structure. They might have only been on Terra Nova, but the training area could easily have been Hyperion.

Hmm, is it me, or is this place designed to train marines to fight on the territory of Gun and the Jötnar?

Next to his parents, there was no group of people Jack

trusted more than his friends on Hyperion. The Jötnar had become family to him, especially during his troublesome childhood. He would have stayed in the APS Corporation if it hadn't been for the encouragement of his Jötnar friend Wictred, who after taking part in battle for the first time had developed a taste for combat. He looked up into the trees and thought back to the hunting trips he'd taken with him and his kin.

Yes, the trees. That is where they will go.

Wictred, the son of the famous Jötnar commander known as Khan, and Hunn, the Champion of Hyperion, were the first Jötnar to pass the entry requirements that so far had managed to block access to his kin. In theory, the Jötnar were allowed to join the Corps, the same as any other citizen of the Alliance. In reality, however, Jack was convinced the increased language and technical skills requirements had been put in place to ensure no Jötnar would be able to pass the tests to enter the Corps. It had taken a great deal of coaching by Jack to get them both in, but they'd succeeded against all the odds. The sight of a multi-legged machine interrupted his thought of his friends. It reminded him of the things he'd seen nearly two years ago.

Machines!

His first reaction was to open fire, but he remembered his training and the voices of their instructors. The sight of a single enemy was not an offering by the gods. It was frequently used as bait, or might simply be a scout. Intelligence was the key, and he needed more information before he pulled the trigger.

"Over here," he said quietly and then twisted to indicate for the two cadets to get down as low as they could. Thai Qiu-Li didn't hesitate, but the second, a feisty woman in her late twenties from Kerberos, refused to listen. Her name was Karen, and they'd ended up arguing more and more over the last few months, neither accepting the authority of the other. Instead of staying down, she ran past him and vanished into the undergrowth.

"What the hell is she doing?" Jack murmured to the remaining cadet. She shrugged in reply, lifting up her rifle in case of any surprise visitors. Almost on cue, there were shouts in the distance, followed by a burst of gunfire.

"Damn it, come on!" he snapped, and the two lifted up from their hiding place and followed Karen's trail into the wooded area. Jack had spent many years tracking and hunting with the Jötnar and had no trouble following the route she'd used. They came to the edge of a clearing, and he automatically stopped and took cover, ever wary of the dangers presented by such a location.

"What is it?" Thai Qiu-Li asked.

Jack examined the surroundings and the ground out in front of them. He nodded to the lightly trampled ground. The plants had been flattened, but there were no more footsteps moving out to the other side of the clearing.

There was a single empty magazine discarded on the ground from an L48 rifle. Jack could see from where he stood that it still contained ammunition. It must have been knocked from her weapon rather than her needing more ammunition. That meant it could be only one thing.

"An ambush!"

He twisted his head around, instantly wishing he had Wictred or Hunn with him. Their senses were incredibly attuned, and there was little chance of any creature or machine ever sneaking up on them.

We have to keep on though. We're on a tight schedule, he thought, remembering the priority for the mission was to secure the communications array within the allotted time. Points would be deducted for losses, but not meeting the main objective would result in a failure of the final test.

"Jack," Thai Qiu-Li said as she moved around the clearing. She was quiet and stealthy, much better than Jack actually. She made it half way around before stopping. She froze as if something had just been pumped into her veins. Jack looked at her with a confused expression, but spotted her slowly lifting up her rifle and taking careful aim. Jack knew what was going to happen and turned his head a fraction, just in time to see the shape appear behind him. Jack saw it with his peripheral vision as his head was still pointing to the side of the clearing. He rolled over to his side, lifted up his rifle, and pulled the trigger in one smooth motion. The muzzle flash from the training rounds was impressive, yet it took half a magazine before the multi-limbed training drone dropped to the ground lifelessly. Images of the machines he'd fought aboard the medical ship a long time before came rushing back to him. Worse were the memories of the torn and mutilated bodies.

"Stay down!" he cried, still suspicious of what was happening.

The briefing had been to locate a missing team at the communications relay inside the jungle area, and these machines must have been sent out as scouts. Now that he had used his weapon, he had announced their arrival. They had two other three-man teams on the same mission, yet Jack was the only one with any kind of field experience in the jungle. While the others were undoubtedly scanning the ground, Jack knew full well that the real dangers lurked in the trees. As if on cue, Thai Qiu-Li called out to him.

"Up there!"

The young cadet pointed her rifle up and opened fire, hitting another of the machines square in its center-mass. The training rounds were actually low velocity, rubberized projectiles that struck with a dull thud. The machine must have been waiting patiently in the lower branches for them to pass by underneath. For a second, Jack wondered how it could do that without causing injury to the cadets, but then remembering this was the final test. It wasn't unusual for cadets to leave with broken bones and limbs. There were rumors that occasionally cadets were even killed in this part of the test. He doubted that, but he didn't want to find out by having the thing landing on him.

"Good job," he said calmly.

The device flashed several times and fell to the ground, its sensor suit registering the hits from the weapon and mock smoke pumping from its flanks, as if it had sustained major internal damage. Jack remembered how they were destroyed in reality and recalled that the things were capable of fighting on, even after sustaining heavy damage.

"So, Jack, what now? Where is she?" asked Thai Qiu-Li.

Jack looked around their position but could see no more signs of the machines. He was tempted to stay and look for their missing cadet, but he knew the mission was the priority.

"She's trained for this. Right now, we have four minutes left to reach the objective, or the mission is lost. We finish the mission, and then we go back for her."

"What?" Thai Qiu-Li snapped.

"You heard me. This mission would be critical to a colony. Remember, the communications array is the only way we have of sending out a distress signal to the passing ship. If we fail, then every single marine and civilian on this rock will die. We are all expendable for this one."

Thai Qiu-Li shook her head in disagreement.

"We can still do this and save her. You think you'll pass

by abandoning half your crew. Didn't your father do that on Euryale back in the Uprising?"

Jack had always had a tough time with his father. In the last few years, he'd started to appreciate the man had faced a tough time, yet the stories he heard continued to rankle him. It was true, his father had left his unit, but only when the battle was won, and because the rest of the military was abandoning a Jötnar unit who were still aboard an enemy vessel. Spartan had saved their lives and won the loyalty and admiration of every single Jötnar.

"Not cool, Thai, not cool at all. Now, get off your ass and follow me!" he growled viciously.

He instantly regretted his anger. It was something he could only assume came from his father's side, as his mother seemed far better at controlling her emotions than Spartan ever had. He moved around the clearing, moving quickly but always checking his peripheral vision for possible signs of the enemy. Ideally, he'd be using a sensor package to look for possible mines and traps, but they both lacked the time or equipment for such niceties. The only gear either of them had was their rifles and two spare magazines. Neither wore armor or carried any kind of communications gear. Jack surmised it was to ensure the test came down to the skills, training, and aptitude of the cadets. After all, they'd be trained to improvise, adapt, and to overcome any and all obstacles that lay in their way.

It can't be much further, he thought, as he pushed through the thick undergrowth.

He lacked a map or any navigation gear, but from the briefing an hour earlier, he was convinced they should have been much closer to the target than they appeared to be. But just two more steps, and he moved from the cover and into a sparsely covered area that lay directly in front of a dark gray tower. Around the eight-meter tall structure were a number of low walls with sandbags all around them. The tower contained no windows, but the highest level brimmed with antennae and some form of pintle-mounted weapon.

Thai Qiu-Li narrowly avoided crashing into him, dropping to one knee as she examined the site.

"This is it, right?" she asked, looking for confirmation.

Jack nodded slowly and checked his watch. It was the only other gear they were allowed and gave him nothing useful other than to know how long was left until the end of the mission.

"How much time is left?" she asked nervously, as if she expected they were already too late.

"Ninety seconds, it's gonna be close."

"Let's do this, then!" she said resolutely, but unlike their missing comrade, she didn't rush off and instead waited to see what Jack advised.

"Follow me and stay close, okay?"

With a quick nod, the two covered the open ground, twisting and turning as they checked for signs of trouble.

Jack ducked down in front of the first wall while Thai Qiu-Li move onward to the tower. It was a simple cover and move technique but with just two of them, their options were limited. She moved to the doorway and peered in. Jack couldn't see inside, but he did see her lean around the corner and give him a hand signal to follow. In one swift motion, he leapt over the wall and landed down next to her.

"You could just have easily walked around it, you know?"

Jack smiled.

"Where's the fun in that?"

He pushed past her and entered the tower, not before checking the frame and floor for signs of tampering. Thai Qiu-Li moved in behind him, stopping as she passed through the door. Jack sensed trouble and moved sideway while lifting up his rifle. A man stood behind her with a mock blade held to her throat. It was a rubber imitation of the combat knives used by the marines, but the blade on this one crackled with electricity.

Damn, a stunner! Jack thought angrily.

It was a special type of training weapon that could deliver a powerful electric shock to whomever it was used against. They both had already been exposed to the weapon, and the effect had not been appreciated. It left red marks and usually knocked out the cadet cold.

"Stop, move inside and I'll gut her!" said the man firmly.

Jack recognized his face. He was one of the assistant instructors from the previous day. He wore camouflaged pants and a thin green top. His face and bare arms were covered in a greasy paint, making him look as though he'd been sleeping in the jungle for weeks. As Jack watched him carefully, another man appeared in exactly the same style of clothing. This one carried an L48 rifle, one that looked suspiciously like the one taken from his fellow cadet.

We need to finish this very fast, unless I want to repeat the course!

He glanced briefly at his watch.

Thirty-six seconds!

He'd heard rumors about cadets that failed the final test. Recruitment levels were high and the Corps was able to be very choosy about their new warriors. He wouldn't be kicked out, but he would likely have the chance to enter at the rank of corporal, or even worse, he might end up in an administrative role. He looked at the two men and considered what he'd heard.

"Five seconds! Put down the gun!" said the man, his tone raised.

Jack's mind was firmly on the mission though, and he did not want to lose. There'd been rumors that cadets would have to retake the tests and courses with major career penalties. What really irked him was that he knew he'd been through tougher times. Yes, he'd been out on hunting expeditions with Wictred and even involved in a few clandestine operations with the Jötnar. But it had been his six months with APS Corp that really opened up his eyes to the kind of viciousness that still remained beneath the surface in the Alliance. He'd met and encountered it on multiple occasions, and each time he'd made it back in one piece.

There's only one thing to do!

He moved the barrel down and slightly to the right. As he did so, the other two men relaxed a little, enjoying his surrender to their superiority. Then he opened fire. The rifle kicked with each shot as he shot into Thai Qiu-Li and the man. The first round struck her left upper arm and twisted her about. With that small window of opportunity, he unleashed scores of rounds that hammered home into the fronts of the two men and knocked them both back. The clothing of the two men flashed to indicate they were out of the scenario, and they stumbled to the ground. Thai Qiu-Li was wounded but not dead. She slumped down, nursing her bruised arm.

"Get up there!" she barked as he edged away.

Jack needed no further encouragement and leapt to the narrow spiral staircase, pulling himself up as quickly as he could. By the time he reached the highest level, he could see the counter on his watch had just ticked down to single figures.

Damn, this is gonna be close!

He looked around and found a raised pedestal in the middle of the floor. It was about waist height and contained a single button in its center. Jack didn't hesitate and jumped forward to strike the button. A loud klaxon hailed through the undergrowth as he and Thai Qiu-Li completed the task allotted to them. Jack leaned against the wall and sighed. It had been hard work, but he was still surprised at how few people they'd encountered on the test. He'd heard stories of desperate last stands and all kinds of weird endgames that often took place. It was then that Thai Qiu-Li appeared at the top of the staircase, still holding her arm.

"Well, did we lose?" she asked disappointedly.

Jack lifted his head slightly in confusion.

"No, didn't you hear the klaxon?"

"Of course," she answered indignantly, "but that isn't the end of the scenario. Remember the briefing?"

Jack was annoyed at being called out, but the mere suggestion they were not finished sent a chill through him. He'd rushed up without checking the area around the tower and was now starting to feel vulnerable in this high tower. He thought back to the parade of cadets and the mission briefing.

"Uh, the map showed the landing pad and the communications tower with the relay. The operation is for the Marine units to send out the distress signal. We've done that."

Thai Qiu-Li raised her eyebrow in a questioning look.

"Really? Don't you remember the last part? You know,

the bit that pays the big money?"

Jack looked at her with a confused look before she reached into her pocket and withdrew a small metal object. She placed it on the plinth next to the transmission button. He examined it carefully before feeling incredibly stupid for forgetting the final stage. He banged his fist onto the metal plating of the tower. The undergrowth around their position shook, and he was sure he could see metal shapes in amongst the foliage.

"We have to hold the transmission tower until rescue arrives." He then pointed at the object.

"The bonus is to keep the object at this point until rescued," he said so slowly that it made him sound slow witted. He then looked back at the jungle.

"Wait, isn't that the part of the test that no cadet has ever been won before?"

Thai Qiu-Li shrugged. A gentle crackle interrupted them from somewhere in the tower. It was the voice of the commander of the training exercise, a harsh instructor known as Captain Blucher who had been called in to run a special series of tests.

"Primary objectives have been completed. Stay alive and wait for the pickup. Rescue cobras are en route in fifteen minutes. Good luck. Out."

It was a brief message, and Jack wondered if he'd done enough. He recalled hearing about this part of the test. Survival was a key part and wasn't required for completion to pass, but he had no interest in half measures. He thought of his father and the stories he'd told him of his battle throughout the Uprising; battles against machines, monsters, and religious fanatics. Jack looked to his comrade-in-arms and then out to the jungle once more.

We can do this! he thought resolutely, and to the surprise of Thai Qiu-Li, he shouted as loudly as his lungs would allow him.

"Marines! Fall back to the tower!"

He then moved to the tower-mounted weapon and checked it over. He looked at it carefully, quickly identifying it as an early twin mounted L48 rifle with box magazine and long-range optical sight. He lifted the handles and checked the mechanism before looking back to Thai Qiu-Li.

"It all looks good. Can you operate the weapon mount?"

She nodded quickly.

"Good, you provide top cover, and I'll watch the main entrance. We can do this."

With those few words, he ran down a number of steps, turned back, and called up to her.

"Your weapon, you have any spare ammo?"

Thai Qiu-Li shook her head as she pulled the clips from her jacket and tossed them down. She turned back to the weapon, and after checking the magazines for dummy rounds; he went back down the steps and to the ground floor. He noticed the bodies of the two men had vanished.

Okay, that's a little disconcerting, he thought, before remembering it was nothing more than an exercise.

They'd probably just packed up and left once their job was done. Even so, their firearms lay on the ground in a neat bundle. That was when the jungle appeared to come alive. Mechanical arms flayed as two of the machines lurched from the cover and made for the doorway. Jack got a good look at them and could see they were far less menacing than the war machines he'd faced in real combat. Even so, they still moved quickly and made it halfway before the dummy rounds from the top gun mount struck them. Both were eliminated less than four meters from the doorway.

"Nice shooting!" he shouted, grabbing the discarded weapons and ducked back inside the entrance to the tower. The jungle started to shake again, and this time he had time to raise his own weapon. A rifle emerged first; it was an L48, the same type that he and Thai Qiu-Li were using.

"Hold your fire!" he shouted, hoping his friend could hear.

Luckily, there was no gunfire, and instead of a machine, four marines appeared. Two were men in their twenties, both covered in grime, and looking about warily. Next to them moved the great bulk of two Jötnar.

"Wictred, Hunn? You made it, huh?" he exclaimed in surprise.

At the same time, dozens of the machines emerged

162

from the undergrowth and rushed them. All five of them turned their guns on the enemy while Thai Qiu-Li poured down fire from above.

"Good work, Jack!" shouted Wictred. "You've moved us into another dead end!"

The two Jötnar roared with laughter, holding down their triggers with obvious glee. Jack shook his head as he added his own gunfire to theirs.

There's nothing happier than a Jötnar warrior in the middle of a battle!

CHAPTER SEVEN

The last real battle fought by the Confederate Marine Corps was in 338CC on the capital world of Terra Nova. In the final desperate action by Admiral Jarvis, she sent the heavy infantry, Vanguards and Jötnar into a direct assault at the Palace and engaged traitor forces loyal to the Echidna Union. The battle degenerated into a close quarter bloodbath until the heroes of the Marine Corps, including Major Daniels, Sergeant Lovett, Lieutenant Spartan, and the Jötnar were able to smash the Echidna Union once and for all. The casualties were massive on both sides, but it did bring the Uprising to a swift end. The Alliance Marine Corps would be the successor to its illustrious predecessor.

Great Battles of the Marine Corps

The new uniform for Teresa was far from ideal. Gone were the fatigues she was used to, and instead the black trousers and loose jackets that were now standard. The belts were worn around the waist but over the jacket to hold it in. At first, she was less than impressed with what appeared to be a scruffy alternative. Gun, on the other hand, had been forced to make do with what he had. His only concession to the Corps was the beret he wore jovially on his head. Luckily, the Jötnar tended to wear militaristic clothing and armor even as civilians, and he reminded her of exactly what the old Jötnar Battalion head looked like in the War. She'd had only a few minutes in her new quarters before rushing to the training hall towards the stern of ANS Savage. Gun marched noisily beside her as they moved through the new smelling warship.

"She's fresh," Gun said with little real interest.

Teresa said nothing and concentrated on making her way to her destination. Gun didn't care one way or the other about the ship. It meant little to him whether it was an old ship covered in rust, or one directly from the shipyards. All that mattered was what it had done and what it would do. The fact that it was new meant it had only potential to its name, nothing more. He watched Teresa as they moved and nodded slowly to himself, well aware she was thinking of just one thing.

"You're worried about Spartan, aren't you?"

Teresa kept moving and tried to avoid his eye contact. It wasn't a subject she really felt like sharing, particularly with somebody like Gun. He had definitely changed in the last years, but he could still be very gruff and avoided most of the niceties of conversation. When they'd first met, he'd know only a few basic words and most of those were to do with weapons, violence, and battle. Over the years, he'd become more and more articulate and was now able to hold complex and detailed conversations. There was nobody outside of her own blood that knew her as well as he did.

"It just doesn't feel right," she said finally, almost blurting out the words. "It wasn't long ago that we were both planning APS operations. Now the company is being stripped, our people are being relocated, and we're standing on a brand new Navy ship with hundreds of marines waiting for us."

They moved on a few more steps before she spoke again.

"None of this feels real to me, not one bit, Gun."

He nodded, thinking he understood what she meant.

"You mean rejoining the Corps while Spartan is missing?"

Teresa immediately felt guilty as he explained it in detail.

"APS is dead, nothing you can do about that. What can you do to help find Spartan? He is somewhere, probably causing trouble, and having a good fight. This expedition is a good step, and it will mean you are doing something to help. You have three children who need you as well. Spartan would want you to show them strength and courage. We will find him, don't worry. We will not stop until he is back. Understood?"

Teresa looked at Gun with his oddly shaped body and great size. It was strange to think that back on Prometheus he and his kind had been the jailers of the place. Although it hadn't been by any choice of theirs, she had seen many of her friends and comrades die at their hands before they gained their freedom and independence. Now all she saw was a friend. She took a along breath and rounded the final corner to their destination.

"So, our new battalion. From what I hear, they are as green as they come."

Gun laughed.

"Let me guess, you want to ship them into shape?"

Teresa gave a short, grim smile.

"Commander, when I am finished with them, they'll put the fear of God into every other marine in this expedition."

Gun nodded happily, glad that for at least a moment he had the old Teresa back, for however fleeting a moment it might be.

* * *

The T'Kari Raiders moved about the bridge of the Raider ship as they continued to take control of the vessel. At least, that was how it appeared to Spartan. He kept a close eye on them and their weapons, as well as what he could see outside.

"So what's the plan?" asked James Lovett.

Spartan and Khan were still on their feet; the rest of their depleted team sat on the floor to the side of the room. Each maintained a careful eye on their surroundings as they contemplated what to do next.

"That depends on a lot of things," answered Spartan while watching the T'Kari he was sure was the leader of the group.

"Such as?" asked Lovett.

"Well, for starters, where the hell are we, and whose ships are those?" snapped back Khan.

He pointed at the myriad of dots on in space. They all looked out through what was presumably the artificial screen, trying to identify them. Most were no more than dots, but a handful close enough they could be made out. The nearest of them all was brightly colored and thickly ribbed along its length. The rear was bulbous and fitted with multiple engines. Studded shapes ran along the top and side at regular intervals. The front looked like a crater or the open end of a pipe that disappeared into the dark interior.

"I've never seen a ship like that before," James Lovett said.

"Me either. Looks like an assault ship of some kind."

They continued watching as dozens more of the same ship design moved into position around the first. From the gaping fronts of the ships emerged formations of smaller craft. Spartan nodded at the emerging craft, as the ship seemed to match his suggestion.

"Fighters?" asked Khan.

Spartan shrugged.

"Who knows? Could be fighters or maybe transports. Either way, they aren't ours. I'm counting at least fifteen of those ships. How big are they?"

Spartan and Khan both watched with interest. Without a known vessel nearby, it was impossible to gauge the actual size of the vessels. Spartan concentrated his attention on the small craft and spotted three windows running along the front of each of the wedge shapes.

"Okay, assuming the small craft are roughly the same size as Thunderbolts, I'd say those ships have to be bigger than cruisers."

Khan nodded in agreement, but before he could speak, a familiar shape moved alongside the other vessels. This one looked very similar to the ships that had tried to seize control of the New Charon system, prior to the T'Kari breaking down the Spacebridge the enemy had used. It was a similar size to an Alliance cruiser but wider and shaped like a prehistoric fish from Earth. Thick metal plates ran across its hull in between the thick ribs that were very similar to those of the larger carrier type vessels. Now that they were close, Spartan could see that the carrier vessels were almost fifty percent larger than the ships that had blasted their way into New Charon.

"Spartan!" Lovett called out.

He turned his head and spotted two of the T'Kari approaching. Both had their weapons slung on their shoulders, much like a marine would. Even so, Spartan lowered his hand to his own weapons, just in case. Unexpectedly, a sound came from the leader of the Raiders. At least, they assumed he was the leader.

"This is the harvesting fleet of the Masters," he said through his translator.

Lovett stood up angrily and looked to Spartan.

"So they could understand us all along?"

Spartan ignored him and instead took a step closer to the Raider.

"Who are you, and what the hell is going on here?" he demanded.

Khan moved to his right while the other five marines lifted their rifles to their hips. It wasn't a direct threat of violence, but it made their intentions perfectly clear. Only Porter remained on the ground. Even so, he was easily able to operate his rifle and joined in with his comrades. The T'Kari bowed slightly and beckoned for the other T'Kari to approach. They moved toward him, forming up in a neat line. They wore the damaged and worn armor they'd first seen upon arriving on the Raider ship. The leader tapped a button, and the helmet opened up to reveal a scarred T'Kari face.

"I am Tuke, I guide our surviving people in captivity," he said through the translator.

Porter tried to lift himself up, but it required the assistance of the others to help him to his feet. Spartan took a step closer to Tuke.

"What are you doing here?"

He looked at Spartan and then to his comrades before continuing.

"We are T'Kari slaves. We were captured by the Enemy, and they forced us to fight."

"How many of you are there?" asked Khan suspiciously.

"We have eight ships and three hundred and twelve T'Kari."

Khan looked to Spartan.

"Well, what now?"

Spartan looked at him and appeared confused. He walked closer to the large window and out to the ships. He could see more of the T'Kari ships and recalled the captured ship that had been seized by Captain Thomas of ANS Devastation. He looked back to Tuke.

"What were you doing when we found you?"

He inhaled from his respirator before replying; his high-pitched voice drowned out by the suit's speaker system.

"The Masters are suspicious. They believe your people are interfering with the T'Kari. We have been collecting information on your people and your ships."

Yeah, that sounds more like it, thought Spartan.

172

"For what reason?"

Tuke looked to Khan and then back to Spartan.

"To help them prepare for the cull of your species."

Khan, Spartan, and his six comrades looked at each other with a mixture of surprise and horror at his words. The idea of war was one thing, but something as primitive as a cull made them seem more like cattle than people. Spartan pointed to Tuke.

"You're saying these Masters are getting ready to attack us? To kill our people?"

He shook his head.

"No, they are already prepared for the cull. We have been sent ahead of the fleet to halt our kin before they can close the Rifts."

"You serve them willingly?" called out Isamu bitterly.

Tuke looked directly at the young APS operative.

The Enemy have our families onboard their factory ships. If we refuse, they will be processed. Either we do this or they will take more and do the same with them."

He looked down, shame clearly on his face.

"We have no choice but to obey them, but we do as little as we can. It isn't much, but it will take them longer."

Spartan stepped in front of him, reaching out with his hand. He placed it on his pale flesh, lifting his face to look directly into his.

"Not true, until today you had no choice, but now things have changed. Now tell me about these Masters?

Who are they? What do they want, and lastly..."

Khan stepped up to the pair of them and grinned.

"Yeah," he started, "where do they live?"

The T'Kari pressed a button on his arm, and a three-dimensional model appeared. It showed what looked like a great spoked wheel that rotated around a glowing central hub.

"We are here," he said, pointing to one of the glowing shapes on the outside of the wheel. He then pointed to another shape on the outside of the wheel.

"The home of the Enemy is here. All are connected at this point," he explained while pointing to the middle of the wheel.

"What is that?" asked Spartan.

"Helios," replied the T'Kari, this time without the translator. Though alien, Spartan was convinced he could detect almost reverence in his voice. It was just a word though and hadn't answered Spartan's question.

"Helios?"

"It is the center. The Enemy is finding a way to reach it again since his banishment."

"That is what this fleet is for?" asked Khan.

Tuke shook his head.

"Yes, the Enemy is looking to find a way back to Helios and the Network."

"And then what?"

"Then the great cull will begin, and he will have his

revenge."

* * *

The lines of fresh marine recruits did nothing to dispel the gossip Teresa had heard about this Marine unit. She might have been promoted and reinstated into the Corps she'd left many years before, but this group made her almost feel it had been a punishment detail. There were grumbles and murmurs as the two moved into the training hall. Gun sniffed as they moved inside.

"Smells like paint, no sweat," he said disappointedly.

Teresa knew full well that it wasn't the sweat. It was the fact that this place hadn't been used properly. He was a strong proponent of sweating in training rather than bleeding in combat. Though she recalled he seemed to like the bleeding part perhaps a little too much.

Here we go again, she thought ruefully.

Teresa examined the walls and noticed they were actually inside the landing bay itself. Additional security walls must have been fitted or lowered for use in training. It was a useful use of the limited space in the cruiser, and a timely reminder of how things had changed. Teresa had spent most of her time aboard Marine Corps amphibious transports like Santa Maria. They'd been civilian ships with heavy modifications for carrying a thousand marines, all of their equipment, shuttles, and even a large training space for them to prepare for combat. Both she and Spartan had spent the best part of a year onboard one as they were trained into marines, prior to the fighting on the Titan Naval Station. A young Captain saluted smartly as she approached the lead group.

"Sir, Captain Michael Llewellyn at your service."

Teresa looked at him carefully. The man was slightly shorter than her, and she was no giant. He was balding and seemed to have a little too much fat around his waist for a marine of his rank. His pale face was podgy, and he appeared to be sweating even though he was doing nothing more than standing still. Teresa saluted. She'd read the notes on the unit on their way over, and it was less than inspired reading. The entire command unit for the Battalion had been involved some kind of fraudulent activity and were up on a court martial. Fresh officers were being drafted in as quickly as possible, but the eight hundred marines, spread over the two crusader class ships, ANS Savage and ANS Sentry, were considered the runt of the Corps. She wondered why they were even being sent on the operation, when surely they need dependable units for such a critical mission.

"Captain. Let me introduce Commander Gun, leader of the Jötnar."

Gun cleared his throat.

"Captain, I am assuming command of the Battalion," he said firmly.

The man appeared visibly shaken at both the sight of Gun and also the unexpected news that a Jötnar had been given the authority to operate in such a way. He looked back at Teresa, seeking clarification.

"That's correct. As a former member of the Corps, Commander Gun has been granted provisional command of the Battalion until a more permanent replacement has been found."

She then turned and faced the four assembled companies in the training hall. Each of them wore the new style of black uniforms, along with their dark berets on their heads. There was something about the new style and color that left her feeling uneasy. It wasn't the Corps that she had known.

"Marines, my name is Major Morato, and I have been sent here on orders from High Command to whip you into shape. The Commander and I have seen the reports on your previous officers and also of your individual squad performances."

She nodded to Gun, who instead of nodding in agreement, decided to join in.

"I have read the reports, and I am not impressed, not at all. I've fought with Army, militia, Marine and Jötnar units, and this one inspires me the least!"

He walked out in front of them all and gave each of the four companies a long stare.

"The Marine Corps has a long and illustrious reputation

in the Alliance, and the Confederacy before it. I saw what your forbears did on a dozen worlds, and they were mighty."

The noise from the back of the hall increased, and Gun sensed restlessness. He looked at them and stamped down with one of his oversized feet.

"What? You don't like the truth?"

A marine from the back shouted out.

"We don't take orders from synthetics!"

Dozens more laughed at the attempted insult. Teresa cast a concerned look at Gun, not for his safety or even honor. No, she was worried about his rage, and what he might do with the marines.

"Really?" he said quietly.

Teresa stopped in her tracks and watched him carefully. *You've done it now, you fools. When he's quiet, he's most dangerous.*

"Yeah!" shouted another. A women off to the left joined in, "We're marines, not mutant monsters. Where are our human officers?"

Gun walked along to the first company laid out on the left of the training hall. All at the front were silent, but he could see the amusement on their faces; a few, not many, showed outward contempt. He spotted one and pointed.

"You, will you follow my orders?" he barked.

The woman looked startled but jostled on by her friends, she shook her head. Sensing victory, a few more joined in with the shouting and insults. Gun pointed to

Teresa.

"What about the Major? Will you follow her orders?"

There was a short pause before a voice at the back said what most of them were thinking.

"She's no marine. My mother could do better!"

Laughter burst out in the hall, but Gun had been watching carefully. He'd identified the rough direction of the voice and now isolated it down to just four people. He looked at them from the side of his eye and then found his target. A tall man, easily two meters tall with dark, tanned skin, black hair, and a sneer across his face.

"You, step forward!" he growled.

The marine spotted him but didn't move. Gun took this as an invitation to exert his discipline, but instead Teresa waved him off. She marched directly into the middle of the group of assembled marines. For a moment, it looked as if they would stand their ground, but when within three meters, those at the front separated. She pushed on, her back straight, and her head held high. Her figure was athletic, helped by daily workouts in the gymnasium, and her long black hair flowed behind her. Her tanned skin against the black uniform gave her an almost exotic look that oozed control. She pushed on until reaching a knot of young marines. The tall troublemaker stood in the center of the group and leered at her. She looked puny next to him, but her body language suggested anything but.

"Private, what did you just say?" she asked, her voice

dripping with venom.

The man looked nonplussed, however, and Teresa noticed the marking on his face. At first it looked like a tattoo, but then she saw it was actually the tattoo of a scorpion, the symbol of one of the infamous crime families from Kerberos. She'd come across them with her work in APS and knew full well the ramifications of what might happen. Gun watched her move with amusement, recognizing her posture and what was to come. The marine leaned forward slightly and tensed his muscles as if he expected trouble.

"I said my mother could do a better job than an ex-marine and a synthetic Biomech!"

Teresa feinted a punch, one that the man was evidently expecting. He lifted his hands while betraying his arrogance with a look of leering pleasure to his face. Teresa dropped to one knee and swept his leg from behind the knee. She moved with the speed and grace of a time spent working as an exotic dancer in the long distant past. As her foot made contact, his leg bucked and he collapsed backward. In a flash, she leapt upon him with her knee pushed down onto his chest and her right hand raised ready to strike. He looked up at her, doing his best to avoid her chest that was now directly in front of his face. She stayed there until she could feel his body relax. With a flick of her body, she was upright and nodded to the two nearest marines to help him up.

"There's no such thing as an ex-marine," she quipped.

This seemed to get the attention of a large group off to the left, and at least a few whooped with delight and clapped their hands. As the man was brought back to his feet, she could tell he wanted to say something. She just stood there, straight, and commanding. Teresa refused to give ground, and the man could sense it. His shoulders sagged and he gave in.

"Sir," he said smartly.

Teresa turned her back on him and moved back to the front. Though now blind to possible retaliation, she could see Gun off in the distance. If there had been even the slightest chance of an attack, he would have let her know. The impression given, however, was one of utmost confidence, and it wasn't wasted on the four hundred marines now watching her nervously. Once at the front, she turned back to face them.

"Now. I've fought more enemies than you've even read about. I battled Zealots on the Titan Naval Station two decades ago, machines and Biomechs on Hyperion, and boarded ships dating back to the Great War. I shot, stabbed, and cut my way through hundreds of enemies and have never known defeat."

She started to walk along the front of the assembled marines.

"Commander Gun is a hero to the Alliance. He was the first of the Biomechs to break the shackles of the Echidna leadership. He fought alongside us, as did his people, and turned the tide. He has killed hundreds of enemies, most with his bare hands, and all in the name of our people!"

She stopped alongside him and looked at his features carefully. She wasn't alone either, and most of the marines watched his great hulk in awe. Few of them could have seen one before, and the fact that the most famous one them all was on their ship must have been quite a surprise. She turned and faced them all.

"The Alliance is in a crisis. We are at the start of a golden age, yet there is something gnawing at us. A great enemy lurks around us, sending agents to our colonies, inciting rebellion and war. We will find them, and we will destroy them. This expedition is the first stage in that process."

There was no reaction from the audience, and Teresa noticed that so far she hadn't mentioned anything about them, or what their role was to be in this great new undertaking.

"We will reach the Helios Gateway in three weeks. That is how long I have to get you whipped into shape. Who knows what we will find, but any combat unit needs to be ready. You are out here as part of your first assignment as a complete battalion. Half of you are fresh out of boot, and the rest have only seen security detail. Today that changes."

She paused, noting that their expressions had already changed from boredom to that of intrigue.

"The 17th represents a third of the total Marine force for this operation. If there is to be any major combat, then you can expect companies from the 17th will be in the thick of it."

She took another deep breath and continued, sensing she was making progress.

"I know you've had command problems, but from today that changes. I intend on turning this Battalion around into a lean, aggressive fighting machine. One that can hit the ground running with the best the Corps has to offer!"

To her surprise she received a cheer of approval. Gun smiled at her and nodded.

"I have been looking at the record for this unit and am astounded to see that you are missing a number of key officers and NCOs. We intend on finding replacements as soon as possible."

She paused, knowing the next words would be shocking to enlisted personnel. She started to speak but then decided it would be better to hear it directly from Gun, the new commander of the Battalion.

"Over the next two weeks I will assess you for skill, leadership, and ferocity. I want marines that can match Biomechs in hand-to-hand combat and outshoot the T'Kari. You'll be fast, inventive, and dangerous. The best of you will be promoted within the Battalion!"

The marines looked stunned. It was clear they had been

waiting bitterly for a large number of officers to arrive from outside the unit to fill the gaps. The command scandal had ripped the heart out of the unit, and this proposal meant they would have input over their own Battalion.

"Now, one platoon from each company will stay here for evaluation. The rest of you can return to your barracks. By the end of today, every single platoon will have been tested, and we will assign your new Sergeant and Lieutenants."

A few of the existing sergeants stepped forward to protest, but Teresa spotted them and waved them back.

"As for those of you currently serving in this capacity, you will also be assessed. There is no room for anything but the best here. The 17th will operate based on merit, nothing more. I will now hand you back to your new Commanding Officer, Commander Gun."

With those final words, Teresa, now Major Morato finished her first speech with the troublesome members of the 17th Marine Battalion. Gun stepped into the space where she had been standing and erupted into a loud, almost violent speech where he extolled the virtues of aggression and improvisation to the enraptured marines.

Captain Michael Llewellyn, the commander of 2nd Company saluted as she walked toward him once more. She stopped in front of him and looked him up and down as before, still finding it hard to believe the man had reached the position he was in based on the way he looked. It was only then that she spotted the framework above his shoe. It was a fine carbon-fiber structure that continued up his trouser leg. She lifted her head back to face him and nodded to his foot.

"What happened?" she asked.

Captain Llewellyn looked down at his foot as if he had no idea what she was referring to. At the same time, he tugged on the pants above the knee to reveal more of the carbon-fiber structure.

"Oh, this old thing? Yes, I lost the leg to a booby trap on a hostage rescue mission five years ago. I was a Lieutenant back then, and my platoon ended up caught in an ambush on our way. I lost two marines that day," he explained with a sigh, "...and my leg."

Teresa understood his pain with regards to combat losses and traps. She'd seen the after-effects so many times before.

"What about the mission?"

The Captain smiled back at her.

"Oh, we got the seventeen hostages out without a scratch on them. The four Zealots were taken out too."

Teresa nodded.

"It's never easy. Still, I bet those seventeen thank your platoon every day since."

The look on the Captain's face appeared to agree with her. He then looked to the marines still lined up in the hall.

"Sir. Only a handful of the officers for the 17th

have arrived through the Prometheus-Orion Rift. We are understrength and only the 1st Company has a full complement of officers. I've lost half my NCOs though. Some because of this scandal, and the rest, well, the Corps never sent them. We've been given the dregs of the Corps and left to rot out here."

Teresa smiled at him.

"Well, Captain, it is just as well we're going to be testing everybody here."

"What about the replacements from Terra Nova? They were due within the week. The Battalion isn't complete without them."

Teresa shook her head.

"No, Captain. We ship out in just a few hours. For the purposes of this expedition, we will have to rely heavily on our experienced officers and NCOs. We will recruit new NCOs directly from the marines on these two ships. I trust you will ensure they are all up to speed. In the meantime, I need to see to the marines onboard ANS Sentry. Good luck, Captain."

She marched out of the training hall with a feeling of both relief and concern. The documentation on the Battalion had been far too liberal with the truth. The command structure was shattered, and she'd never seen such a green force before. Ideally, they needed to spend another three months working together, along with new officers. She walked out into the corridor and wiped her clammy face with the back of her hand.

Oh well, the best way to get somebody ready is to get them to do the job!

She straightened herself and continued down the corridor toward her quarters. As she passed a small number of Marine and Navy personnel, they stopped and saluted. It was something she had not experienced for a long time, and though at first it seemed tiresome, it quickly started to grow on her. She almost reached the habitation section of the warship when she bumped into a single officer. He wore the markings of the Intelligence Division. He turned and faced her as she approached, saluting almost in perfect motion.

"Major," he said first as he indicated to her doorway, "May I?"

Teresa inhaled and then nodded.

"Of course, come in."

She opened the door and walked in, closely followed by the officer. The quarters were spartan. There were no decorations of any kind, just a bed, small washroom, and some storage units. There wasn't even a desk. She turned around to face the man who had now shut the door behind her. He withdrew a device from inside his long black coat and placed it on the bed. It flashed once and sent a blue pulse through the room before settling down to a low level flash on its top.

"I am Colonel Cornwallis, Alliance Intelligence Liaison

for the Helion Expedition."

Teresa looked him over. He was tall, probably just over two meters and had pale skin and dark hair to contrast with his jet-black uniform. He sported a mustache, an affliction that was becoming increasingly rare in the Alliance military.

"Major, I've just been sent a priority flash direct from Intelligence Director Johnson."

He leaned in close to her face.

"It is about your family...on Carthago."

Teresa's heart skipped a beat. Her three children were all in the military now, with just her grandparents and a few distant relatives left on Carthago. The planet was a troublesome place, full of angry citizens, and a great deal of poverty. She shuddered to think what had happened.

"What is it? Why not just send a message?" asked Teresa, trying her best to stay calm.

"Twelve hours ago a military vessel smashed through the atmosphere and crashed into the third city, the home of your grandparents. The casualties are catastrophic. It will go public within the hour."

Teresa was shocked, yet the former executive officer for a major private security firm felt something wasn't right. After trying to calm down, she shook her head and tried to analyze the information carefully.

"It's an accident, so why send you?"

The man grimaced at her words.

"Very true. Your relatives are confirmed among the missing, but that isn't why I am here. The problem is that no vessel hit the city. There are radiation traces for kilometers in every direction. We suspect it was the work of..."

Teresa cut him off.

"Terrorists?" she asked.

The man nodded slowly.

"Yes, it looks like atomics were involved. The worst affected area is actually the military barracks and spaceport. Two entire Marine battalions were in the blast zone. The Director told me you should know."

Teresa looked at him and found herself struggling to decide which piece of news was more painful. The fact that her grandparents were dead, or that Carthago might be ready to explode into revolution once more. Teresa shook her head angrily.

Not again!

CHAPTER EIGHT

Slavery would never rear its head in the Alliance, and for many, its past ill effects would never be encountered. The machine smashing festivals of Kerberos were often the only reminder of the days where corporations had attempted to subvert workers with the use of intelligent machinery. It was the military, however, that managed to circumvent the laws concerning slavery. Where did synthetic warriors fit into the system? Local and regional commanders made varying use of manufactured warriors with varying degrees of success. With the meeting of cultures in the Orion Nebula came new ideas and new approaches to the exploitation of others.

History of Slave Labor

It was on the sixth day that something finally changed in the fleet. They'd been forced to maintain position with the fleet as the large command ships created temporary

Rifts every few hours. Each time the vast Armada traveled through them, and with each trip, Spartan could feel they were moving further from home. Even worse was the fact that the Rifts were opened and closed by the ships themselves. Either they stayed with the fleet or they waited in space, with no chance of getting back. Spartan had wasted hours watching the hundreds, possibly thousands of ships in the great fleet. They hadn't dared moved from their precarious position, and instead had been left to wait, hoping against hope that at some point they might move from the holding position and onto somewhere else. It had been Tuke that recognized the place they had arrived at. To Spartan it looked like any other system, no different to the more than forty they had now traveled through. This one was known to him, and according to Tuke, it was one of the ancient Nexus that his people had used long ago. Spartan recalled their conversation and his promises that he could navigate at least part of the Network from here.

I hope you're right, Tuke, because if you screw us, we'll die out here, he thought nervously.

It had finally happened, and the bulk of the fleet was now moving through the massive Rift created by the command ships. Tuke had explained that the fleet traveled through the worlds of what he called the Slaves; a term he suspected coined by the enemy for those he warred against. They implanted technology, agents, and supplies while attacking military installations, seemingly at random. Spartan had a few ideas as to why they were doing this but had so far only discussed it with Khan.

"Nearly done," said Tuke.

Spartan, his comrades, and the T'Kari watched nervously as one by one, each of the ships moved through the Spacebridges until just they remained.

"You are sure we cannot return to New Charon?" he asked for at least the tenth time in the last few days. He knew how far they had come, and also what the answer would be; yet still he asked. Tuke shook his head in a frustrated fashion.

"No. Since we left, the Rift had been destabilized. That can mean only one thing; our comrades found it and shut it down. It doesn't matter anyway. We have no way of traveling back to the Rift, only their ships have the ability to create short distance Rifts. We have to find another way home."

"But you do know the route to the enemy's homeworld if we can access your old Network?" asked Spartan.

Tuke nodded and replied quietly, somehow forgetting that his suit used a fixed volume for the translators.

"Yes. If we can reach this place, we will be able to enter the Network again. I cannot promise how much is still intact though. Large parts were held open artificially, only some of the Rifts are natural. To return to New Charon will take many weeks, and we may have to pass through the

Enemy's domains unless we can find safe routes through. It is a very long time since we dared use the Network like this. Who knows what we might find, or if we will even make it out alive."

Tuke looked to his T'Kari comrades, and one by one they looked at Spartan. He wondered what they were thinking but knew from experience that they gave nothing away unless pressed. Lovett and Khan arrived; the rest of the team was resting in the room opposite the bridge where they had set up temporary sleeping quarters.

"We're ready," Khan said firmly.

"Good," replied Spartan who then looked back to Tuke and pointed at the screen.

Lovett and Khan were both carrying their weapon across their bodies as if expecting trouble. In reality, it was simply because they wanted to be ready for trouble, even though there was little, if anything, they could actually do. Khan gave Spartan the nod.

"Okay, Spartan, let's do this."

Spartan in turn looked to Tuke.

"Power up the engines and take us away from this place. If we can't go home, we'll do the next best thing. Find where they live and bring back intelligence. Anything is better than just floating out here with the rest of their fleet."

Khan grumbled.

"Or bring back their bodies," he muttered.

Spartan grinned and watched in awe as the fast and advanced T'Kari vessel accelerated toward the nearby Spacebridge. If they hadn't explained it to him, he would have assumed it led back to where they started. According to Tuke, this particular Rift would bring them to a dead Nexus where dozens more Rifts awaited them. The T'Kari had an odd look to him as he explained their destination, and Spartan suspected there was more to the place than Tuke was letting on. As they entered the tear in space and time, the vessel shook and the colors around them changed to a dull blue. It took a few seconds for Spartan's eyes to adjust before he could make out the triple stars in front of him and the derelict remains of a vast space station.

"Now that is impressive!" said Lovett, more to himself than anybody else.

The structure was shaped much like the station orbiting Prometheus, but this one was infinitely larger. Around it floated a number of smaller stations, each showing the same levels of destruction and devastation. Spartan looked to Tuke.

"What happened here?" he asked.

Tuke took in a long breath.

"This was one of our trading systems, the first sector ever colonized by the T'Kari. It was destroyed over two hundred of your years ago."

Lovett looked at the objects, concentrating on what appeared to be vast derelict ships.

"Who did this?"

"We did," announced Tuke, to the surprise of Spartan, Lovett, and Khan.

"What?" Khan snapped back.

"It is true," Tuke explained. "Rebel factions tried to split away two centuries ago. There was a great war, and our weapons devastated this entire sector. Now nobody lives here."

Spartan was the only one still watching the main window display and the vast station. As he looked at it, he noticed shapes moving amongst the crippled sections.

"Are you sure about that?" he asked.

Tuke followed the direction he was watching and then tapped several buttons. The image magnified, showing the particular section, as well as several small ships that could have been just a hundred meters from the structure. Red symbols on their hulls marked them out as belong to something, but what Spartan couldn't tell.

"Your people?" he asked.

Tuke shrugged, mimicking the gesture used by Spartan.

"No. I do not know them."

"Very interesting," Spartan said, scratching his chin. He turned to Khan and Lovett.

"Get the team ready. I want to check this out."

* * *

Teresa waited at the observation level that looked down into the training hall. It was technically in the early hours as the ship was running on Terra Nova time, as was normal throughout the Navy, and most of the ship was quiet. Unknown to any but those immediately below her, this was a well-planned training mission that had required modifications to the internal layout of the ship. Over the last week, she'd drilled the marines, and knowing there were only two more weeks left before they reached the Helios Gateway made her nervous. Captain Llewellyn waited alongside her, as well as the gruff drill instructor for the ship, Gunnery Sergeant Hacket. There was a great deal riding on this operation, not least to see how the marines were progressing.

"No Commander Gun?" asked Captain Llewellyn with surprise.

Teresa shook her head.

"No, he's working with the marines on ANS Sentry. You've seen what some of them are like and Gun has, well, a rather unique way of instilling discipline."

Gunnery Sergeant Hacket heard the last part and laughed to himself. Any other marine would have stayed silent, but this old warhorse of a warrior felt comfortable around Major Morato, and in the time she'd been aboard, he had found more and more to like about her and her methods.

"Something to say, Gunnery Sergeant?" asked Teresa.

The man looked up at her and simply grinned at her.

"Nothing much, Sir, only that the Commander is just the kind of guy we need. I've been saying for years that we should be using the Biomechs to improve the quality of our marines. Instead, we get safety nuts from logistics telling us what we can and cannot do. Don't do this; it could hurt them. Don't do this; it could harm them psychologically. We both know about combat, Sir. If you don't work like a bastard, you'll be buried, and fast. Now this Gun, he ain't no tactical genius, but he's tough, has seen action, and won't take shit from anybody. This is a new unit, and we need people like him to get these slackers into line."

Both Teresa and the Captain were taken aback by the vulgarity from Hacket. He noticed them both but refused to apologize. It was something that only a well-decorated gunnery sergeant could even consider to try. Not that it mattered though, Teresa was only interested in getting the unit ready for whatever uncertainty awaited them through the Helios Gateway. She'd been through enough unknown scenarios in the past to know that preparation was key. She didn't care what the jarheads themselves thought of her.

What were those names? Teresa thought, remembering what she'd heard from the other men in the unit. Yes, *Iron Bitch was one. Ball Breaker was another.* There were others she suspected but that was fine, just as long as they didn't try using them around her. She looked back at the training hall from their position on the observation level. Captain

Llewellyn moved closer to her.

"Have you seen the latest bulletins from Carthago with the protests?"

Teresa nodded slowly, surprised at the change of subject. She was always suspicious when anybody mentioned Carthago.

"Yes I have, it looks like order has been restored though."

The Captain looked down to the hall for a moment longer before continuing. His voice was softer than normal with a hint of melancholy about it. Teresa suspected he was about to reveal something, quite possibly serious.

"My ex-wife lives there," he said calmly.

Teresa didn't know quite what to say. She'd received confirmation that her grandparents were dead, yet she couldn't bring herself to share such private and personal information with somebody like the Captain. It was something she would have to deal with in her own time, ideally when she was reunited with Spartan. She'd already sent secure messages to her three children, but with them all now in the military, it was impossible to easily speak with them. She looked to the Captain and noticed him still looking at her. It wasn't that she didn't trust him, no; it was more that Teresa was now second-in-command and needed to maintain a distance from her officers. Familiarity was fine in the lower ranks, but right now, she needed respect and discipline if she was to turn the 17th around.

Luckily, the Captain looked back to her with a sly grin.

"They couldn't have hit a nicer a person," he added sarcastically.

Try as she might, Teresa couldn't quite keep herself from laughing. Gunnery Sergeant Hacket seemed less than impressed. Like most of the men in his position, he thrived on discipline, and by all account, was one of the best in the entire Marine Corps. Teresa regained her composure and checked her watch.

Three more minutes.

"I kind of understand why they are protesting on Carthago though," explained Captain Llewellyn, with a tentative hint of a question in his voice.

"Of all the colonies and planets in the Alliance, Carthago is the one that has never recovered. I was looking at the images from the press. The cities still look the same as they did in the Uprising and even going back to the Great War."

Teresa knew all of this only too well. She'd been born there, after all. Carthago was one of the roughest and most troublesome parts of the Alliance. There were people there that hated the Alliance just as much as the Zealots and the Echidna Union before it. She'd experienced racism, intolerance, and poverty while living there and had little interest in spending any more time there than was necessary. Even so, she saw no reason to share this kind of information with him. In fact, it was proving useful to learn as much as she could from all around her.

"Gunnery Sergeant, what do you think?" she asked.

The experienced marine looked to her, his expression frozen like ice.

"Sir, I leave politics to civilians. The citizens of Carthago are a tough, nasty bunch. They are well motivated and make damned good marines," he said firmly, looking back to the training hall, "but they don't make good citizens," he finished.

Teresa warmed to him at those words. As a citizen herself, she found his simple summary to be surprisingly accurate. There were few that would argue that Teresa was a good citizen. She was fiery and had little time for politics either. But as a marine, her service had been exemplary. Captain Llewellyn watched her for a moment before speaking again.

"I heard rumors that the crash site on Carthago was contaminated. Some are saying it was the work of planet-based terrorists, not hijackers of a spacecraft. I'm not surprised. There have been bombings, kidnappings, and hijacks in that area since I was a kid."

"Who knows?" she replied, doing her best to change the topic.

At the same time, she was trying to avoid thinking of the conversation she'd had with Intelligence Director Johnson. The two were firm friends, and he'd been trying to gauge the mood in the Corps with regards to the growing violence on Carthago. The words that stuck in her mind were his description of the planet itself. He'd said the citizens were losing hope. Starvation in the outlying towns was becoming prevalent, and few traders from the other Alliance colonies were stopping there anymore. Anger and resentment of Alliance authority was increasing. He had told her that a large number of state departments had been attacked, and discontentment was continuing to spread.

Focus, she told herself, *there's no point worrying about things you can't change.*

"Major, ten seconds," said the Gunnery Sergeant.

Teresa looked back into the hall and the scenario laid out before them. The hall had been transformed to look like it had been attacked. Boxes were overturned and equipment lay strew everywhere. A number of dummies lay on the floor to represent marine casualties, and a thin layer of smoke hung throughout the hall. To all intents and proposes, the hall was the landing bay of a ship, and it had just seen a firefight. Behind the improvised cover was one of the most experienced platoons from ANS Crusader, the flagship of the Navy and home to the best marines in the Corps. Forty-two marines, dressed in a rough approximation of the clothing and armor worn by the T'Kari Raiders, waited quietly. It wasn't perfect, far from it actually. But his was the best she'd been able to arrange at such short notice, and in the low light of the open space, it looked real enough. The lights on the walls flashed red and the emergency klaxons started.

"Now it begins," said Captain Llewellyn quietly.

They watched patiently as the first minute ticked by without a thing happening. The T'Kari fidgeted and adjusted their positions as they awaited the marines. One group pushed ahead, placed something on the ground in front of their positions, and ducked back into cover. Then the first squad rushed in. They were hastily dressed and fumbling with their rifles. The squad had clearly staggered out of their bunks, grabbed their weapons, and rushed to the sound of danger. All weapons for the four embarked companies were equipped for training rounds only and could only be checked by examining the settings on the weapons. They actually used live ammunition in the coilguns as the weapons simply emitted metal slugs. The power selector of the weapons themselves determined the velocity and therefore the lethality. For training purposes, they would move at just over a hundred meters a second and with the same force as a baseball. Only when they were within a few days of the Helios Gateway would the weapons' live fire mode be activated.

Unless we need it earlier, Teresa thought.

"Look at them," complained the Gunnery Sergeant.

He watched with amusement as the first of the Marine squads was cut to pieces by a single volley of gunfire. The projectiles from the T'Kari coilguns struck with force, and the bruises would definitely be felt for a few days to come. They each walked away from the training hall with defeat showing clearly from their body language. Teresa's secpad vibrated, and she looked down to see four marines were flagged as KIA already. Not that she needed the update; it was quite clear what was happening down below. She shook her head, disappointed but not entirely surprised at the result. There would be casualties in a scenario such as this; it was a surprise attack, after all.

"It's a simulated boarding action, and they are the first on the scene. Let's see what the next squads do."

As if to answer her question, a heavy exchange of gunfire erupted from the multiple entrances to the remodeled training hall. She counted two squads of marines, and they were taking their time. Instead of rushing headlong, they'd secured the one side of the hall and were spreading out to take advantage of any available cover. Their gunfire was relatively ineffective, but they were keeping the T'Kari busy.

"At this rate, it will take an hour to clear the hall and another fifty casualties," the Gunnery Sergeant said bitterly.

Teresa had read his dossier and could understand his irritation. He'd seen a long and active career, only to take a permanent injury in his lungs that had moved him off frontline combat duty. She'd seen him training with the other marines, and he was out of breath in the same time as the newest recruits. Even so, she'd never seen him give up. She looked at him and smiled, but in a way that implied sympathy rather than pleasure.

"If fifty casualties are what it takes to secure the ship, then fifty is what we will lose. The important thing is for them to block access to the rest of the ship."

She pointed at the marines.

"Look at them. They've blocked access completely and are working methodically to contain the threat. They are using marine bodies as armor, instead of leaving it to the ship. It's costly, but it is doing the job."

He looked at her with a measured look of respect. It was hard to find officers that understood what needed to be done, while retaining loyalty and respect of the enlisted marines. The job of an officer was to make these kinds of calls. He knew her reputation, but that meant little to him, what really mattered was what he saw in front of him.

You're as hard as the reports said you were, he thought wistfully, looking back at the training scenario.

The two Marine squads were making slow progress. But what intrigued Teresa was that a third squad had elected to completely avoid the training hall and was actually heading for the lifeboats on the starboard side of the ship. For a moment, she considered canceling the mission, in case something out of the ordinary occurred that could risk the lives of her marines. She hesitated, but something about the squad caught her attention. Either they were leaving in a hurry, or they had a plan. Once in the lifeboat, they detached from the ship and disappeared from the view of the internal camera feeds.

"What the hell?" muttered Captain Llewellyn.

"That's okay, leave them!" called out Teresa, her right hand lifted to halt him.

"I want to see where this goes."

She lifted her secpad and dragged the camera menu to the center. A simple tap brought up external feeds from the dozens of cameras fitted around the ship. It showed two lifeboats from the same side as they drifted into position above the service hatches and into the ship.

Interesting.

The first waited and then rotated to face its starboard door to the metal hull of the Alliance ship. It opened up to reveal the marines, each wearing fully enclosed PDS body armor suits. They must have had no internal pressure inside the lifeboat as they exited calmly, with no pressure blowout. In seconds, the entire squad was in position on the hull like a group of fleas on a dog.

"What if they blow the hatch and depressurize the section?" asked Captain Llewellyn.

Sergeant Hacket shook his head.

"No, the outer section are double-sealed, and there are internal safety seals and shutters installed. The worst that can happen is they manage to open the inner and outer shields simultaneously. The area would immediately seal. It takes less than a single second for the lockdown procedure."

Teresa pointed at her secpad.

"Even so, it doesn't matter. Look."

They examined the display and watched as one of the squad opened an external hatch, and they pulled themselves through the open space and inside the vessel itself.

"Where the hell are they?" asked Captain Llewellyn.

Like all good NCOs, Gunnery Sergeant Hacket knew his surroundings well. More so, than it would seem the Captain had given him credit for.

"That is one of the outer service chambers. It's to allow for maintenance work outside the sealed sections of the ship. If they have the right security access codes, they can get through to the outer door control station off to the right."

Teresa smiled as he explained the layout of the ship.

"Exactly. If they are smart, they will have an entire squad in position to hit the boarding part in the flank and cut them off from escape to their vessel."

As she explained their plan, the two squads in the hall itself had pushed ahead nearly two meters. Her secpad showed four more casualties, but there was an equal number of T'Kari KIA as well. Even so, the enemy was regrouping around what looked like the carcasses of two marine fighters. There was an open killing ground in front of it that would make reaching them nearly impossible. To make matters worse, they had brought up a heavy weapon and were putting down considerable automatic gunfire.

"Look!" said Hacket.

The side door to the hall slid to one side, and out emerged marines, each with their weapons raised to their shoulders and moving silently. A tall man led them and used hand signals to move them into position. Eight made it before they were spotted. The marine dropped his hand, and they each fired. The close ranged firepower from an unexpected position caught the T'Kari completely by surprise. Five were cut down instantly, and the survivors were forced to move back toward the corner of the hall. Those that had been pinned down pushed ahead, securing the position from where the heavy gunfire had been coming from. In seconds, the three squads merged together into a wide line and pinned the T'Kari into the last quarter of the training hall.

"Well, it looks like they've done it," said a surprised Captain Llewellyn.

"Not yet," answered Gunnery Sergeant Hacket.

They watched, as one by one the T'Kari raised their hands and then lowered their weapons. Each moved from cover and toward their waiting foes. The marines lifted their weapons in apparent pleasure at the victory and cheered. Additional marines entered the hall, some fully armored, others less so. There were even three marines still in their underwear, carrying nothing other than their firearms.

"The fools!" muttered Teresa as she watched them commit their biggest mistake.

Gunnery Sergeant Hacket lowered his head and looked to her, nodding in agreement.

In the middle of the celebration, the marines from ANS Crusader who so far had played the part of the T'Kari so fearlessly, turned on the marines. They rushed at the nearest enemy, proceeding to punch, kick, and wrestle with whomever they could reach. By the time the newly arrived marine reinforcements knew what was happening, the entire hall had degenerated into a massed brawl. Teresa sighed at the sight and tapped a button on her secpad. The lighting activated, and the training hall lit up bright blue as the lights increased in intensity. At the same time, she connected with the sound system and spoke directly through the secpad.

"End of exercise, cease fire!"

Most of those fighting stopped, but nearly a dozen continued the life or death struggle with their fists and feet. Teresa was forced to call out once more before the other marines intervened and stopped the scuffle.

"Marines, return to your quarters. You will receive your assessments directly from your unit commanders."

Before looking to the small group with her, she watched the marines down below. Most were leaving, but it was the shape of the tall marine that had led the squad outside of the ship that interested her the most. She finally turned to

Captain Llewellyn.

"Who is that?" she asked, pointing at the figure.

"The tall marine?"

Teresa nodded, but the Captain said nothing for a moment. Teresa looked back and watched with surprise as the marine removed his helmet, revealing long, flowing red hair and a darkly tanned face.

"Ah, that's Corporal Arina Nova," he said slowly.

Teresa watched the tall woman as she spoke to the marines about her. She was easily the height of the tallest men in the unit and moved with the authority of a marine with years of experience.

Interesting.

She looked to Gunnery Sergeant Hacket and then to the Captain.

"I like her. Send her and the NCOs from her squad to meet me in the ready room."

Hacket saluted and marched from the room, leaving just Teresa and Captain Llewellyn at the observation point.

* * *

Teresa brought up the list of potential promotions on the desk in front of her. The electronic display was built into the surface and gave the impression of a paper-based system. She looked back to her secpad and dragged each of the dossiers she was interested in from the small units and onto the desk. As each one landed, it expanded to show greater detail as befitted the space available on the desk. She was flanked by Gunnery Sergeant Hacket and Lieutenant Pollock from logistics, who was responsible for the record keeping and administration of the unit. A knock came at the door, and after replying, it opened to reveal the Sergeant currently on guard detail.

"Sir, Corporal Arina Nova."

Teresa nodded, the boredom of the last two hours finally starting to shift. She'd been working through pages of promotions, and this was the first one out of the ordinary.

"Good, send her in."

The Sergeant saluted and stepped back outside. In walked the tall, beautiful Russian women. She looked even grander close up than she had at a distance, and for the briefest of moments, Teresa was taken by surprise and said nothing. She looked back down at the woman's dossier and checked her details. She was twenty-four, yet had only join the Marine Corps a year ago. Her background was colorful in the extreme, with reports of several violent incidents on Prometheus, as well as three moons. Teresa suspected a troublemaker, but she wanted to see for herself. The Corporal stood firmly to attention and saluted Teresa who returned the gesture.

"As case, Corporal," she stated, nodding to the chair in front of the desk. Arina sat down and looked directly ahead to Teresa. Her face betrayed a calmness that didn't suit her age or background.

"Your dossier makes for, well, very interesting reading," said Teresa.

"Thank you, Sir," replied the Corporal.

Teresa did her best not to smile at the comment and continued.

"Even so, your background doesn't interest me in the slightest. What does interest me is your ability to lead marines. I can see that you have only recently completed your Marine training. Your aptitude tests are off the scale, yet trouble seems to be following you."

Teresa paused and then stood up. She walked around the table to the side of the woman. Even though Arina was sitting down, she still almost reached the short height of Teresa.

"I am reorganizing this Battalion. Those with the right skills are being moved into units more appropriate for their skills. I saw what your unit achieved in the scenario, and you've demonstrated the level of aggression and leadership that is perfectly suited for a role in my assault platoons."

Teresa looked at Arina, again noticing the calm approach she maintained, even when being questioned by her superior. Teresa leaned in closer.

"1st Platoon, 1st Company, is the best unit on this ship. Even so, the unit was stripped in the scandal and has left me with few commanders. It is in need of a sergeant. Somebody with the fire, leadership, and skills to lead the best the 17th has to offer. It is my intention to make the 1st Platoon of the 1st and 5th Company in the 17th as an assault unit, just like we did back in the Uprising. Vanguard armor is available and underused right now; that is going to change. I want the entire 1st Platoon trained and ready to use it. Any ship used by the 17th will always have access to at least one strong assault unit."

Arina was impassive, but Teresa couldn't tell if she was deliberately trying to stay calm, or if this was simply the way she normally behaved. She looked over the young woman and couldn't but admire her physique. She was tall, muscled, tanned, and could easily have been an athlete or dancer. She wasn't thin or scrawny like many of the female marines, and if it were not for her ample bosom and long red locks of hair, she could easily have been mistaken for a lightly built man.

"Well then, Corporal, are you interested in playing a more important part in your Battalion?"

Arina looked at her with a glimmer of pleasure in her eyes.

"You want me to command 1st platoon, 1st Company, Sir? I'm just a new marine, Sir. I've not even seen combat yet."

Teresa looked at her, registering the honesty in the woman's eyes.

"I was an exotic dancer with debts and problems when I joined the Corps. In less than a year, I was in combat on the Titan Naval Station. You learn fast in the Corps, and people with your skills and leaderships abilities are few and far between. This Battalion is just as new as you, Corporal. You will all grow up together."

She waited for a moment and watched the Corporal as the news sank in. It took just a few seconds before the woman was nodding and seemed to accept the gesture for what it was. Sensing the change, Teresa decided to move to the details.

"Okay, you will operate under the command of Lieutenant..."

She paused as she checked her documentation. The administrative clerk leaned over and whispered.

"Lieutenant Glouise River, Sir."

Teresa looked at the officer with irritation. She didn't like being spoken to in such an off-hand and casual manner, especially when in front of new marines she needed to command.

"Yes, Lieutenant River. Do you think you can manage that? It will mean teaching your skills to the three squads of marines. You will maintain the discipline of the unit, help with their training, and advice the Lieutenant."

Corporal Arina positively glowed at the news.

"Sir, it would be my honor. Why me though, Sir?"

Teresa nodded politely.

"Good. Well, you've demonstrated command skills, initiative, and aggression. I need all of these things but especially for 1st Platoon. We might be the newest battalion in the Corps, but I intend on making this the envy of every battalion we have. 1st Platoon will be the best trained in this unit, and I want you to make it happen. Choose your corporals wisely and get them drilled."

Arina sensed it was time to leave and saluted smartly before leaving the room. As she marched out, the Lieutenant from logistics made a motion to speak. Teresa ignored him and instead turned to Sergeant Hacket, a man with whom she seemed to have developed something of a rapport.

"Your thoughts?" she asked him.

Hacket snorted as he considered his words. He was an old pro, unlike most of the marines of the ship and had reservations about all the new marines in the Battalion. He looked to Teresa.

"She's got spunk, I'll tell you that. She's tough, and can lead. But there's something else."

Teresa looked into his eyes, but it was like looking at the head of a shark. His dark, merciless eyes betrayed nothing.

"She wants it, and badly. If you're after an assault unit, I reckon she's the best we have."

It was a simple confirmation of what she was already thinking. Teresa didn't expect the unit to somehow transform overnight from four hundred raw marines to an elite unit, but she did expect them to work hard at it, so when the time came, they would come through alive and victorious.

"Good. Now let's sort out tomorrow's schedule. I want to work on their hand-to-hand combat skills, and I think I know just the person for that."

Sergeant Hacket looked at her with amusement. He knew she was talking about Commander Gun, the giant in the Battalion, and the one warrior he knew even he couldn't bring to the ground; at least, not without trickery or fancy weapons.

"Major," he said slowly, "I like the way you think."

Teresa smiled, and for a brief moment forgot about her worries with her family and the mission to Helios. Right now it was just her and her marines, and for the first time in a long time, she felt at home.

CHAPTER NINE

The death of Admiral Jarvis took place prior to the founding of the Alliance. Yet the cult of her leadership and sacrifice became entrenched in the Alliance Navy. The founding of the Admiral Jarvis Naval Station at Terra Nova was part of the growing tradition. Even those who had never seen the commander of the Confederate Navy knew her by the graduates of her Academy, and the continuing reminders of her final battle in the names of colleges, ships, and memorials.

The Fall of Admiral Jarvis

The approach to the large space station took almost two days, much longer than Spartan could ever have expected. When they had arrived, the station looked just a few hours away. In reality, the moon-sized structure was much further away. To make matters worse, they were forced to approach on minimum power, coasting to the target rather than accelerating and alerting those already present. They had drifted to the station, along with the multitude of debris that moved throughout this part of the system. Over that time, the mixed assortment of T'Kari and humans had thoroughly mapped the structure, as well as the positions of the machines that had been detected on the surface. After navigating through the ruined dock of the station, the T'Kari Raider had taken up a position only a short distance from one of the long abandoned industrial loading platforms.

Spartan and Khan stood on the landing ramp of their shuttle and looked back to the shape of the T'Kari ship waiting over them like a sentinel.

"Spartan, we're good here. I'll have the shuttle brought aboard and prepped in case you need a hot extraction," Lovett said over the intercom.

Spartan waved in a kind of mock salute to the ship and looked out into the ruins of the station. Tuke, the leader of the T'Kari Raiders stood alongside them and gazed upon the ruins of his people's old colony with a completely expressionless face.

"Are you sure they built this?" asked Khan. There was wonder in his voice.

It was rare for Khan to feel anything like this for such a place, but even he couldn't deny the grandeur and sheer scale of it. The basic shape was like a gigantic ring, hundreds of kilometers in diameter. From the outside when viewed from their ship, it had shimmered with a silvery color. Now that they stood upon its solid foundations, they could see the inside was actually dark gray and gloomy. Where fields, plants, and gardens had once stood, there were now featureless spaces of masonry, metal, and rubble. Very few of the buildings remained undamaged, and broken armored suits and equipment from a war fought long ago still remained; as if every warrior had been sucked away from the station, leaving nothing but their equipment behind.

"This was the site of the last battle for dominion of this place," Tuke explained.

The shuttle ramp slid back into the small T'Kari craft, and just as quickly as they had arrived, it lifted itself up and moved back along a pre-determined path to their ship. It had been Spartan's plan to keep the shuttle on the ship, but as Khan watched it go, he started to feel trapped on the uninhabited station. Spartan remained silent, but Khan then looked to him. He had a question forming on his brow.

"Who won?" asked Khan.

Spartan watched him, noticing how Khan always became more animated at the description of the greatest battles and struggles. In many ways, the warrior was more like a child, though over the last two decades he'd changed substantially. Even so, the rage was always just below the surface, and it was important to remember he was barely older than his nineteen year old son.

Just like Gun, Spartan laughed inwardly, thinking of his old friend back home.

Tuke lowered his head in shame.

"Nobody won here. We fought until just a few hundred remained on each side. The climate, air, and power systems were shattered, and the Biomechanical creatures used on both sides had killed almost all the civilians. We agreed to a truce and turned our backs on this place."

"And you never came back? Not once, in two hundred years?"

Tuke nodded.

"When we left, the others collapsed the Rift. Another way in would have to be found. Over time, the details for many of these tunnels in space were lost. Some by accident, other deliberately to keep our people safe."

Khan pointed to the part of the station almost seven kilometers away. A shattered spire pushed up from the surface, and a large vessel waited nearby. It was different to any of the ships they'd come across so far, roughly the size of an Alliance frigate. It was stationed almost half a kilometer from the station, yet from this distance looked massive.

"What about them?"

Spartan looked in his direction.

"Yes, I think we managed to make it here undetected. Now we just need to get close enough to see who they are and what they are up to."

Tuke beckoned to the right.

"There is an underground transportation system two hundred meters away. It is just below the surface and will keep us out of their sight. Not that they will be looking for us."

Khan grinned.

"Yeah, why would they?"

The three walked through the ruins of the station, each glancing at the myriad of bodies and equipment littering the ground. Spartan couldn't remember the last time he'd seen such devastation. The lack of a viable atmosphere had kept the place in a state of almost perfect preservation, all of this time. They wore their fully sealed armor and carried firearms at the ready. A wide ramp led to the underground section and blackness. Even so, there were a number of dim lamps, perhaps enough to light a quarter of the underground structure.

"Where is the power coming from?" asked Spartan.

Tuke looked to the stars and moved down into the blackness of under ground.

"The suns. This entire facility uses massive amounts of solar energy. The storage capacitors will keep functioning even after a thousand years. I'm surprised more of them are not working."

The three continued forward through the rubble, continually checking for signs of trouble. Rather than announce their arrival, they made use of their suits' inbuilt night vision modes. They moved further inside the structure, picking their way past the damaged vehicles and broken weapons. It took nearly four hours for them to cover the distance until they finally reached the point where Tuke stopped. He waited and looked about as though expecting trouble before looking to Spartan.

"Directly above us is the old control tower. It was used for coordinating the landing of supply ships and aircraft. The scavengers are three hundred meters from the tower."

Spartan nodded and moved to the dark entrance to his right. The door had been torn up by a violent action at some point in the past and lay in pieces on the floor. As he moved inside, he tried to avoid looking at the dozen corpses of T'Kari civilians. Their skeletal remains served as an important reminder as to both the hostile environment on the defunct station, as well as the violence that had occurred there. That was when Spartan appeared to have an epiphany.

"Tuke, there's no atmosphere and minimal power, yet we have gravity?"

"Yeah," muttered Khan, as though he'd been thinking the same all along.

Tuke tilted his head slightly and to the ground.

"At the heart of the station is a microgravity generator. It is self-sufficient and provides a gravitational core at the center."

Spartan looked confused and thought of asking for clarification before remembering that the last time he asked a technical question, he just ended up feeling stupid.

No, he thought, *if you don't know already, why bother asking now?*

They moved through the opening and past what looked like some kind of mechanical walker. It reminded Spartan of the Vanguard armored suits he'd helped develop in the War. The big difference, however, was that these looked like machines rather than equipment that was worn. Tuke saw him looking and nodded gently.

"Yes, these are some of the machines we used to use in times of war. They were quick to construct and very effective. Until the other side started to build them."

Yeah, I wonder where the idea for those machines came from.

Spartan could see parallels with their own uprising two decades ago on the derelict station. They had almost lost to the Biomechs and the Zealots, both of whom fought for what became known as the Echidna Union; an entity that Spartan was starting to believe was nothing more than a construct of this Great Enemy that despoiled worlds and created wars. As quickly as they had moved onto the slope, they were out in the open. The bright light from the triple stars was very different to the stars of Alpha Centauri, and Spartan's mind started to wonder what other parallels there were with this world and his own. They moved past shattered masonry, and a question formed on his lips. That was when he spotted the machine.

"What the hell?" he said involuntarily.

The machine was the size of a building and firmly planted on the ground. It looked like a mining machine with its variety of tools and attachments extending in all directions. Hatches all around it were moving while wheels and parts also moved. Powerful arms pulled in sections of metal with surprising care and deposited them inside. A dull red glow seemed to light up the inside of the machine, and glints of the light leaked out wherever gaps or seams showed in its odd shape. Tuke looked at it with recognition showing on his face, even through the visor of his armor. Spartan and Khan ducked down behind the almost limitless debris and watched it work. The machine moved at a crawl as the arms loaded in recovered materials of all kinds.

"Uh, Tuke, what is this thing?" asked Spartan, this time with less patience.

Tuke looked up and spotted something above them before he was able to reply. He sidestepped and then ran to where Khan waited. He looked back, half expecting something to have caught up with him, but he was safe. Tuke looked to Spartan who was now about fifteen meters away and behind a smashed wall.

"It is a harvesting machine. The Enemy sends them to conquered territories to bring back resources. We have seen them before. In the past, a large number arrived at one of our moons. The last images we ever saw of that place were when our warriors destroyed them. A few hours later the colony was gone."

Spartan looked back at the machine and noted that it seemed only interested in collecting machines or technology of some kind, never simple raw materials.

"Because that is what they do, or because you interfered with them?"

Tuke looked at the machine and then shook his head slowly.

"They never take everything. We treat them like scouts. They stay for a few days and then leave. If we interfere, we must face the consequences."

Spartan didn't like the sound of that.

"What kind of resources?" he asked quietly, suspecting the worst. "People?"

Khan replied before Tuke could speak, much to their surprise.

"It's storing information on your technology, isn't it?" he asked.

Spartan was startled by the simple and rather obvious deduction.

Of course, he thought. *With the T'Kari defeated, this great Enemy could spend as much time as it wanted to collect information of weapons, equipment, power, and electronics. Surely they are already advanced enough though.*

"Why bother? Surely they are more advanced?"

Tuke looked to Spartan.

"Yes, and they want to make sure it stays that way."

Suddenly it all became clear to Spartan. At least, he thought it was clear. The machines were here to obtain intelligence, not the technology itself. With the fighting over, the enemy wanted to see how far the T'Kari had progressed, presumably to help understand the strengths and weaknesses of them.

"So maybe they aren't quite as powerful as you thought?" he asked with a grin.

Tuke looked away and back to the machine as it continued its work.

"No, we suspect they do this simply to ensure we do not become too strong or advanced. No T'Kari has ever actually seen the Enemy himself, only his soldiers. There are some that believe the Enemy keeps us weakened and at war with our neighbors to stop us turning on the real threat, themselves. Others think they use us like crops, to harvest for raw materials and technology."

Spartan tried to digest the conflicting ideas but neither seemed likely to him. Except for the part about keeping them divided and fighting each other. The more he thought about it, the more he appreciated the simple logic. He felt vibrations through the ground and looked up to see a biomechanical creature of the kind he had only dreamed of. It stood five times taller than Khan and consisted almost entirely of dull metal. It was bipedal, and its head reminded him of the demon-like structure of the Echidna creature on Hyperion. It looked directly at Spartan and opened its jaw. No sound came out, but this could easily have been down to their being no atmosphere to carry the vibrations.

"What the hell is this?" shouted Spartan unnecessarily. With them all wearing suits, they were communicating via intercom, and the internal system was forced to compensate to avoid them all being deafened by the volume.

Khan didn't even bother speaking. Instead, he dragged his forward curved blade from its sheath on his armor and prepared to strike. Spartan lifted his weapon and took aim directly at what he assumed was the thing's head. Even Tuke brought out a weapon so that all three were armed and ready to face off against the monster. It opened its mouth once more and then made directly for Tuke. At the same time, a glint of light from the distance showed a group of three more. They must have been alerted because a craft was swooping down to collect them.

"Spartan?" called out Khan.

It was a question that implied concern, more a question to know what the plan was. Khan was never one to back down in a fight, and certainly not one against a powerful enemy. Spartan looked to him and back at the quickly approaching machine. They waited, but none of them opened fire until Spartan gave the word. The machine stomped closer still until it stopped within ten meters of Spartan. Now stationary, they could all see that it was completely mechanical, but it was impossible to see what lay inside the thing itself. It bent down to look directly at Spartan.

"Here they come," said Tuke stoically.

Spartan glanced to the side of the machine to see the craft carrying the other three of the machines. It was moving at great speed and heading directly for them.

"Hold your fire," Spartan said calmly.

He could see that just one of the machines would be more than a match for them. The three reinforcements would likely destroy them in a matter of seconds. All he could think was that if they appeared to pose no threat, they might avoid a confrontation.

"Now...move back, slowly."

He took a step back, and the machine watched him carefully, tracking his every move as he inched away from the metal beast. Tuke and Khan did the same, even though Khan muttered angrily to himself as they did so. They continued back until reaching the underground exit they previously emerged from. No sooner did they enter the blackness, and the machine turned and moved back to the collecting machine. It approached from the side and placed an attachment onto it.

"Interesting, they are using the collecting machine as a kind of tool and when we appeared to be no threat, they left. Have you seen them do that before?" he asked Tuke as the three waited in the darkness.

Tuke nodded his head.

"Yes, there is footage of these creatures on one of our outpost stations. We call them the soldiers. They are the machines that fight for the Enemy. They are the closest we have ever come to reaching him."

"They fight for the Enemy?" asked Khan.

"Yes, they were not built by us. They are controlled and used by the Enemy wherever he wishes to strike. It is rare to see them, but wherever they travel, there are sure to be ships nearby. They are the hand of the Enemy and cannot be defeated."

Spartan's intercom unit clicked inside his armored helmet.

"Spartan, Lovett here. The ship, it is moving in closer to the station."

"Understood, get the weapon systems online and watch them. If they appear hostile, you know what to do."

"Ahead of you there," came back an almost sarcastic response. I've got three turrets tracking your position. Give the word, and we'll rain down fire on their shiny heads."

Spartan grinned to himself as he imagined the expression on Lovett's face. He then checked his L52 Mk II carbine and activated the high power mode. He could feel the gentle vibrations through the carbon fiber housing as the capacitors charged to their maximum capacity.

"Affirmative," he replied, content that he was ready. He then looked to Tuke.

"If those are foot soldiers of the enemy, then we cannot let them leave. They've seen all of us, and they are stripping this place of valuable information, maybe even technology."

"I...don't understand," he replied. "They have been here for years. We are too late to stop them learning all that we already know."

"Maybe," said Spartan quietly, "there is another reason though."

Khan nodded at this part.

"Yes, they are the soldiers of this great Enemy. It's time they learned about us, and that we are not their playthings."

Spartan pointed to the rubble all around them.

"I won't let them do this to a single other world. We need to stop them, and this is a good place to start. We might even get some information out of them."

Tuke looked surprised, even shocked at his words.

"Information, from where? They will not talk."

Spartan laughed at his words.

"Talk? All I want to know is do they die?"

With those last words, Spartan moved back out into the open and directly toward the machine. It turned its large metallic head and stared at him. Spartan continued walking toward it, and to all of their surprise, it took a step back. Khan emerged from the darkness, slung his blade, and raised his L52 as well. The ship floated above them, and from beneath its bulbous structure, the other three bipedal machines dropped down to land alongside their comrade. Although of the same design, each had subtle variations of posture, color, and movement. Even more noticeable were the scorch marks and deep scratches on their bodies. Spartan smiled at them from inside the safety of his amour.

Yeah, you've seen some action, haven't you?

He lifted his carbine to his shoulder and took aim at the head of the first machine.

"Lovett, you ready?" he asked, almost whispering over the intercom.

"Oh yeah, all four are lined up and in our sights. The turrets are good to go."

Spartan smiled to himself. He could see Khan with his peripheral vision moving out and to his side, his own weapon ready for the battle. Though Spartan was outnumbered, and facing an unknown but powerful enemy, he felt comfortable with his old comrade alongside.

"I'm tired of hearing about this enemy. They cause wars, and makes us fight each other, and for what? If they are that worried about races allying together, then they can't be as strong as they want us to believe. Right?"

Tuke said nothing, but Khan seemed quite excited.

"Spartan, let's do this!"

Without waiting for another word, the Jötnar warrior

opened fire on the bipedal machine. The L52 Mk II
carbine ripped chunks from its metal hide as Spartan's
own weapon joined in. Their gunfire seemed petty until
the massed cannon of the T'Kari Raider added to their
own torrent of fire. Khan roared with pleasure as the four
machines were torn apart before their very eyes. Only
Tuke appeared concerned, but neither of them bothered
to look at him. If they had, they would have noticed the
expression of fear and horror that covered his face. It
wasn't the horror of the violence that shocked him. No,
it was the fear of what was to come; now that they had
turned upon the Gods his own people feared so much.

* * *

Like all twelve warships in the expeditionary fleet, the crew
and marines aboard them were being drilled and trained
continually. It was standard practice to conduct training
scenarios aboard ships, and many of the marines might
learn all their basic drills on ships rather than barracks
and naval stations. ANS Savage and ANS Sentry were
the only ships in the fleet that had conducted more than
thirty drills, and as the emergency lights flicked off, and
the normal lighting returned, they reached the thirty-first.
Every one of the exhausted marines staggered back to
their quarters, or to the small number of shower blocks
sited throughout the vessel. To the naval crew stationed

aboard, it was just another drill, but for the marines it was yet another test initiated by their new commander Gun, and his ever-present second-in-command, Major Teresa Morato.

Inside the shower block, a small group of exhausted marines stood as they washed the sweat and grime from their bodies. The warm steam filled the room and reduced the visibility to only a few meters in any direction. They all looked so worn out that they barely even noticed each other. It was normal for the male and female marines to make use of the coed facilities together, as they did with all other facilities on the warship. There were now only three days remaining before the expedition reached the Helios Gateway, and the intensity of the training continued to increase with every hour. The door opened and in walked Sergeant Arina Nova. She moved to her locker and unbuttoned her Marine Corps fatigues and boots before sitting down on the bench and sighing. She never realized that this kind of responsibility could be so exhausting. Her underwear felt like a wetsuit, and every centimeter of the fabric clung to her like glue. Now that she'd stopped exercising, the coldness of the air permeated throughout her body. She tore off every piece until she stood there, bruised, tired, and aching.

Gods, I can't take much more of this, she thought.

Arina stood up and felt as if she was twice as old as she actually was. She covered the short distance to the block and stepped inside, moving up to the furthest showerhead from the entrance. They were short, metal stalls, and each one partially shielded to offer a modicum of privacy from the others that were busy washing. Arina moved past the other marines and stood in front of the showerhead, rubbing her bruised body gently as the scolding hot water ran over her. The bruises weren't so much the problem though; it was the dull aching in her muscles that she just couldn't shake off.

What the hell is up with the Major? She's been riding my ass for weeks now. I know she wants us ready, but is all of this necessary?

Arina had woken in the middle of the night to find her arm and leg muscles throbbing with pain every night for the last week and was determined to try and sear away the ache before she left for her quarters. She'd tried all manner of remedies, yet the pain from each day's trials was taking its toll on every single one of them. She would have complained to Major Morato, apart from the fact that the officer joined in with the physical training. It wasn't something she'd seen before, and though the pain was uncomfortable, the sight of her commanders doing the same grinding work at least made her feel it wasn't just her.

The large open plan block was gently lit with a dull orange glow that cast hazy shadows anywhere the steam and mist was allowed to settle. The light itself bore down from the ceiling-mounted lamps fitted behind secure transparent panels. Arina put her hands to the outer wall and felt the cold metal as the water ran down her back. It was relaxing to just stand there, but she knew she couldn't stay there all night. There was always tomorrow and yet another exercise.

"Sergeant, you okay?" asked a familiar voice nearby.

Arina turned her head, the water continuing to strike her face and run down through her long, red hair. It was Corporal Kata Hiko, the mechanic and tech specialist for 1st Platoon. Like Arina, she was stripped naked and stood just inside her stall. Arina looked about, checking she hadn't drawn attention to herself.

"I'll live, Kata. It's just the last combat-drone scenario against 3rd Company. The Major wanted us to compete with the company, even though we were only a third their number. My body is in pieces."

She waited, letting the water run down her. The sound of the water dripping down blotted out all but the noisiest of sounds. The next moment Kata's hands were running down her back and kneading her spine with surprising skill. Arina stayed still for a moment, enjoying the sensation before turning to face Kata. The other marines continued washing, each in their own worlds as the hot water washed away the day's work.

"No, not now," she started before looking about the place, "and definitely not here," she said, though a little colder than she intended. Kata looked taken aback. Arina tried to smile, but the pain in her muscles turned it into something that closely resembled a grimace.

"We can't. This isn't the time or place, and we are getting close to the Helios Gateway. I need to get some rest, or I'll be dead in the morning. We're up in two hours, and we have EVA assault practice…and Commander Gun will be running the drill. You know how patient he is!"

Kata moved her hands away from Arina's smooth skin and nodded politely. She stepped back and moved to the stall directly opposite Arina. She continued facing Arina so that she could look on at her nakedness as she washed.

"Don't you think this Major Morato is pushing us a little too hard? I heard two more were put in sickbay today because of the training drills."

Arina shook her head violently, shaking the water from her hair. It was the one thing she had retained from her previous life before the Corps. Though in combat she was obliged to tie it back, she liked to let it flow long and loose, as frequently as she could get away with. She moved to the end of the shower block and stepped out to grab one of the many towels clipped to the wall.

"No. You know what the 17th was like before they arrived. Most of our officers were gone and our units a shambles. If you ask me, we were just going to be used as a reserve battalion to replace losses on the other four Crusaders."

Kata looked surprised at her response, but before she could speak, a group of three men in their twenties arrived and moved inside. They all glanced at Arina as they passed, each ogling her naked form and long, bright red hair.

"Keep your eyes on the shower, gentlemen," she said firmly and to their surprise.

Arina had only been a Sergeant for just over a week now, and already she was settling into the position quite well. She wiped her face, and after a quick rub down moved to her locker where her underwear and black Marine Corps fatigues waited. She made no sound as she moved to the locker; the only noise being the water from the others now showering. The most recent group of marines started to wash and discuss the events of the previous day. It was mainly the aches and pains of training, with the odd reference to gossip they'd heard throughout the ship. It was nothing Arina hadn't already heard. As she listened carefully, Kata stepped out, her small-framed body looking out of place next to the three men that had recently arrived.

"She is pretty hot though, for a major, don't you think?" asked Kata.

Arina looked at her with amusement. It didn't really matter what she thought about their commander, because one way or the other, as a marine, and an NCO at that, she had to remain professional. This wasn't the kind of conversation she could have with any of her fellow marines. She had responsibilities now and turned away from her friend, back to the cold wall. At the same time, she did her best to hide her smile.

Yes, Major Morato is something else, she thought, imagining the last time she'd seen Major Morato bellowing orders at the marines. She shuddered slightly and shook her head, surprised at her own thoughts.

For God's sake, woman, keep your mind on the job, and off her ass!

All the while Kata watched her, trying to work out what could possibly be keeping Arina so occupied. She'd known Arina since they'd met at boot camp, and the two of them had been in an on/off relationship ever since. As she looked at her, she realized she was feeling envious, perhaps even a little jealous, and it was a feeling she didn't enjoy.

CHAPTER TEN

ANS Devastation was the first to be built of the second tranche of Crusader class ships. Lessons learned from the first models in her class were incorporated into the design, as well as additional technology discovered and adapted by Alliance scientists during the Uprising. The most significant change of all was the addition of bow-mounted particle beams that replaced the powerful railguns. Many criticized the sudden change of armament, but the improvements did allow the Crusader class to tackle larger and more powerful ships. Even more importantly, engagements could now be decided in minutes and sometimes even in seconds. The memories of Admiral Jarvis and her hours long duel over the Titan Naval Station would hopefully never have to be repeated.

Ships of the Alliance

Major Teresa Morato, Commander Gun, and Captain Llewellyn stood to the side of the observation point off the starboard bow. Normally, they would have observed a phenomenon such as the Helios Gateway from the safety of video screens inside the ship, but this was an occasion for which transparent metal and their own eyes were required. A number of other Marine and Navy officers were present. Teresa looked at each of them and back to her two comrades. Over the last weeks, Teresa had been forced to lean upon the young Captain more and more, due to both his knowledge of the eight companies of marines under her and Gun's command, as well as his surprising skill at motivating and training them. Her first impressions of him couldn't have been more wrong. She beckoned to the odd distortion in front of them.

"Have you ever seen one like this before?"

Gun seemed less than excited at the sight of the massive distortion in space. It looked like a reflective sphere but the size of a small moon. Around the Rift were a small number of T'Kari ships. She counted three of them, and was about to turn her head away, when she spotted a fourth moving past one of the Alliance military ships. Teresa suspected these were the much vaunted T'Kari scouts, or Exiles as they called themselves. She recalled the briefing and the report she'd read afterward that outlined their exploits in this sector. Apparently, they watched for signs of the enemy's agents as well as keeping the Helios Gateway secure.

"Why try and hide it, when you can easily see the

thing?" said Gun.

"Just look at it. Are you trying to tell me our enemy, you know, the one that created Biomechs, war machines, and started wars is incapable of finding a distortion like that with generations to look for it?"

Captain Llewellyn smiled at her words.

"Commander, according to the report, the Rift is invisible until activated. The only way to find it is to get hold of a T'Kari that knows the location and force them to activate it. Apparently, not even Ayndir has the location. It is a secret entrusted to the Exiles only. At least, that's what the report says. Even so, the T'Kari threw the switch for us about an hour ago. Once we're through, they will close it again."

"And then they will know where it is."

Captain Llewellyn nodded, "Perhaps. But is there any other way?"

Gun didn't seem to have an answer for that. Instead, he looked back at the Rift.

"So if it works, and they close it behind us, how will we get back?" he muttered.

The Captain pointed at a black color T'Kari ship. It was small, no larger than an Alliance cruiser, yet the way it moved suggested power and agility. As they watched, it twisted along its length and then moved into position between two Crusader class ships.

"Two of the scouts are coming with us. They can

activate the Spacebridge to bring us back."

Gun shrugged. "Yeah, heard that before. Is there a backup plan?"

Teresa looked up at Gun's face. He looked grumpy, and something was clearly bothering him. She thought about asking but decided against it. Gun was a proud warrior, and being asked such a question in front of the other marines would be problematic. She'd never seen him embarrassed but could quite imagine it would be noisy, angry, and potentially violent. Captain Llewellyn sensed the mood and decided to move the conversation elsewhere.

"What I'm more interested in is what we are going to find on the other side."

The sound of the ship's public address system sounded throughout every deck onboard the warship. As usual, the audio was tinny and thin sounding, as though the speaker units themselves were faulty or broken in some way.

"Now hear this," started the voice. Teresa instantly recognized it as the sound of the ship's XO.

"Entry to the Helios Gateway begins in fifty minutes. I repeat; we will enter the Rift in fifty minutes. All naval crewmembers are to report to their stations. Marine commanders will prep their ground forces. Good hunting."

Teresa almost smiled to herself. They were supposed to be on a mixed political, scientific, and exploration expedition, and yet the order for their forces was 'good hunting'. It hardly seemed right for what should be a peaceful trip. The Captain saluted to them both before making to leave.

"Well, I had better get back to my unit. Are there any changes I need to know about?"

Gun said nothing, leaving it to Teresa.

"No, the plan is the same as before. All marines will be prepped ready for ship-to-ship operations. Make sure the shuttles and landing craft are ready, and go through the kit checks. Oh, there is one thing."

The Captain raised an eyebrow in question.

"1st Platoon has been consistently scoring the highest in all drills and scenarios in your company. Is that correct?"

He nodded without a moment's hesitation.

"Good. I want a squad from 1st Platoon to meet me on the landing platform in twenty minutes. They've already been drilled on close escort and security operations. I understand Sergeant Arina Nova has proven her worth on multiple occasions?"

Again the Captain nodded.

"Excellent, the Sergeant will command the squad as our personal escort while in this part of space. Where we go, they go."

Gun even looked surprised at her announcement.

"You expecting trouble?"

Teresa tightened her forehead as she imagined the situations they'd been in before.

"Trouble? Have we ever been anywhere where we

haven't run into trouble?"

Gun seemed amused at her response, but she failed to notice and continued speaking.

"No, thirteen marines and a Sergeant like Arina are just the right amount of security I think I could make use of. What about you?"

Gun laughed at the suggestion he might need protection. Teresa remained stern-faced, and for a moment, he worried she was serious. If true, it would be the greatest insult he had heard for a long time. He knew Teresa too well though.

She is joking, he agreed.

"Don't worry about me. If they have anything they can throw at me that might do any damage, you'll have much bigger things to worry about."

Seeing they were finished, the Captain saluted once more and marched off to leave the two of them to watch the Rift. More of the expedition's ships were moving into position, with the heavier Alliance ships taking the lead position. Even so, there were kilometers between each vessel. A distance great enough that even the thermal energy from a breached reactor would cause no damage.

So, they are taking no chances today.

Teresa didn't like being cut out of the loop. Though she was second-in-command of the Battalion, she kept finding important information didn't seem to make it down to her. The command of the operation lay with

Admiral Anderson, and little information had come down to either her or Gun in the last week.

"I take it you've received nothing from the Admiral?"

Gun shrugged in reply.

"Typical. Is he doing this with the other battalion commanders, or is this treatment just for us?"

Gun wiped his forehead with the back of his hand.

"The 17th doesn't get much respect in the fleet. It was only activated three months ago and isn't ready."

Teresa shook her head, "No, that isn't true. It wasn't ready. It is now."

Gun looked at her and recognized the look on her face. She was determined; he could see that just from her eyes. He looked back at the mysterious Rift and then to the ships.

"This reminds me of the old days, you know, back when we fought the Zealots. Good times."

Teresa looked at him and sighed.

"Good times. Are you kidding? Come on. Let's get back to the troops. It's speech time before we go through."

Gun nodded and the two walked away from the magnificent view and made their way back through the many walkways and corridors to the rear. The design was very different to earlier ships, with the front half of the ship containing the power units, CIC, crew quarters, and weapon systems. The rear contained the mission modules, marine quarters, and hangars. As they moved through, it became obvious when they reached the section further back; the number of navy crewmembers diminished while marine numbers went up. Of more importance to her though, was that the weapons, ammunition, and equipment was stored further back. It took almost five minutes for them to reach the large landing bay area they'd used so effectively for training. Teresa marched in directly behind Gun, stopping in front of four complete companies of marines. Gun turned to her and smiled discreetly.

"They look different, don't they?"

Teresa remained expressionless as she examined the columns of marines. Each stood smartly to attention in their black armor. Gone were the days of warriors in camouflage. Instead, every single one of the marines was clad in black like some fearsome demon of ancient lore. The only concessions to the camouflage of the past were subtle gray streaks that slightly broke up their shapes. Across their chests were the dependable L52 Mk II Carbines, but she did recognize a small number of L48 rifles used by the sharpshooters that dated back to her time in the Corps.

"Impressive, very impressive," she muttered gently under her breath.

Gun nodded to them all before speaking.

"Marines, today is your first operation, and it will be in a part of the galaxy never before explored by humans!"

To Teresa's surprise, the marines erupted in a rapturous

cheer at the news. Information about combat postings and operations were always popular, but she was completely taken aback by this attitude. Then she remembered.

Damn, didn't we tell them?

She watched Gun bathe in the adulation of his Battalion as she tried her best to look pleased. He didn't even have to speak now; he just lifted his muscled arms to the air and roared. The more they cheered, the more she found herself thinking of Spartan and where he might be. Just a few seconds contemplating that, and she was already resolved to do what needed to be done. Her face changed to one of anger.

We'll get control of this Helios and its Rifts. I don't care if we have to kill of thousand of these things to do it!

It was only then that she realized she was threatening the life of an enemy, yet so far she had no idea who this enemy was, or even if there would be one. She'd been so busy the last few weeks preparing the marines that she hadn't even given it any thought.

Calm down, woman, you don't need to go looking for enemies. They always manage to find you!

* * *

Admiral Anderson stood quietly and watched the main viewscreen as they moved in closer to the Helios Gateway. The fleet was in position, and he'd kept them stationed at a safe distance while the Alliance science ship ANS Kepler performed a series of detailed scans. They were positioned inside a large debris field from a long destroyed planet or moon. The largest object in sight was a rocky planet with apparently no name. It had been logged along with all other data and returned to fleet HQ. For the last hour, a torrent of data had arrived, of which only part matched the Spacebridges constructed by Alliance scientists. Unlike most Naval officers, Admiral Anderson wasn't just an experienced combat officer; he was also actually a highly skilled scientist and engineer himself and had been the commander of Prometheus and its science stations for a number of years.

"Interesting, very interesting," he said, reading the latest batch of data.

"The power levels are off the charts," the Chief Engineer said, doing his best not to be surprised at the technological proficiency shown by the Admiral.

"Yes, this Rift has more in common with our own system back at Prometheus. We can only assume the distances between this Rift and Helios are equally as impressive as our own journey here."

The Chief Engineer scratched his forehead as he examined the raw data.

"Uh, not necessarily, Admiral."

He leaned forward pointed at a particular column of numbers.

"Ah, you're right, this part of space is being contested by three astronomical objects. The forces present must require changes to the power signature of the Rift generator. The level of technology to build this thing is impressive."

The Chief Engineer brought over two screens of visual patterns and placed them over the new reading. He pointed at the images to the left before continuing.

"I think there's more to it than that. If we overlay the data from this area of space, you'll notice the gases; forces that make up this sector are almost identical to Prometheus. We always assumed only the rarest of places could be used to create stable Rifts at extreme distances."

He looked back to the Rift and the number of small stations and platforms built amongst the ruins of a moon. Their sensors had detected nothing but debris upon their arrival. It was only when T'Kron and his scouts had sent the signal, and the generators had powered up, that the Alliance vessels had detected the platforms hidden in the debris field.

Platforms hidden from view, to activate and control a Spacebridge, that seems familiar, he thought, considering the Anomaly discovered in the middle of the Uprising. It had also been operating with similar platforms stationed around it.

"I think you might be right," he said. "Perhaps this Helios will provide the answers we need on constructing, maintaining, and managing our own Spacebridge

Network."

From his position on the combined bridge and CIC, he could see the rest of the fleet assembled and waiting to go. ANS Victory was the assigned flagship of the force, for no reason other than she was the newest of the enlarged third tranche of Crusader class warships. Even more importantly, she was commanded by the redoubtable Captain Jane Parker, former executive officer of ANS Devastation, and hero of the battle for New Charon. ANS Crusader may have been the namesake of her class, but Victory was the most powerful ship in the fleet. It was an impressive force but not too massive. He counted the other craft, confirming in his head that all of them were present.

It's hardly the fleet we used at Euryale, but it should be more than enough.

There were no great troop transports or battleships in this force. In fact, the most substantial warships were ANS Victory and the other five Crusader class warships. They were there to provide the muscle, as well as carry half a battalion of marines onboard each ship. They were not alone though; there were also the much smaller T'Kari vessels as well as the same number again of civilian transports. He was forced to remember the meeting he'd had with Chairman of the Joint Chiefs, Rivers. The force was a token in numbers to both wave the flag and also demonstrate the strength of the Alliance. Any more vessels, and the expedition would look more like an invasion fleet.

"Well, gentlemen, this is it. Are we ready?"

Around him stood the highest ranking individuals in the fleet. As each of them nodded in agreement, he examined them carefully. There were many new faces, but some he recognized. There was Brigadier General Daniels, the recently promoted Marine officer in charge of the ground element of their force. Slightly younger than the Admiral, he was one of the most experienced military commanders in the expedition, and if he remembered correctly, an old rival and friend of Spartan.

Spartan, he thought back to the old Marine officer. *What are you up to, and where the hell did you go?*

Next to him waited Captain Jane Parker, the new commander of ANS Victory. As always, her cropped red hair made her stand out just as much as her pale blue eyes. Admiral Anderson wasn't fooled, and he was well aware of her reputation aboard ANS Devastation. It was rumored that she ran a tight ship, with no room for arguments or negotiation. Anderson turned his attention to the space distortion as the Rift started to take form. It was unlike any he had seen before. It was a more a storm in space, as opposed to the almost mirrored glass effect seen on the stable Rifts used by the Alliance.

They had better keep it stable.

"Admiral, the T'Kari have activated the Rift, and it is clear for entry," announced the ship's XO.

Admiral Anderson nodded but said nothing immediately. Unknown to the rest of the crew, he had been privy to one final briefing with the T'Kari scouts and the highest-level commanders in the Alliance military. He recalled the schematic they'd shown him of the T'Kari control mechanism for the Rift. They'd explained how each of the races had coded their own Spacebridges to Helios via unstable Spacebridges, a system that granted maximum security for each of them. Without the race specific control data, the Rift would destroy anything entering it. According to T'Kron, the codes were the most prized secret of their race, an heirloom that each of the races guarded with their lives.

They'd better hope this thing is working then, he thought, imagining the carnage that would occur if his ship entered an unstable Rift.

He'd traveled through the Spacebridges enough times now to know how much he disliked using them. There was always the doubt in his mind that something might go wrong, or that it might close down with him halfway through. Even so, he'd been one of those behind their development, and he couldn't deny the benefits they'd given them all.

"Can you put them on the main screen?" he asked, with a commanding tone to his voice.

The main display running along one side of the room transformed into a forward view from the ship. Part of the bow was visible, and it formed a slightly curved frame from the space distortion itself. They all looked into the spherical shape and the wild patterns and shapes that flickered across its center.

"Very well, proceed. Send in the scouts," he ordered curtly.

The officers in the CIC worked like a well-oiled machine, and in less than a minute, the two T'Kari ships moved toward the Rift. Admiral Anderson watched them carefully as they moved closer and closer until they finally reached the distortion.

Here goes nothing.

It all happened as if in slow motion, each of the craft touching the tear in space, and then vanishing in a brief flash of light. There were no noises, ripples, or shimmer from the Rift, just the emptiness that had been there before. Not that there would have been a notable effect from inside the ship out in space. Even so, Anderson was concerned. He looked at the rest of the force, and the final two T'Kari scout ships waiting in the center of the fleet. Nothing happened.

"Uh, Admiral, we're not getting a signal."

Anderson looked at Captain Parker.

"What do you mean, 'no signal'?"

The Captain of the flagship appeared unfazed at his comments and pointed to the Rift.

"A short burst transmission confirming their arrival is

the last thing we received. Then silence."

"What about their status indicators and the beacons they took with them?"

Captain Parker raised her shoulder and shrugged.

"Nothing, Admiral. Either they are unable, or they are unwilling to respond."

Anderson felt a familiar chill running up his spine.

No signal? What if something on the other side destroyed them? This Helios Gateway could be no less than a tunnel into the heart of a star.

"Could they have traveled somewhere that could have destroyed their vessels?"

Commander D'Vani, the Chief Engineer shook his head and answered for her.

"No, Admiral. The signal we received was an automated response that was triggered upon arrival and after running a series of almost instant diagnostics. There is a partially damaged feed packet, but the computer is having a hard time with it."

Admiral Anderson shook his head angrily.

Damned typical, he thought angrily as he started to pace. It was an old and annoying habit, yet he found it hard to think when simply standing still. Finally, he stopped and pointed to the communications officer.

"Get me T'Kron!"

The young officer wheeled about in her chair and motioned with her hands as she established a link with the waiting T'Kari ships. The images of their commander appeared.

"Admiral," T'Kron said through his translator unit.

Anderson took a short breath and glanced back at the main screen and the Helios Gateway. The sound of voices from the officers in the CIC increased in volume as the situation turned from a holding pattern to one of possible danger. Alarms sounded at multiple stations, yet Admiral Anderson blocked them all out. They were something for the ship's crew to concern themselves with. As he looked back to the communications screen, he did spot the weapons indicators that showed the warships weapon systems were being charged up as a matter of course. He closed his eyes briefly, took in a breath, and looked into the eyes of T'Kron.

"We've lost contact with your scouts. Do you have anything that can help us?"

T'Kron seemed unconcerned, but he did turn and speak with somebody in the background before answering his question.

"No, Admiral. Something must be stopping their signal. They must be in trouble. We must send in the fleet to help them."

Admiral Anderson shook his head once more, "No, T'Kron. Two scout ships is one thing. I cannot risks thousands of crew and marines on two scouts. I need more information before we send in more."

T'Kron tilted his head slightly to the side and spoke in his own tongue. The translators did nothing, and he could only assume he was speaking with his own people. He spoke in an agitated tone, and the shapes of two, perhaps three other T'Kari could be seen moving about. Voices in the CIC caught his ear, and he turned to look directly at the Captain of the ship.

"Admiral, the T'Kari ships are breaking formation," announced Captain Parker.

"I think they're heading for the Rift itself."

Anderson turned his attention to the main screen and watched as the two ships used their maneuvering engines to break formation. He brought down his fist on the nearest console unit. The heavy impact shocked the young ensign that was working nearby. He looked back at the communications screen and the face of T'Kron.

"You need to maintain your position, T'Kron. If there is something that could risk the fleet on the other side, I need to know before I send in more ships."

Instead, the alien shook his head, a gesture he must have learned from his human contacts.

"No, Admiral. My people are few, and these Exiles are my brothers. We have watched this place for generations. I will not leave them to their fates. Either I go after them, or they will be lost and abandoned by my people, and by yours. No, you can join me, or wait and see if we return."

He moved away from the display and concentrated on

his own crew before returning for just a few seconds.

"My Exiles are revered amongst the T'Kari. The consequences of leaving them to die alone could be... uh...problematic." Then he was gone.

Anderson was angry, yet with no way of forcing T'Kron to listen to him, he felt compelled to act. He turned his attention to his own forces that were waiting in a perfect stationary formation of warships. Strung out behind the Alliance ships was the slightly larger formation of transports and science vessels. The only movement to be seen was that of the two T'Kari ships breaking formation and being followed by two pairs of lightning space superiority fighters. Anderson looked at them, knowing that any decision he made would risk the lives of thousands of men and women. There was also the chance that leaving the T'Kari to go on alone would cause a long-term problem for the two peoples, and one that could make New Charon, or T'Karan as they called it, untenable.

You idiot, T'Kron, if this causes casualties, I'll have your head!

With that last thought, he reached for the intercom unit and connected directly to the commanders of every single ship in the fleet.

"This is Admiral Anderson; prepare to move through the Rift. All ships to battle stations."

Captain Parker looked confused. She spoke to her XO and then turned to Admiral Anderson.

"You want us to go in? Without sending drones or scouts in first?" she asked.

Anderson nodded slowly.

"Yes, there is one thing worse than losing the T'Kari out here, and that is losing them because we refused to act. Do it."

The Captain moved from her position in the center of the room and nearer to the Admiral. Though slightly shorter, her presence was commanding, and she refused to back down, not yet.

"Admiral, I must protest. We could be sending the entire fleet into a star. We must obtain more information first!"

Admiral Anderson shook his head and beckoned for General Daniels to come away from the screen he was watching. The three of them stood in silence as more reports came in from the fleet.

"I agree with the Captain. The fact that we've just lost contact with two T'Kari ships is information enough, is it not?"

Captain Parker's attention was on something else. She was watching the Rift on the mainscreen. It flickered and flashed as the two T'Kari ships made their final approach. She lifted her hand and pointed to the distortion.

"We're too late!"

As if they had never been there, the two T'Kari ships vanished. Unlike the previous two ships, the transmissions continued to be sent and were displayed in small windows on the main screen. The three senior officers watched in interest as the feed cleared slightly to show a large dark object surrounded by a red color. Admiral Anderson grimaced at the sight.

"Tell me that isn't a star!"

Then the image cleared up as quickly as it had arrived. The outer hull of the nearest T'Kari ship filled the screen. Admiral Anderson started to relax, that was until the ship moved away and revealed a vast open red star system filled with objects. The quality was still poor and digital interference left odd artifacts and tearing throughout the image. At first the large shape to the left looked like a celestial object, and just as he could make out the shape, the video feed froze and then vanished.

"What the hell was that?" he snapped, "Bring it back!"

The CIC burst into activity as the situation changed in a matter of seconds. The technical crew worked on the communications traffic while the rest did last minute adjustments to prepare for whatever might lie on the other side.

"Crew to your stations!" barked the XO in a gruff voice. The sound echoed throughout the open space via the wall mounted public address system; it would be repeated throughout the entire vessel. "I want fighters in the air. All ships open your gun ports and prepare for battle," he added.

The image from the corrupted video feed returned

to the mainscreen. It filled a third of the unit, yet drew the attention of anybody that looked upon it. It showed three T'Kari ships arrayed in a line and facing toward a large pentagonal shaped object. A bright line ran from this shape and intersected the T'Kari vessel. What caught all of them by surprise was that the T'Kari ship had been cut in two by whatever the line was.

Gods! Anderson thought bitterly. *When will this all end?*

He looked to the crew and noted they were concentrating on their jobs, all but him, Captain Parker, and General Daniels. *What can I do?*

A corrupted video feed displayed on the main screen. It was T'Kron.

"Admiral, we have encountered the Helions. We need your assistance, they are…"

The image vanished and was replaced by static. Anderson closed his eyes and exhaled, fully knowing the ramification of his next words. He nodded toward Captain Parker and General Daniels.

"We have no choice. We have to go forward!"

Captain Parker looked at him and nodded slowly. She understood the difficult decision he had just made, but not even she could quite imagine exactly what they would find.

Here we go, he thought, as the vessel shuddered slightly. It was the feeling provided by the main engines as they powered up. The crew was already strapped in, and two

Navy officers beckoned to the commanders to take their place before the engines fully activated. Admiral Anderson needed no persuasion and moved to the left-hand side where he was helped into a side-facing seat. By the time General Daniels was in position, the engines were on full burn and the ship moving towards the Rift.

"Admiral, this is the right decision. We have an obligation to the T'Kari on both sides of the Rift."

Anderson nodded.

"Yes. It isn't the T'Kari that worry me though," he answered before Daniels could say any more.

He looked about the CIC and at the men and women of the Alliance Navy, most of who had never known war; certainly not like the kind of struggles he and the General had experienced. He had watched ships explode after being struck by multiple nuclear warheads, had recoiled in horror as vessels were exploded by the colossal power of particle weapons. Even worse, he had seen the carnage at first hand when two capital ships had been forced to fight long duels with railguns that left hundreds dead or maimed.

It's my crew, he thought ruefully to himself. *If we have to fight, then we'll fight like Admiral Jarvis.*

"Admiral, thirty seconds!" called out Captain Parker.

Anderson simply nodded; watching as the shape of the Rift loomed ever closer. In front of him a holographic model of the fleet appeared directly over the central table unit. It was positioned so that the commanders could monitor and coordinate the actions of multiple warships in military situation. The Rift flickered and flashed. The Admiral held his breath as ANS Victory, the flagship of the Alliance-T'Kari Helios Expedition moved through.

So it begins.

CHAPTER ELEVEN

The Great Uprising went by many different names over the history of the Alliance. While technically a civil war, there were many colonies that managed to avoid the fighting entirely. To these people, the Uprising was a common term. Those more closely associated with the terrible bloodshed on Proxima Prime, Kerberos, Euryale, and Terra Nova referred to the period as the Civil War or the Proxima Emergency. The least remembered name was the Revolutionary War, a term only ever used by the few surviving members of the Echidna Union.

Reports of the Proxima Emergency

Jack still couldn't believe they'd passed the final test and returned from their passing out parade. He'd been training for nearly a year, and now that the basic part of the process was over, the relief had drained almost all of his will from his body. An entire day had passed since then, and every single marine was looking forward to some R&R. Not Jack though. He'd just received news of a critical private video communication from his mother. That had been an hour ago, and he was still waiting for it to be vetted and cleared before he was allowed access to it.

"Come on, Jack, it can't be that bad, otherwise somebody would have been down here already," suggested Wictred.

Jack smiled back at his friend, but it did him no good. Not knowing was far worse than any bad news, and he was expecting the worst. He looked at the data file and checked the information stamp that all digital media was equipped with. He instantly recognized the signature of his mother, Teresa Morato, but also two other imprints that marked it as having been read before reaching him.

Bastards, he thought bitterly.

Not that he was surprised; it was standard practice after all, for all communications of this nature to be checked. But what was surprising was the time it was taking. He thought of contacting the commander of the station, but then decided against it. He'd already accumulated two black marks during his training, and trying to bypass the chain of command for a personal message would hardly do him much good.

That doesn't stop me doing a little fiddling with the data myself though, does it?

He brought up a window containing a series of personal

files and binary applications that he'd brought along with him. Wictred spotted the change in his body language as he combined the encrypted data file with two of his special tools.

"Jack...what are you up to?" asked his friend.

Wictred, being one of the younger Jötnar, had less patience than any of the group. In fact, Jack often considered his friend to be more of a juvenile than most human teenagers. Even so, he was smart, if a little unpredictable. He moved closer to Jack, his larger body easily dwarfing the shape of his friend. He and Hunn were nowhere as big as the fully-grown Jötnar, but they were still substantially bigger than any humans.

"Ah, running a few tools, are we?" he added in a hushed tone, as if implying mischief.

Jack threw him a quick glance.

"This message is important, just look at the stamp. My mother wanted me to see it immediately, and yet some pencil pusher is delaying it."

"Maybe it is time related? Your mother is back in the Corps, so maybe she's on a mission?"

Jack stopped and looked at him. He squashed his lips together as he concentrated. It didn't take long though for him to turn back.

"She knows procedure. If it was that important to maintain secrecy, she wouldn't have sent it."

Plus she knows full well I won't let it lie!

With a final button press, he started a series of powerful brute force attacks on the file.

"There, I should have access within the hour."

"Hmm," snarled Wictred, unimpressed, "maybe you can finish getting ready now?"

Jack nodded curtly and stood to adjust his uniform for the last time, making sure her shirt and tunic were tucked in correctly, and then did his best not to laugh at Wictred and Hunn. Whereas Jack was wearing his black Marine Corps cadet uniform with the belt on the outside the jacket, the two Jötnar were desperately trying to emulate his look without looking ridiculous. Their uniforms had been custom made, much to the annoyance of the quartermaster who had at first declined to modify clothing for them. In the end, they wore their traditional armor and clothing, but with a modified waistcoat that allowed them to move their oversized chest and arm muscles without tearing the fabric apart.

"What do you two look like?" asked Jack with laughter in his voice.

Footsteps from outside their quarters signaled the arrival of three more cadets. The first to enter through the open door was Thai Qiu-Li. She burst out laughing at seeing Wictred fumbling with his waistcoat, or what was the loosest approximation of one on his large frame.

"You need to hurry. We're supposed to be out of here in the next seven minutes," she explained with feigned urgency in her voice. Jack stopped and looked up at her.

"What's the hurry? It's only a party."

"Only a party?" Thai Qiu-Li replied.

"He's not wrong," Wictred said. "We're in the middle of something here."

Thai Qiu-Li looked at them both with a coy expression.

"Aw, do you two need some more time alone?"

Jack grinned and made for the door before realizing he'd left his belt on his desk. He grabbed it and thrust the end through the loops on his jacket. With a firm tug, he pulled it around his Marine Corps jacket. He threw a sideways glance at his friends when finished, as though he'd been ready all along. Neither looked particularly ready, but in his experience that was as good as they tended to look. He nodded to himself and did his best to hide a grin. Hunn didn't notice, but Wictred spotted the corner of his mouth moving.

"Hey, you think this is funny, Jack?" he asked bitterly.

Jack stood up straight and pulled at his jacket.

"Hell, yes. If you could see yourselves, right now!"

Wictred and Hunn looked at each other and then both laughed and nodded in agreement. Wictred moved first, made for the door, and stepped out into the corridor. Hunn moved to follow him, and in just a few seconds, the whole group was moving along the main corridor. It was wide and much better finished than the interior of the ships they'd spent time on over the last year. As they continued, the six marines reached a crossroads section that was also packed with lots of other uniformed marines. In the distance, the sound of loud music thumped through the thick walls of the station.

"Jack, you ready for this?" asked Thai Qiu-Li.

He looked at her, opening his mouth to speak but was stopped by the sight of a large group of almost a dozen Alliance Navy officers and cadets. They were all smartly dressed in their dark navy uniforms, long coats, and peaked caps. It was a very different look to that of the Marine Corps. It was the two black-haired individuals that caught his eye, however. Wictred saw the exchange of looks and put his hand out to stop Jack from moving forward.

"What is it?" asked Thai Qiu-Li.

"Matius and Ingo," muttered Jack under his breath.

All of them were now looking at the Navy officers. It looked like they might leave, but one of them laughed, and in an instant were walking towards the marines. When they were close enough, the marines, Jack included, lifted their hands smartly and saluted at the young officers. The two black-haired lieutenants in the middle of the group snarled at Jack, their disgust immediately apparent. A young man with a dark, tanned face and dark eyes shook his head at him.

"Nice to see you again, brother," said Jack calmly.

The man stood next to him with the same dark eyes

and complexion took a step forward.

"What the hell are you doing on a Naval base?" he asked angrily.

Wictred lifted a hand in a passive gesture.

"My friend, you seem unburdened by intelligence. Can you not see his insignia? Jack has just completed his passing out ceremony. He is now a marine."

The man looked to Wictred and shook his head.

"Friend?" he stuttered. "I'm not your friend. Nobody wants a Jötnar animal for a friend."

Both Wictred and Hunn growled at this insult, and it took Thai Qiu-Li and her other two marine comrades interceding to stop a brawl. Jack, on the other hand, just stood by and gazed into the dark eyes of his half-brothers. They'd never been friends. At best they'd got along, but as he'd reached his teenage years, and his father Spartan had spent more time with them, they had become embittered.

"Matius and Ingo, I didn't come here looking for a fight," Jack said.

Wictred choked on his own laughter; he knew too well the tone in Jack's voice.

Matius stepped forward and directly in front of Jack. He was just a few centimeters shorter than Jack but held himself as straight and tall as he could manage. His face was tight and his cheek muscles tense. He looked at both sides of Jack's face, sniffing as though identifying the trace of something foul.

"What is that?" he asked sarcastically.

Jack closed his eyes and breathed in a slow, single breath. "Funny. Like I said, I'm not looking for trouble."

Matius smirked at his half-brother.

"I don't see what our mother sees in your father. You're just as simple and vulgar as he is. No wonder you all joined the Corps."

Jack had stayed calm for long enough, but the insult to his father, himself, and now his friends was more than he could stand. Every muscle in his body wanted to strike, and it took all his self-control to stand his ground. He may have succeeded until Matius, now confident he had Jack under his control, took it a step further. He reached out and grabbed Jack's collar with his right hand.

"Good lad, you know your place. You'll always be the runt in our family. A pathetic little…"

That's it! Jack thought; his anger now unleashed.

Jack thrust his left hand over Matius' arm and brought his hand and forearm back under his, locking Matius' arm. With a quick wrench, the arm creaked, and Jack had him under his control. It wasn't enough, and try as he might, he couldn't stop his right hand from forming a fist. He struck Matius hard in the jaw with a swift uppercut that almost knocked him out cold. Still Jack held onto his broken arm.

"You insult me, my father, my friends, and now the Corps? You bastard!"

With that, he released his half-brother's arm and

delivered a powerful kick to his groin, sending Matius staggering back two meters and into his group of friends before falling to the ground in pain.

"Did you see that?" snapped Ingo with her hand pointed directly at Jack, "He just struck an Alliance officer. That's a court martial offense!"

Jack turned to Wictred who just grinned back at him. Thai Qiu-Li and her two friends looked as though they were going to join in, but Jack waved them off.

"No, this is between us. Don't get involved."

Thai Qiu-Li looked to her left and her right, but neither of her friends seemed very keen on staying back. Both were female and in their twenties. Like all the marines, they were physically fit, strong willed, and ever eager for the fight.

"No chance," spat Thai Qiu-Li as she unbuttoned her brand new Marine Corps jacket.

"You attack one of us, you attack all of us," said her tall blonde friend with surprising ferocity.

Matius lifted himself to his feet and spat blood to the floor. He spoke to his brother, and an angry exchange broke out between them and the other cadets. One of the older officers stepped back with their hands raised, as if suggesting he was backing off. Matius swung at the man, but he ducked to avoid the impact and then walked away shaking his head. Jack looked at the group carefully and checked the stance and position of each. He counted nine remaining, and every one of them appeared keen. Matius was definitely the ringleader, but there was one other, a taller man with broad shoulders and a scarred face. He must have been in his early thirties, yet was still a cadet.

"Matius, don't be a fool. I do not want to fight with officers," Jack called out so that anybody nearby could hear.

There were now a good number of marines and navy cadets, plus a smattering of junior officers. The music from the hall just twenty meters away increased in volume, and it seemed to pump up the adrenalin of all those present.

"Then you shouldn't have come!" Matius shouted back.

With that last statement, the nine rushed toward the marines. Jack, Hunn, and Wictred lowered their stances and waited for the rush. Thai Qiu-Li and her two friends moved off to the right as if not taking part, leaving the three on their own and exposed. The largest of the navy cadets reached Jack first and attempted to smash the smaller man to the ground. Jack sidestepped and moved a step ahead to jam his knee into the man following. The attack caught the man completely by surprise, and he dropped to the ground with a groan. Wictred grabbed two men around the chest and bear-hugged them, his massive arms stopping them from moving and forcing the air from their lungs; that left Matius and five others for Hunn to deal with.

"Jack!" Matius shouted as he spun around.

Instead of facing him, the young marine moved his back foot to the right and twisted so that he could land another strike on the next man before they reached Hunn. His attack was fast and violent, sending yet another man to the floor. Four more leapt at Hunn, and either through skill or luck, they managed to force him to the floor. Jack tried to help, but Ingo grabbed him and held him back. He looked at him and shook his head.

"Not today, brother!"

With an open palm, he struck him shoulder and sent him flying backward. It wasn't enough to take him out of the fight, but it did move him back far enough to allow Jack to leap on the nearest man pulling at Hunn. At the same time, Ingo crashed into a group of onlookers and managed to bring them into the brawl. A fist struck his face, and he was knocked down, just in time for his brother to arrive on the scene.

"Who did this?" he said.

Ingo rubbed his forehead and wiped the sweat from his face. He reached out and pointed to the rolling melee on the ground.

"Our bastard brother."

Matius' face seemed to contort even further than it had at the onset of the fight. Months, perhaps years of frustration at their unwanted sibling boiled up to the surface, as he rushed back into the fray. He threw himself at Jack, and the two rolled to the floor while the two

Jötnar flailed about in the middle of an increasing group of fighters. They looked like a pair of bears surrounded by yapping dogs, yet neither seemed concerned. In fact, as Jack rolled on the floor, he was convinced the two were having the time of their lives as they threw marines and navy cadets about. His vision blurred, and he spotted Matius lifting his hand for yet another strike. He could feel pain in his forehead.

That asshole must have landed one! he realized incredulously.

As the strike approached him again, he batted it to the side so that Matius struck the ground with all his force. His fist made a sickening sound, much like the sound that had occurred when Jack had fractured his right arm. He screamed out in pain, and Jack took that as an opportunity to flick up and kick his leg out from under him. Matius collapsed to his side and left Jack standing alone with a smirk on his face. Ingo rushed back in, a chair lifted over his head and followed by three men, each wearing navy crew uniforms. Jack didn't realize what was happening until they were on him. Thai Qiu-Li and her two friends jumped in front of him, blocking the path and grabbed, punched, or grappled with the new arrivals. Jack looked about and nodded with amusement.

"Now this is a fight I think Spartan would be proud of."

His moment of smug self-satisfaction was stopped by a firm punch delivered from an angry looking sergeant. The man's face looked like a weathered rock, and his bark was louder than any, shouting in the open space that was now filled with fighting Alliance personnel.

"Enough!"

Jack rolled to the ground, a searing pain spreading through his head. It joined the other sharp aching pains that seemed to be coming from all around his body. His instinct told him to move, and he rolled to the side in time to avoid a black leather boot from striking his chest. With all his remaining strength, he lifted himself back up, shook his head, and swung his fist.

"I said, enough!" shouted the Sergeant who pushed the punch aside with his left forearm and then delivered three swift punches into Jack's stomach. He doubled over and dropped to his knees, gasping for air. A loud thud from five meters away indicated the end of the fight with the Jötnar. Wictred turned to look at Jack with a grin the width of his face. He spotted Jack wheezing and made to approach the marine that had struck him. A look of recognition appeared instantly on his muscled face, and instead of advancing, he stood his ground.

"Better," said the Sergeant in a calm yet assertive tone.

Over a dozen people lay injured or knocked out on the ground, including one of Thai Qiu-Li friends who kept rolling about on the floor groaning. The Sergeant ignored her and turned to face what were now nearly hundred people. He shook his head angrily.

"You people are an embarrassment. Half of you have only just graduated the Navy or Marine Corps academies, and now you're brawling like common thugs or even worse, pit fighters."

He spat at the floor in disgust.

"Hell, at least pit fighters do it for a living."

He looked at them all and soaked in the details. There was some blood, but he was pleased to see that there didn't appear to be any major injuries other than the odd broken bone.

Wounded pride, more like.

"This incident will be investigated, and the facts will come out, mark my words."

He straightened up, his back as level as a piece of wood and lifted his chin.

"I'm Sergeant Stone, and I'm here to tell you that today is your lucky day. All leave is cancelled. Your little soirée is over. You can get yourselves back to your quarters and into your combat gear."

The atmosphere in the room changed completely. Instead of facing off against enemies, the cadets and officers each turned their attention to the veteran Sergeant standing before them. He watched them, pleased to see that at least this news seem to get their attention. A few started to run for the door, but a loud cough from the Sergeant stopped them cold.

Here it goes.

"As of thirty minutes ago, all Alliance military units were activated. That includes the 8th Battalion. Every vessel and tactical unit stationed aboard this base will be leaving in the next hour. Get your gear and wait for your next orders."

There was a stunned silence until a female Navy officer called out.

"What's happening, Sergeant?"

"We're going to war, that's what's happening. Thirty minutes ago an exploratory mission was attacked on the distant edges of T'Karan. There is no more information, but trust me, it will come. All you need to know is that the fleet is assembling, and all Marine units from Prometheus and Prime through to Terra Nova have been activated. Now, jump to it, people!"

The room quickly emptied, and even the wounded vanished, but they must have been carried or helped. Jack and his comrades didn't notice, and they approached the Sergeant.

"Sergeant...I..." started Jack.

The Sergeant looked at Jack, starting with his feet and then moving up until reaching the young man's bruised face.

"Son, you need to sort out this rage. You're Spartan's son, aren't you?"

Jack nodded.

"Yes, Sergeant."

"Yeah, I thought as much. I never met him, but I know him by reputation. He was a hot head like you, but he learned the value of discipline and self-control early on. If you want to be half the marine he was, you need to bottle it. Save it for the enemy, and believe me, there are plenty of them."

He lowered his voice as, speaking just to himself.

"There always are."

Wictred moved up to Jack, looked at his bruises, and then to the Sergeant. Although he had been involved in the fighting just as much as anybody else, he failed to see that he'd done anything wrong. In fact, by the look on his face, he seemed to think he had behaved rather well.

"Well, well. Sergeant, you have Jötnar warriors in the Corps now. If you need more help, just contact our leader. Gun will not let the Alliance down," he then looked over to Hunn, "He never has."

The Sergeant shook his head.

"Ladies, this is all very touching, but right now you're on my wrong side. Now, get your fingers out and fall in. I need marines kitted up and ready to go, and fast. Hell, the Corps needs you ready."

Sergeant Stone marched away from them toward the corridor leading back to the bow of the ship. He looked over his shoulder and spotted the small group making slow progress in the opposite direction. He stopped and called out to them.

"This isn't over, Private Morato. You struck a sergeant in the Alliance Marine Corps. Well, you tried to strike. I suggest you spend the time from now and your hearing to fix your reputation. You might want to watch your back as well. Navy officers have plenty of time on their hands, and nobody likes getting their arm broken by a jarhead."

He walked out of the room, and try as he might, found it almost impossible to hide the glimmer of a smile. Jack looked to his friends who stood around him. Everybody else had gone, even his siblings who must have escaped at the first opportunity.

"What's going on?" asked Thai Qiu-Li.

Jack shrugged.

"The Sergeant didn't give much away," Wictred answered in a slow voice.

The public address system siren sounded, quickly followed by the voice of the station commander.

"Now hear this, now hear this."

Wictred smiled and tilted his head towards the sound.

"Here it is."

The muffled voice continued, "All Alliance personnel are to report to your ships. Marine units are to assemble on platforms seven-twelve."

Jack looked at his group of friends and smiled.

"It looks like we're going to war!"

He marched from the room and into the corridor, without even checking if the others were following. Thai

Qiu-Li, Wictred, and Hunn stood there in silence. Thai Qiu-Li's two friends had already gone. She'd noticed them go, with one holding on to the other, but the news from the Sergeant was more important right now.

"I need to go," she announced, leaving in the opposite direction to go and check on them. Now just the two Jötnar remained, and they looked at each other. Wictred looked impassively at Hunn who now just smiled. He was known as the Champion of Hyperion, and had won the title after defeating ten of his brothers in a bloody and violent contest. Where Wictred was young, impulsive, and excitable, Hunn was far less predictable. Most of the time he was calm, but his rage knew no bounds. His mouth changed from almost a smirk to a wide smile. He reached out and grasped Wictred's arm.

"Brother, we became marines just in time to save the day!" he laughed.

Wictred cocked his head and laughed but not as enthusiastically as Hunn. He thought of the stories he'd heard from the first of the battles fought by the original generation of Jötnar. Hundreds, perhaps thousands had died in the service of the Confederacy. He loved war as much as any Jötnar, but he was convinced it had to be different this time.

"Yes, but this time we will show them how to fight a war. We are no longer cannon fodder."

Hunn looked surprised at his comments. He thought

about them for a few seconds. "You are right. It is time to lead men into battle. We need promotions, and fast!"

Yes, thought Wictred, *promotions and responsibility will give us units to command. That is how we will change things for the Jötnar.*

* * *

Tuke approached the ruin of the four alien bodies with trepidation. Khan and Spartan shared no such concerns. Their fallen enemies lay smashed and broken from the powerful gunfire released by the T'Kari Raider. Spartan moved to the closest of the things, tapping its head with his foot. The shape was easily the size of Spartan's armored torso and beautifully intricate and ornate. Tuke moved up to him, bent down to take a look, and stepped back.

"What's wrong?" Spartan asked.

Tuke's translators took a moment to catch up with his quiet words.

"The Enemy, I've never seen one of his soldiers... never so close."

Khan joined them and kicked the metal head. Tuke recoiled but neither could establish if it was concern or fear.

"It's just big soldiers, nothing special about them."

Tuke shook his head.

"No, you do not understand."

Spartan spotted a fluid running from a number of holes in the metal of the head. It didn't surprise him. After all, he was already very familiar with the idea of biomechanical creatures. What did surprise him was that the hand-sized holes in its arms and chests revealed nothing other than scorched metal and electronics. He looked to the armored form of Khan, giving an expressionless stare back from inside his suit.

"So? It's an armored bug."

Spartan reached down and examined the thing even closer.

"No, it's more than that. This entire warrior is mechanical, a bit like the machines we fought on Hyperion. But the technology used for these is a league ahead."

Khan moved to the other side of the fallen warrior and kicked at the shattered side of the armored helm. Several chunks of metal broke off, yet he still couldn't get inside. To the shocked expression of Tuke, he pulled out his own savage looking blade and embedded the hardened metal into the ruined shape. With one heavy foot on its head, he pulled on the handle, and it finally tore open. He gazed inside and smiled.

"Interesting. Very interesting," he said calmly.

Spartan and Tuke moved around to examine the damage. The first thing Spartan noticed was a gyroscopic suspension system that was fractured. It had been encased in a heavily reinforced and ribbed unit that was fused inside the thickly armored helm. Fluid oozed out and ran down the metal of the machine and to the ground. Part of the thick goo touched Tuke's foot, and he immediately stepped back, looking about as though expecting trouble. Spartan turned his head but remained down at the machine.

"Tuke, my friend. You need to calm down."

With that last sentence, he pulled at the gyroscopic unit to reveal an armored egg that was also fractured. He reached inside and pulled on the outer wall; it easily broke apart, revealing damaged grey matter. He stood up and shook his head.

"Brain matter. This is just like the AI cores that the enemy tried to use to control our ships."

Tuke seemed surprised at his words.

"You have seen this done before?"

Spartan nodded slowly and pointed at the shattered helm.

"These AI Core units are brains that are used to control equipment. The enemy managed to put this tech in the hands of the Zealots and their followers. Their equipment allowed the biological unit to connect directly to our ship's computer systems and take control of them.

Spartan then kicked the fallen machine.

"This guy is something else though. Why bother putting in a brain directly into a soldier? Seems a lot of work when they can grow warriors like my friend here."

Tuke was the only one that failed to see the problem.

"These soldiers are not common troops. The Enemy is a master of technology, but he has just one weakness, his numbers are finite."

"Finite?" replied Khan sarcastically.

Spartan turned from the machine and back to Tuke.

"What do you mean?"

"According to our histories, the Enemy is ancient and immortal. We have faced their commanders in battles a hundred years apart, and still it is the same leader. The myth surrounding them tells that they do not die."

Spartan raised his hand and shook it in disbelief.

"Wait a second, Tuke. Are you telling me that this Great Enemy of yours is a biological race that's cocooned inside machine bodies?"

Tuke looked confused.

"Did you not already know this?"

Spartan looked back at Khan with a large grin on his face.

"Khan, my friend. It looks like we've seen the face of our enemy, well, his brain anyway!"

Khan lifted his curved blade and brought it down on the damaged gyroscopic assembly and casing. It crunched through metal, electronics, and brain matter, sending chunks of debris scattering around them. He roared with pleasure at the same time.

"That's one less to deal with!" he howled through his suit, walking over to the next fallen machine. He lifted his weapon high, poised like an executioner above a condemned man.

"Now, let's see what we can find inside you."

As the blade came down, Tuke turned away, showing his back to the shattered machines. There was no sound in the airless environment, not that it really mattered. It was clear to both him and Spartan what Khan was up to. As Tuke looked away, he noticed a glimmer of light out in space. It was different to the other objects up there in the night sky, and for a moment he watched it, entranced by its movement. Then it changed course and his pulse quickened. He turned back to Spartan and Khan who was still busy smashing away with his weapon.

"Somebody is here!" he said fearfully.

Spartan looked up in the same direction as Tuke, but Khan was far too occupied destroying the machine to notice what they were doing. The shape of the T'Kari Raider was clearly visible, but more worrying was that the bright shape was moving toward it. Spartan connected directly to Lovett on board the ship.

"Lovett, have you seen it?" he called out.

The two shapes were now moving as they positioned themselves, for what could only be some form of engagement. As Spartan watched them, he became acutely aware they were out on a derelict station with no other forms of transport, or support. A cold feeling of fear traveled up his spine. He discarded the thought. The sound of Lovett's voice returned, much to his relief.

"We're on it. I don't know how the hell they managed to get so close. Either they were here all along, or another Rift must have opened up nearby."

Dozens of bright flashes erupted along the outside of the new arrival, as if struck by a battery of weapons. Spartan hoped, but knew deep down, there was no way the T'Kari Raider could have maneuvered into an adequate firing position in such a short time. By the last count, it had taken almost a minute for the capacitors to charge for the main guns.

Let's just hope they were still charged from the bombardment earlier.

Tuke looked at him briefly; his visor was up and revealing his worried expression behind the armored glass. Spartan looked into his eyes, yet again was astounded at how similar they were to his own people. Other than muscle tone and coloring, they seemed to be identical to humans. Even in the middle of such a dangerous situation, he was reminded of a documentary he'd watched just a few months ago that contained interviews with top Alliance scientists, as well as T'Kari. Neither had been able to come up with a satisfactory explanation for the similarities or the origins of the species. Most were convinced it was a parallel development based on similar conditions, but others went for a more grandiose idea. The more religious were using it as an argument for their intelligent design by a creator, while others thought it might suggest a third party that had been involved in planetary seeding and genetic engineering. Spartan noticed Tuke was speaking and shook himself out of his stupor.

"Spartan, we are in trouble!"

The T'Kari crew are powering up the weapons. You need to keep your heads down until..."

He stopped speaking, and a sound of distorted voices bounced inside Spartan's helmet. He shook his head and tried to reconnect. There were multiple channels that connected both to the ship and directly to the remaining members in Spartan's team. For a brief moment, he managed to reach Lovett, but his voice was drowned out by a digital tone.

"Jamming!" Tuke called out.

At the same time, the T'Kari warrior moved away from the most recent scene of destruction on what remained of the old station. He dropped down behind a shattered wall and looked back up to the starships. Spartan stood his ground, waving his fist toward Lovett and the others.

"Lovett, get out of there!" he bellowed, but with no connection, there was little chance anything would now get through to them. Khan had now turned from his smashing spree and looked up in time to watch a series of flickering shapes moving between the two vessels.

"What's happening?"

Spartan shook his head, amazed that his friend had

managed to miss almost everything that had happened in the last thirty seconds. He could see Khan was breathing heavily and must have worked himself up quite a bit destroying the machines. Sometimes Spartan forgot how much hatred there was from the Jötnar toward those responsible for creating them. At first, it seemed it was down to the Echidna Union and their Zealot followers but now he had learned of this ancient race; he could only imagine the rage in his blood. The Jötnar had suffered greatly and were still considered outcasts throughout the Alliance. Tuke waved to get their attention.

"We have a visitor, and he's heading right for our ship."

Both Khan and Spartan watched as the ship moved even closer to their borrowed Raider. As it came closer, the ribbing and outline became clearer. Tuke recognized the shape and called out on the intercom in an excited voice. After a short delay, the translator explained.

"It is one of the carrier craft from the fleet. They must have sent back a scout."

Khan slammed his armored foot into one of the felled machines, "Maybe, or they received a signal from these things asking for help."

"Perhaps," answered Tuke.

Each looked up at the ships, wondering what was happening. That was when the T'Kari Raider vanished in a bright blue flash that obscured its hull completely. Spartan staggered back as he thought of Lovett and the others on the vessel.

Maybe they abandoned ship, he hoped, but he knew that it took more than a few seconds to get off an unfamiliar vessel. Another series of blue flashes moved around the vessel from bow to stern before fading away to leave nothing but a cloud of fine dust and the newly arrived warship.

CHAPTER TWELVE

ANS Victory was one of many powerful warships that continued the proud name. The first had been a British 42-gun ship from the sixteenth century. Five more ships were to bear the name until reaching the most famous Victory of all, the eighteenth century 100-gun first-rate ship of the line. It was this mighty warship for which ANS Victory was built to honor. Where HMS Victory led Admiral Nelson's fleet to victory at Trafalgar in 1805, the new ship was built to take the fight to enemy ships or planets with its complement of half a battalion of marines. The incident at Helios would test the modifications to the Crusader class to the limit.

Ships of the Alliance

ANS Victory appeared in the blink of an eye at its destination outside the planet Helios, the nearest planet to the burning hot star at the center of the system. It was a trouble-free journey through the Rift, and as usual, there was no discernible split from the space back at T'Karan and their destination. The mighty ship made no noise in the cold void of space, yet it looked like an angry beast, bristling with armor and weapons. Nobody would make the mistake of assuming this metal machine was anything but a weapon of war.

No sooner had they arrived and the internal alarms were blaring. Every single station in the CIC seemed to be hit with a stream of messages, alerts, and warnings from throughout the ship. Admiral Anderson watched the tactical display as one by one the entire Alliance military force arrived. None of the civilian ships followed, just the six Crusader class warships and the four T'Kari scouts that were already there. It wasn't the new star system that caught the Admiral's eye; it wasn't even the odd red hue that seemed to be everywhere. No, it was the massive pentagonal structure that filled the mainscreen.

"I need a full scan of that object. What the hell is it?" he demanded.

As the officers rushed about, he continued looking at it. General Daniels was the only other officer watching; the rest were busy at their stations.

"Looks manmade to me, maybe a station?" he suggested helpfully.

As he spoke, a detailed three-dimensional schematic of the shape appeared. The ship's tactical officer, Lieutenant

Jesse Powalk explained the details as the information was added, one layer at a time.

"It's massive. The computer estimates the total diameter at close to eight hundred meters. It is definitely artificial and generating a powerful gravity well. It must be occupied."

A black grid appeared on the model and distorted around the shape of the structure. Color areas then appeared at certain points.

"This is the XO, all hands to battle stations," the ship's executive officer called out over the public address system. The order was barely required as every single Navy and Marine crewman was already at their station and waiting for their orders as they moved through the Rift. As the XO though, it was his job to ensure the ship was operating at maximum efficiency. The lighting inside the vessel was now dull red and gave the impression they were already in a shooting war.

"Yeah, It's definitely occupied, Sir, five to six hundred life signs. Wait, there's a power surge."

On the model a number of bright blooms flashed along parts of the station.

"Brace for impact!" shouted the XO over the intercom. It was an automatic reaction to the news and reached the crew at just the right moment. Seconds later, over a dozen indicators lit up on the model.

"Weapons fire!" cried the Lieutenant.

Admiral Anderson looked back to the mainscreen where the vast pentagonal shape was sending stream of projectiles out and toward the newly arrived ships.

"Communications, get greetings sent out on all frequencies!" snapped the Captain.

"And light up those projectiles! Get our turrets moving!" added the XO.

His words were unnecessary, however, as the tactical officer and his team of experienced crew was already busy activating the many defensive systems throughout the ship. It took only a few more seconds before the stream of rounds from the station reached the T'Kari ships that had pushed out far from the Alliance warships.

"What the hell are they doing?" snapped Captain Parker.

Admiral Anderson watched the tactical display with calm precision. He could already see their position, and it was clear to him what was happening.

"They are moving into defensive positions around their lost ship. Look, the first scout vessel is in two halves."

As he pointed at the nearest ships, the first rounds from the station arrived. Round after round hit the T'Kari scout ships, and with each impact a piece of metal armor was ripped off. Anderson wiped a bead of sweat from his face and then called out to Captain Parker.

"Bring us into position ahead of the T'Kari. I'll bring up Crusader and Serenity to watch our flanks. We have to keep the weapons fire off them until they can recover their wounded."

"Aye, aye, Sir," she replied smartly.

The idiots. They are either unable to defend themselves, or they refuse to do so.

It only took a few deft hand movements to connect directly to the commanders of the other ships. Each followed his commands without argument, and in seconds, the ships were all moving. With a lurching feeling, the great warship powered up her main engines and pushed out and past the smaller T'Kari warships. Anderson looked at the images of the Crusader class warships and couldn't but be impressed with their speed and power. He just hoped they could keep them alive long enough to either withdraw or find a way to stop the violence.

Good, first job is to protect the ships. Second is to stop this insanity!

"Admiral, we're in range of their projectile weapons. Our rules of engagement are confused, can we return fire?" asked Captain Parker.

Admiral Anderson looked up to the mainscreen and shook his head. Much as he wanted to open fire, he was loath to turn a violent first encounter into a full-scale war; at least, not yet.

"No. For the sake of damage to our ships, I cannot risk a war. Our mission parameters are clear. We are to investigate Helios, clear the Rift, and maintain the security of the Alliance. We cannot leave backdoors into any regions of space we have access to."

General Daniels nodded at his words, "Yes, the last thing we need is to turn another race against us. We need the Helions on our side, or at the very least neutral."

Captain Parker looked unimpressed at the response and turned back to her XO with whom she had a curt confrontation. Anderson commanded the fleet, but the operations of the ship belonged to the Captain. He looked briefly at the tactical screen, along with General Daniels.

"This is taking too long," said Anderson, now realizing the T'Kari must be in a worse state than he'd imagined.

"I don't like this," said the Marine officer slowly.

Anderson nodded.

"I agree."

He then called out to the CAG, the single man responsible for command of the fleet's fighter squadrons. Normally, he would coordinate just the fighters from ANS Victory, but today he was controlling the position of the fighters from each of the Crusader class ships.

"Get birds in the air and put a protective cordon around the fleet. We have to keep the big stuff away from our hulls. The point defense gear can deal with the rest."

The young looking marine saluted and proceeded to move icons about on his large glass vertical display. It was a fast and effective way to communicate directly with each of the pilots.

Anderson looked to the XO, who was doing his best to

keep the crew on task while avoiding damaging the station that seemed so intent on destroying them. He almost called out an order before forcing himself to take a step back. He had the tactical control of the situation from his position in the CIC. The tactical display showed him the status of every vessel under his control, as well as direct communication with any ship in the formation. He tapped the lead T'Kari ship, surprised it actually connected. He breathed a sigh of relief as the image of T'Kron appeared.

"About damned time! What the hell is going on?" he roared.

"Admiral. We are evacuating our crippled ship. They were fired on by the automated systems on the station upon arrival. It is…"

"Enough of that!" interrupted the Admiral, his voice straining with impatience. "Why have you not told them to stop firing?"

The image flickered for a moment and then went black before quickly returning.

"Admiral Anderson, you do not understand. They are broadcasting a general alert in seven languages. It says they are treating all of us as intruders. They will continue firing until we leave. Any vessel moving closer to their station will be attacked with their anti-ship systems."

Anderson shook his head angrily.

"What do you mean, closer?"

"Where our scout was hit. By moving out here to

protect us, you are inviting their wrath."

Anderson's face was starting to redden with anger and frustration.

"T'Kron, get a dammed move on. Look after your people, and keep sending the Helions our messages. This madness must stop. I will protect your ships, but this cannot go on forever."

He paused as he contemplated the situation they were in.

"How long do you need to get your people out?"

"Fifteen minutes, maybe more. Some are trapped in the wreckage. I have teams bringing them back."

"Good, I want updates every five minutes. If we can't stop this fighting, then we will have to withdraw. I am creating a cordon around your ships. If you have any defensive systems, I suggest you use them."

T'Kron nodded and the feed cut.

I need status reports from the rest of the fleet. We need time to sort this out.

He then looked at the tactical display in front of him. His fleet was strung out and vulnerable, and he was acutely aware of how fragile the ten ships were if it came down to a major confrontation. He thought back to some of the greatest battles of the Uprising. In those encounters, he'd witness columns of dozens and dozens of ships moving in to deliver broadsides of railgun shots. The battles had gone on for hours, and the casualties had been terrible.

I'd forgotten how vicious this can get!

"We need to know what the hell is going on out here."

The Alliance ships had already altered their formation, and as expected, the gunfire from the station switched to the nearest of the ships. With ANS Victory at the forefront, the bulk of the fire targeted her flank. Small dimples on every part of the ship moved as the multitude of rapid-fire point-defense turrets opened fire. Each was fully automated and contained multi-barreled kinetic weapons and a mixed visual and radar based tracking system. Lines of tiny rounds streamed away and struck at the approaching weapons fire. Even so, a small percentage managed to penetrate the protective screen and make it through to the thick hull of ANS Victory. Dozens of rounds struck the armored flank. At first, they seemed no more serious than rain falling upon a thin roof. The intensity increased until emergency alarms sounded.

"Captain, the reactive plating is breached!" called out Lieutenant Powalk.

It wasn't as serious as it sounded, as the reactive plating was an additional layer of armor that extended out several meters from the hull. It was thin and equipped with modular explosive plates that detonated when an impact was detected. Though it could only be used once, the modular components were small, each no more than a meter in length and able to stop a large projectile or warhead from causing serious harm when it finally struck the primary armor.

"Keep the guns running. Everybody else, get me information! The armor can only take so much."

Admiral Anderson watched the approaching fire from the pentagonal station at his formation of ten ships. The T'Kari vessels were moving out of the line of fire, and now the heavy warships were doing their work. On the tactical screen were various clouds of projectiles, but the Crusader class ships appeared to be fending off the worst of it.

"Captain, armor is holding," said the tactical officer calmly.

"Good. Power up the primary weapons, but do not fire."

Lieutenant Powalk nodded in agreement. At the same time, the gruff XO examined all the data coming in from each station. He made a mental note of the most important pieces of data before passing them on to the Captain. Commander D'Vani, on the other hand, had already run through scans and looked first to the Captain before speaking.

"Captain, scans are complete."

"Good, give us a précis."

Admiral Anderson smiled grimly at her curt reply. The Commander looked to the Admiral before starting.

"The description given to us by the T'Kari seems close to what we have encountered. Orbiting the star are five planets, all populated to various degrees. We are closest to the first planet in the system. There is a belt at approximately twenty-seven astronomical units from our current position. I'm getting odd readings from it."

"Forget the belt. I just need information on what we have around us."

The Commander looked back at his screen but was instantly overawed by what he could see. Admiral Anderson stepped closer, leaning in to look. He shook his head in surprise at the variety of images flashing by as the Commander classified them by group.

"What is it?" asked Admiral Anderson, expecting trouble.

"Its...it's just the amount of traffic. Our threat indication system has flagged over three hundred vessels within a day's travel already. Not even Terra Nova has this concentration of craft. All five planets are populated have similar traffic levels."

"That is all very interesting, Commander. What I really need to know is the tactical situation."

"I have that, Sir," announced Lieutenant Powalk. "There are four ships on an intercept course for us. They are of a similar size to ours and are escorted by a dozen smaller vessels, possibly fighters. Scans indicate energy weapon capacitors, possibly similar to our own."

He then pointed to the nearest planet that was over twelve hours away.

"Closer to the nearest planet are another thirty plus craft, and they look like they are activating their systems. They are not a threat, not yet. I suspect they are preparing for a fight, just in case."

Captain Parker sighed at the news. She looked at the center of the detailed system-wide model and tapped the station.

"Sir, there's something else."

With those words, he enlarged an image of a region of space well out from their current position.

"Our optics are unable to isolate detail at this distance, but we are picking up a number of collapsed Rift signatures in unprecedented numbers. It's unlike anything I've ever seen."

Admiral Anderson looked at the shapes appearing on their star chart as it filled in with details. At different points through the solar system, Rift after Rift appeared like exit points into a hive.

"I've got over a dozen, including the one we came through, and more are still being picked up."

"So, it is true. Helios really is the center of this Network. No way is this natural. The Helions and their friends must have built this at some point."

"Not just that, Admiral, there is this one right out on the periphery."

The man's finger stopped on an empty region of space. As his finger sat there, a large number of flashing red boxes appeared in an almost hexagonal shape.

"It looks like a distortion to me, and there are massive objects, possibly moons or maybe artificial objects have been positioned around it."

"A Rift?"

Lieutenant Powalk nodded.

"Probably, but a Rift unlike any of the others here."

Captain Parker considered the information for just a few seconds.

"My guess is those are stations, much like this one here, and it is designed to stop whatever is on the other side from coming through. Keep the scanners going. If we have to leave in a hurry, this intel might be all we can get. "

That has to be the entrance to the enemy's domain! So, the T'Kari were right all along. So Helios really is the center of this artificial Spacebridge Network, and they have barricaded the entrance to the most dangerous race out here. She didn't know whether to feel happy or concerned at the information.

She turned to the Admiral, a look of satisfaction now showing on her face only to see grim determination on his face.

"Admiral, I think this is the entrance the enemy's domain. It matches all the facts of the last two years, including the intelligence given to us on the Helions. They fought their last war, and this must be how they keep them from coming back."

"The eighth race," confirmed General Daniels. His

voice sounded doom laden as he answered. Admiral Anderson glanced at his comrade, noting with surprise at how he was taking the news. A moment of doubt entered his mind that he was the right man to lead the marines if things turned bloody.

Too late now you fool, he thought angrily.

General Daniels was right to feel unhappy at the news. He wasn't compromised by the words, but the scars of the ground combat on Euryale flashed back to him. In the years since those battles with biomechanical creatures and legions of warriors, he'd developed a healthy respect for the enemy and the damage and terrors they could bring to a fight. Being this close to what might be their own empire left him feeling almost queasy at the opportunity of sending so many men and women to their potential deaths.

"Good, this is what we came for," said Admiral Anderson.

Captain Parker looked at him, surprised at his words. She spotted the look on the General's face and noted that although he didn't look surprised, he also didn't appear particularly pleased at the news. That was when her brain raced ahead as the facts coalesced in her mind.

So we are not just here to explore. We sent three battalions of marines through the Helios Gate to use as an expeditionary force, surely not?

She looked back at the Admiral, trying to gauge his

reaction to the news. The more she thought about it though, the more surprised she was that she had been left out of the loop. As far as she was aware, the operation was an exploratory mission to map out the Network and to secure access for the Alliance.

"Admiral, are we here to finish the war with the enemy?" she finally asked.

Admiral Anderson looked to General Daniels who politely smiled back at him.

"No, our orders are flexible. Three battalions does provide us with a great deal of flexibility, however."

The young General did his best to avoid choking with amusement.

The ship shook at another volley of gunfire. A computer display flashed and then exploded, the shards of hardened metal and glass embedded into the arms and torso of its operator, a young woman with short black hair and narrow framed glasses. She was knocked from her seat and was helped by two of the Marine guards.

"Get her to medical!" called out the XO as he moved in to manage the situation.

The blast shook her attention from the distortion and back to their immediate situation. She watched the ships on the display, but Admiral Anderson was already looking back at the station.

"So, they have build defenses around all of the Rift entrances, including this one back to T'Karan. They must think we are vessels from the enemy as well."

"Then why attack the T'Kari?" she responded.

Admiral Anderson smiled, "They attack themselves, don't forget. They must have less faith in the T'Kari than we have."

General Daniels finished speaking on his comms unit and leaned over the tactical display, placing his hand directly in the middle.

"What about the station? We can't maneuver anywhere in this system until it is dealt with."

Lieutenant Powalk walked around the central table and was forced to grab the side of the unit as a powerful impact made the ship shudder. He almost lost his footing but quickly recovered and moved into position. He pointed at the shapes representing their own ships and then the point where they had arrived.

"If you look at the distances involved, it's pretty clear this station was built specifically to monitor and control this point of space. Either they want to stop their own people from activating it and traveling through…"

"Or they want to stop the T'Kari from returning. If you ask me, they want this area secured, and if that means firing on the T'Kari, so be it. We need to change the situation and bring force to bear on them. At the same time, we need the T'Kari to make contact and let them know that we come in peace," finished Admiral Anderson.

The schematic of the station was becoming more

and more detailed with every extra second they were in the system. At the center of the object, a glowing orb increased in intensity."

"What's that?" demanded the Admiral.

Captain Parker was already turning to her crew and shouting out so that every single officer could hear her. At the same time, the XO was barking orders to the science team. On the main display, the object appeared to split apart into two-dozen ultra high-speed missiles. Nobody seemed to be paying any attention to either of the senior officers on the ship. Admiral Anderson almost shouting before spotting the objects on the display. It was quite clear why they were all suddenly distracted.

"Hypersonic missiles, estimated time for impact, seventy-two seconds, Captain!" shouted the tactical officer. "Sensors are picking up low yield nuclear payloads on board."

"Atomics!" said the Captain in a hushed tone. They were the most feared weapons used in space combat, as once embedded in the armor of a ship, they could obliterate all but the most massive of warships. The only defense was to explode them outside the structure of the vessel. There would still be a superheated burst from the warhead, but with no air in space, there would be no damaging shockwave. All major warships were heavily shielded against radiation and magnetic pulse attacks.

"Bring them down!" she ordered in a firm, yet calm

tone.

The ship's XO was more concerned with the massive energy build up on the station. He heard the words from the Captain though, and while still looking at the screen, pulled the nearest command intercom from a support bulkhead. Of all of the officers in the CIC, he was the grimmest. His face was pockmarked and rough to look at, and he walked with a slight limp from an injury sustained years before his military service. None of that had stopped him from an exemplary career as a combat officer in the Navy. He cleared his voice and called out over the public address system to the crew.

"Incoming weapons fire, brace, brace, brace!"

Admiral Anderson looked to his side where General Daniels was watching the attack unfold before him. Until nearer to the enemy, there was absolutely nothing for him to do but check on the status of his three battalions, and make sure they were ready for action. He looked on helplessly as he waited for something, anything to do.

"Here it comes!" cried the tactical officer.

On the mainscreen, a great red line appeared, running directly from the station and toward the Alliance warship. It was thick, easily ten meters wide, and reflected from the odd red particles that littered the region of space near the Rift entrance. At first nothing happened, then came the alarms, and shortly after that the sparks and fires. Just a second after this, the entire ship shuddered as if it had just struck a massive barrier.

"Captain, we have breaches on all levels!" cried Lieutenant Powalk.

"Emergency seals are active, and holding!" added the chief engineer.

Before anybody could respond, the CIC flashed yellow, and a dozen computer units exploded directly in front of their users. Admiral Anderson was blasted to the wall with such ferocity that he was unconscious before he even hit the floor of the large open room. More systems exploded in a spectacular fashion, and the XO as well as Commander D'Vani, were also struck down.

"Admiral, missiles are locked on. Do I have permission to…" said an unfamiliar voice, but it was nothing but a dull murmur to him now.

"Admiral?"

His view went black and quiet as more weapons fire continued to slam into the armor of ANS Victory. It was a testament to her backup systems, defensive turrets, and multi-layered armor that not a single deck had yet been breached for longer than the internal seals could operate. At the same time, the auto-repair units pumped sealant into ruptures and cracks in the plates. But nothing could stop the energy from the weapons wreaking havoc in the populated parts of the ship. A great surge of electricity ripped through the enclosed space, destroying electronics and displays with ease. Anyone touching the equipment was instantly incapacitated. Captain Parker moved to the tactical display, doing her best to avoid the injured or possibly dying around her. It showed a great mess of a battle as every one of their ships continued shooting at approaching rounds and missiles.

That's it, we need to get out of this place, T'Kari, be damned!

She pulled the intercom to her lips, but another blast ripped through the ship. Shards of glass from the tactical display disintegrated and flew at her like a cloud. She was dead before her mutilated body crashed into the bulkhead. Of the command crew, only General Daniels was still standing. Just four more officers remained at their posts, including the tactical officer. He wiped his forehead and felt a sting as he rubbed against a piece of fractured glass on his forehead. Ignoring the trickle of blood running down his face, he took the intercom from where the Captain had tried to reach it. She'd left it active for the entire ship to hear.

"This is General Daniels. I am taking command of the ship. Prepare for battle, we are taking the fight to them!"

* * *

Lieutenant Ortega watched the series of explosions rippling along the outer hull of the leading Crusader class warships. He was forced to push maximum power into his lateral thrusters to avoid a stream of metallic rounds that were targeted directly at ANS Victory.

"Alpha Squadron, form up on me. Defensive pattern Delta," he announced over the fighters' intercom system.

The fighters lurched to the right and moved into a figure of eight pattern around the fleet, along with the rest of the widely spaced out squadron behind them. These sleek new craft were Hammerheads, the latest addition to the Alliance Navy fighter arsenals. Only one squadron was active with the taskforce, the rest being the standard twin engine Lightning MK II fighters.

"Now!"

With a brief burst of power, the fighter pushed forward and built up speed. Behind it came the rest of the formation. Their engines glowed as they expended substantial quantities of fuel to accelerate. The Hammerhead fighters were the heaviest and most advanced fighters ever created and had been designed like most of the new Alliance hardware to be multi-use. With four engines and two crew sat side-by side, they were easily fifty percent larger than a Lightning. They carried more guns and ordnance, as well as a mission bay that could carry supplies, heavy ordnance, or even a complete combat unit of up to a dozen warriors. Sea Skua anti-ship missiles were fitted above and below the wings, but what really made the craft stand out were the gun systems. Turrets were fitted above and below the main fuselage, with each fighter equipped with automated weapon systems and 20mm Gatling flak cannons for defense purposes. Slung under the chin was a pair of massive 60mm railguns, each capable of destroying fighters and other spacecraft with ease.

"LT! 7 o'clock."

Lieutenant Ortega twisted his head and instantly identified the threat; a pair of hypersonic missiles was moving at high speed toward ANS Victory. The scanner picked up a dozen more, each of them launched in salvos from the station.

"Fighters, break and engage, don't let them through!"

He pulled the stick back and twisted the thruster control. Small outlets across the fighter spun the craft around even though it continued on its same track. By ensuring the front of his fighter was directed toward the missiles, he could give both the turrets a clear view. His co-pilot, Sergeant Taka Asan removed the safeties from both turrets. They opened fire immediately, sending vibrations through the reinforced hull of the fighter. Four streams of magnetized projectiles licked out and ripped the missiles apart. The next three fighters peeled off and activated their own turrets. In less than ten seconds, all but one missile had been destroyed. Lieutenant Ortega linked to the tactical officer onboard the targeted warship.

"Lieutenant Powalk," came back a short, impatient voice from ANS Victory.

"Lieutenant, one got through!"

"Understood, stay clear, it is all under control."

Over a dozen turrets from two of the Alliance warships concentrated on the missile and disintegrated it less than a hundred meters from the ship. The shattered metal fragments continued at high speed and smashed into the multi-layered armor. Great chunks of metal were ripped out and a seven-meter long gouge scratched the outside as though a massive metal talon had dragged its edge along the ship.

Close one, Lieutenant Ortega thought, as he altered his fighter's orientation back on course. The other fighters in the Squadron reformed and continued along their preset pattern.

"This is an official command order from General Daniels, Alliance Marine Corps. The Navy command staff has been incapacitated in the attack, and as the ranking officer, I am therefore taking over command of this force until the Admiral is fit and able to resume command."

Lieutenant Ortega looked over to his co-pilot.

"Great, old firebrand Daniels is in charge. You know what that means."

Sergeant Asan grinned with grim amusement.

"All forces, you are authorized to use lethal force to defend yourselves. I want that station stopped, and I don't care what you have to do. Weapons free, let's end this before we lose a ship to these idiots!"

Lieutenant Ortega checked his scanner and identified the nearest threat to the fleet. As expected, it was the station; the other ships were a long distance away. Three other squadrons of Lightning MK II fighters were already changing their courses, based on new data from ANS Victory. The same orders flashed on his mapping unit. He nodded to himself before passing the information on to his group of fighters.

"Check your targeting systems; we've been given the honor of assaulting the primary weapon system of the station. Stay close, and keep your defense turrets active."

He looked straight ahead through the reinforced canopy and toward the heavily armored station. Streaks of gunfire from scores of defense systems opened fire, sending lines of projectiles out in all directions. The torrent of gunfire was like flying directly up into a thundercloud. He gritted his teeth and checked the status of his squadron.

"This is it boys. We're going in!"

The fighters maneuvered apart as they moved closer and closer to the target. Off on the periphery, at least six more Lightning MK II fighters attacked the flank of the station with a volley of missiles. Repeated defense cannons shot down every single one.

"Target the weapon systems. Use gunfire, save your missiles!"

They were now only a few kilometers away, and two Lightnings had been destroyed and one of the Hammerheads badly damaged. A streak of metal shards ripped into the left wingtip of Ortega's fighter.

That's it!

He flicked off the safety on his stick and pushed down on the trigger. A dull vibration shook the fighter.

"Fire!"

Three sets of quadruple 20mm coil-cannons opened fire. One set was mounted in the nose while small sponsons on each side of the cockpit housed another mounting. Twelve barrels fired at almost five hundred rounds a minute. They employed the same principles as the coilgun used by the marines, but upscaled to match the fighter's size and power systems. The weapon was actually a simple projectile accelerator, using electromagnets to hurl magnetized rounds at super-high velocities.

"On target, hits scored," his co-pilot said in a calm and almost monotone voice.

CHAPTER THIRTEEN

The Alliance Marine Corps at the time of the Orion Incident had entered the first major phase of its transformation into a fully mechanized force; the old transports and improvised troop carriers now replaced by the latest Crusader class warships. Though the military formations were now smaller, they were also better equipped and traveled aboard state of the art warships. The Vanguard armor that had been used so effectively in the past was in its fourth iteration and being rolled out to select battalions in the Corps. Now designated as heavy battalions, they were designed to operate as an alternative to tanks and other ground vehicles with access to more powerful weapons. They could be used independently or alongside their lighter armored cousins, either on foot or in their brand new eight-wheeled Bulldog transporters.

History of the Marine Corps

Jack entered their quarters first and immediately moved to his computer display. The brute force tools he'd left running had completed, and a light flashed on a dialog box, along with a status indicator. He slid into the curved metal chair with a clunk and leaned in closer. Wictred came in next and went directly to his locker.

"Jack, leave it. You heard the Sergeant. We have to get ready."

Jack ignored him and opened up the first of the partially decrypted files. He checked the indicators and recognized the seals were accurate. It was definitely from his mother, but it was also just three of the seventeen packets that made up the complete file. With a few quick gestures, he combined them into binary container and sent the output through an audio-visual filter. In just seconds, an image of his mother appeared.

"Teresa?" asked Hunn, walking through the doorway and stopping next to Jack's shoulder.

Jack had to skip the first minute, as there was too little data. He finally reached a segment with both audio and video that was working.

"...do not know how long this operation will take. The 17th are a green unit, and Gun and I will have our work cut out... when...do not."

The audio cut out, and the video distorted badly. Hunn started to speak, but Jack lifted his hand for silence and leaned in closer.

"...news about your father. He, Khan, and the others are missing...incident with Raiders."

"What did they say about Khan?" asked Wictred with obvious concern. Khan was his father, and the news was just as new to him as it was to Jack.

The display flashed black and a red box appeared showing a restricted symbol. Smaller text detailed the restriction access that had been made, and an alert was sent out to the tech crews on the station.

"Crap," he muttered, quickly hitting the reset button on the system. He turned around on his seat and looked at his two comrades.

"I don't know what's going on out there, but it looks like a group of our people, probably from APS, have gone missing, and it's something to do with Raiders."

"T'Kari?" asked Wictred.

Jack nodded.

"Yeah, didn't they attack the Jötnar colonies a few months ago?"

Both Jötnar nodded in agreement.

"So, that's all we know?"

Jack shrugged.

The door swung open with a loud bang, and in walked a Captain with a long black coat and dark glasses. At his flanks were four heavily armored marines, carrying L52 carbines across their hips. Jack could see they weren't expecting trouble; none of them appeared ready to get involved in a fight.

"Private Morato?" asked the Captain.

Jack stood up smartly and saluted. The two Jötnar looked at Jack, then to the Captain before doing the same.

"I've been sent to escort you and your comrades to the Admiral. He wants to see you."

"Yes, Sir."

The Captain stepped back outside, beckoning them to follow. Jack looked to Wictred who sighed and followed him.

"Here we go again," he muttered in a low tone.

* * *

The destruction of the T'Kari Raider was still a shock to Spartan, as he lay hidden in the rubble of the derelict station. All three of them were keeping as low and stationary as they could possibly manage. Above them moved some type of landing craft, and it was moving at a slow speed over the surface of the station. Spartan could see its outline through the shattered wall he was hiding behind. They had less than three minutes to hide when the craft had separated from the main vessel. It was now hovering over the bodies of the biomechanical warriors that had fallen in the ambush. Spartan watched, and his level of frustration was starting to grow.

Now I'm getting just a bit pissed off with this!

He had changed though. In his youth, he would have broken from cover and attacked the machine with any weapon he could find. When he'd joined the Marine Corps, he'd been in his late twenties and full of fire and anger. Now he was just three months away from his fiftieth birthday, and he had something to lose. He had a wife and a teenage son who'd now followed in his footsteps and joined the Marine Corps, and so he finally felt he needed to be a little calmer with the decisions he made. Throwing his life away fighting machines was no good when others needed him. As he lay in the rubble, he thought back of his time in the service, and the last few years where the military bureaucracy had culled so many of its active units and personnel in cut after cut. He'd taken the money in the end and started APS, along with Teresa.

You idiot, you should have stayed in the Corps.

Deep down, he knew it hadn't been an option. In times of war, people like him were an asset. With the wars won, he was a firebrand; an officer who was probably way too much trouble than he was worth. He'd managed to get all the way to Colonel before the trouble started. Those from the War always treated him with respect, but there were plenty in the years that followed who considered him gruff and unsuited for the job. Peacetime postings had taken him from the frontlines, and possibilities for promotions or opportunities had faded. Maybe APS Corporation had been a good idea; he'd just left it too long. At least, that was how he liked to think. The vessel moved lower, and a hatch opened up underneath like a long bomb bay. He estimated it must have been at least twenty meters in length, and easily capable of holding hundreds of weapons. It glowed an evil red and dark shapes moved inside.

Oh great, what next?

Spartan instinctively grabbed his assault carbine and held it close to his body. He extended his fingers around the selector, making sure he'd chosen the full-power mode. He didn't expect he would get more than a few seconds to shoot, so every round would need to be as powerful and as damaging as he could muster.

"Khan," he whispered in his helmet.

"Yeah," came back a sarcastic reply.

"You ready?"

There was a short pause.

"Always, why? You want to attack?"

Movement caught his eye, but with great self-control, he refused to move his body. Instead, he moved his retina slowly, almost tenderly. The smaller craft appeared to be coming down lower and was about fifty meters away. A shape flickered, and then he spotted six armored shapes; this time much smaller than the ones that had been killed. These were very similar in armor and looks to the T'Kari Raiders, yet their upper bodies seemed larger and ungainly compared to Tuke's people. Each was encased in armor from head to toe and carrying a large projectile weapon that was connected via a flexible mount to the torso. They moved about the bodies, fanning out to create a protective cordon.

"No, not yet. We can't move unless the odds are in our favor."

He then slowed his speech to emphasize his words, "Do not make a sound."

Spartan was forced to use all his self-control when one of the enemy's warriors, the massive mechanical creatures like the group they'd already come across, dropped down to the surface. This one was slightly different to the dead ones; it was still fully armored but much shorter and squatter. If it had been human, it could easily have been a dwarf, based on the size difference. It was much more heavily armored, with additional plates covering the articulated sections. The head was sunken and protected by a thick metal collar.

What the hell is that?

It looked about and then walked slowly but carefully around the debris. It moved off to one side and behind a partially collapsed three-story building. Spartan couldn't quite see what was happening from his position. He moved slightly to the right and immediately regretted it. Either his foot or his elbow must have grazed the rubble. Whichever didn't matter though, as chunks of dusty material fell down around him. There was now a hole the size of his head to the side, and he could see the eyeless head of the machine facing him.

No, it can't see me. There's no sound here, he thought hopefully.

His intercom whispered gently in his ears.

"Spartan, we have a problem," said Tuke in his machinelike voice.

"I know. Tuke, what's your status?"

"I…I am in position behind a fallen walker. My sensors indicate more of these machines in the area. Whatever we are going to do, it needs to be done quickly."

Spartan nodded mentally.

"Wait, I can see…"

Then the transmission stopped. Spartan used the retina-based control system on his suit to reconnect to Tuke, but the alien warrior didn't respond. There was no sound on the intercom, and Spartan couldn't do anything but hope the T'Kari was staying low and silent. He hoped against hope that the alien fool didn't try to do anything clever.

"Bastards!" snarled Khan.

In an instant, Spartan knew their position had been compromised. The smaller warriors moved about quickly and smashed aside a pile of broken metal, dragging Tuke out. It was like watching a pack of dogs pulling a rabbit out of a warren.

"Khan, do not move!" came from Spartan's lips without even thinking. He knew full well that his old comrade would be itching to jump into the fray. Spartan continued watching the machines, and his blood felt as if it was starting to boil.

"Spartan, we have to help!"

"Don't you dare, Khan!"

They dragged the helpless Tuke toward the waiting metal behemoth. It bent down slightly and moved its head closer to the T'Kari. It then turned to the right and swung back with its right arm. Sharp, heavily powered claws grabbed at him and lifted him up off the ground. The blade cut deeply, breaking and shattering the armor like rotten wood. Gas escaped from the cracks and damage. Spartan knew there and then that Tuke was a dead man. He wanted to leap up, but they were heavily outnumbered. Dying would achieve nothing for any of them.

"What the hell!" he shouted, as one of the six smaller machines pulled metal out of the way to reach him.

He lifted the barrel of his L52 Mk II pulse carbine and blasted it with a single high-energy round. All three barrels combined their output to send the triple charge directly into its center mass. At this distance, the high-speed round smashed cleanly through its armor, out of its back, and into the debris behind it. Spartan pushed himself up, twisting to aim his weapon at the next nearest foe. It fired at the same time as Spartan, and managed to clip his armor along the left elbow joint. The impact was like being hit by a lead weight, and it spun Spartan about. As he lost his balance and fell down, he watched with satisfaction as his target fell backward, missing its head.

"Die!" screamed Khan over his intercom.

With that, he rushed in, firing his weapon as he vanished into the middle of the group. Even the great machine seemed to recoil at the fully armored sight of Khan. He shot one and then leapt at the center of the large machine. Spartan didn't wait, lifted himself to his knee, and took aim at another of the soldiers. A powerful impact struck him hard, and he turned his head to see a second of the massive machines standing over him and grasping his armored leg. Then he was upside down and hanging from his foot; a great deal of pain soared through his limb, and his carbine lay helpless on the ground.

I'm not going like this!

He flailed about and struck at the metal plating on the machine. Not even his most powerful blow could penetrate it. He caught a fleeting look of Khan as he hammered away with his edged weapons, and then he could see space.

My pistol! He remembered.

Without even needing to check, he reached down to his thigh and felt the flat metal plating. A gentle tug and the military issue firearm came away loose in his hand. He aimed it at the blurred shape holding him and pulled the trigger repeatedly.

* * *

Spartan opened his eyes to the sight of nothing but the dull shadows of other prisoners. He reached down and checked the pain coming from his legs. The pain in his left leg was excruciating to the touch. He blinked a few more times, looking around with wide-open eyes. They started to adjust to the grim lighting conditions, and he could see that the people around him were an odd mixture. Some wore military clothing, many nothing more than rags. Spartan opened his mouth to speak, but the dryness in his mouth and throat stopped anything other than a groan from coming out.

Where the hell am I? he wondered, swallowing several times.

He smelled the air. It was damp, cool, and very different to the feeling he'd expected inside a spacecraft. The wall behind him felt cold and slightly rough, maybe shaped from some form of resin.

"Spartan?" He heard a familiar voice.

He looked about, trying to find a sign of his friend. The shadows and hidden faces of the dozens of people in this section made it almost impossible to adequately search the place. He tried to stand, but the pain in his leg kept him on the floor.

"Spartan, over here!" said the voice, this time from his right.

He twisted at the hip, lifted up his bodyweight on his hands, and finally found the large shape of Khan behind two groups of people.

"Khan? Yeah, I see you."

Spartan's eyesight was much better now, and he could see there were holes above them. They were tiny, no bigger than a finger, and sent down a dull yellow glow at equal distances along the floor.

"Stay there," said the old warrior.

With a lot of noise, he staggered over to Spartan and dropped down beside him. His right arm hung down uselessly, and Spartan could see dark shadows across his body. It was only then he realized neither of them was wearing their armor.

"What happened?"

Khan coughed a little and let out a low groan. The cough itself seemed to send more pain through the Jötnar's body. Both of them leaned against the wall. They were like a pair of old men with the aches and pains of bodies three times their ages.

"You don't remember the trip?"

Spartan shook his head.

"No, last thing I saw was you fighting that machine."

Spartan was sure he could see the glint of teeth, presumably Khan grinning. He finally closed his mouth and sighed.

"Spartan, but that was about a week ago. You don't remember getting here?"

He thought hard, desperately trying to remember. He'd

dreamed of all manner of bizarre things. Machines fighting, dogs running off with his keys, and being trapped in an ice cube. The images were all short, as dreams always were, but none of it seemed relevant for what was happening. Again Spartan shook his head.

"No, nothing, I don't remember a thing after the fight. I take it we didn't win?"

Khan coughed roughly.

"Well, Tuke didn't. They pulled him in half before I could kill that thing."

Spartan was surprised, even shocked at this revelation.

"You destroyed that monster?"

Khan tried to laugh, but the pain was now clearly causing him trouble.

"Oh, yeah. The first one was easy. It was the second one that was the real problem. You know, the big, dark red one."

He looked at Spartan as if he should know what he was talking about. Again the two waited, but Spartan simply couldn't remember a single clear image of the events. Khan leaned in close.

"He's the one that took your hand."

Spartan's heart sank at those words. He lifted both of his arms and found the stump of the left arm that stopped at the elbow. He almost choked as he realized the trauma his body had sustained.

"What…what happened?"

"It took your arm and smashed your legs swinging you about."

He sat back and let out a long breath.

"Still, you weren't useless. You manage to bring it down to the ground with your pistol, long enough for me to get there."

"And yet we are still here?"

Khan laughed grimly.

"I might be a great fighter, Spartan, but even I can only destroy so many of them. Another four came after the red one. We both fought, but they beat us down and dragged us to their ship."

"Tuke?"

Khan coughed, "Yeah, he's still on that station. In pieces."

He picked up a rock or piece of metal and cast it along the floor.

"Poor bastard."

The two stared at the other prisoners for almost a minute before Spartan spoke again. As he opened his mouth, he cradled he mutilated arm, trying to avoid looking at where the cut had been. The stump itself was covered in a synthetic material that was as hard as plastic.

"Who fixed my arm?"

Khan spat on the floor.

"Fixed? The animals out there sealed your stump Spartan, that was before they started the questions, in the yellow room up there."

Khan pointed above them and to the small lights. Spartan looked to the light, and then it came back to him, as if a video screen had been showing him the footage. He recalled the bed he'd been strapped in, as machines moved around sticking needles into his upper arm and shattered legs. The part he remembered most clearly was the red machine. It looked like the others on the derelict station, yet this one was a dull crimson and adorned with trophies. As he thought back, he saw images of human, Biomech and T'Kari heads hanging about its torso.

"You remember?" asked Khan, watching his friend.

Spartan tried to speak but leaned forward, retching as his body involuntarily spasmed. If he'd actually eaten anything, he would have vomited. Instead, his body went through a series of painful convulsions and eventually calmed down.

"Yeah, you remember the red machine well enough. He just keeps asking one question."

Spartan panted and it took him almost a minute before he could speak. He took a number of deep breaths before trying.

"Question? Yes, he kept asking me…over and over."

"Where is the Gate to Helios?" finished Khan.

Spartan looked to him and nodded slowly.

"Yeah, same for you, huh?"

Spartan rested back, doing his best to ignore the pain.

He looked to his right and then to the left, counting over forty people in the dark, cold place; the majority a similar size to Spartan, but one thing seemed to unite them.

"They are avoiding eye contact with us, why?"

"They've been here longer than us. I don't think they are strong enough to speak, let alone try and move over to us. I've tried talking to them, but they always look away. Sometimes they cry, but usually they just curl up and say nothing."

A noise in the darkness alerted them. It was the shape of a man. He lifted himself up to his feet, and his silhouette was black and clear underneath the dull light coming from above. He looked over to the two of them and staggered to the nearest wall. As he reached it, he pulled back his head and smashed it as hard as his frail body could manage. His forehead connected with the wall in a cracking motion that must have shattered bone. Not one of the other prisoners even flinched as his body slid to the ground, still, and quiet as death. Khan looked to Spartan.

"It happens every day. This place must make them mad."

Spartan's right fist clenched tightly, and he was convinced his left fist was doing the same. His upper body shuddered as his anger spread through every muscle in his body. Even those in his broken legs did the same. Khan sensed a change, and he turned and placed his great hand on Spartan's shoulder.

"Khan, we're not staying here. We are getting off whatever this is, and we are going to put their heads on spikes. You understand me?"

Khan nodded, but even he seemed less than convinced at the words.

"There is just one problem, Spartan."

"Which is?"

"This place, it's an underground prison. Where will we go, assuming we can get out?"

Spartan seemed unconcerned at that piece of information.

"Prison? So what? I was trapped on Prometheus with General Rivers for long enough. We got out of that one, and we will this one as well."

"True, but you had Gun on your side back then. This is different."

Spartan shook his head.

"No, not really. I have you, and we have something else that they don't have."

"What?" asked Khan, genuinely curious to hear his response.

Spartan tapped his temple.

"I can remember the way we came in here."

It may have been dark, and both of them were in pain. Even so, Spartan was convinced he could see the gleaming, dull teeth of his friend as he smiled. He punched Khan pathetically in the shoulder with his good hand.

"Right. So, what are we going to do, and when are we going to do it?"

CHAPTER FOURTEEN

*The Multi-role Logistics Drone, also known as the 'Mule',
was developed before the Great Uprising and saw its first use
in those early, yet brutally violent struggles. Initially created to
carry equipment and ammunition, some later variants carried
weapons and were used in an assault role. The latest model
of the Mule features a three-day powerplant that allows it to
operate independently in almost any weather conditions. It has
a combat module that can be configured for cargo or weapons,
and sometimes even as a medical stretcher.*

Equipment of the Alliance Marine Corps

General Daniels watched with a satisfied look on his face
as wave after wave of Alliance fighters strafed the Helion
station. Each attack run reduced the defensive fire and
opened the target for more attacks. The Lightning fighters
had been forced to withdraw, following the devastating flak

defenses of the station. Luckily, the new Hammerheads were proving perfectly suited for this job. With their strong defenses and powerful weapons, they'd destroyed over half the turrets. It was the only aggressive action the group of six battered Alliance ships had taken so far. He looked briefly around the CIC, trying to avoid the smell of blood and fear that permeated the place.

"Clear the wounded and get me more crew in here!" he growled.

Marines were already inside, helping to carry the wounded and dead from that part of the ship. He could see on the status indicator on the cracked main display that there were casualties on other parts of the ship as well. It made his next decision much easier to choose. He grasped the intercom, looking back as Admiral Anderson was helped to a chair. Blood dripped from a head wound but he seemed conscious. He was tempted to try and check with the Admiral, but the sight of so many casualties swayed his opinion.

Why are we trying to keep the peace? What peace?

Lieutenant Powalk twisted his head around quickly, instantly catching his eye.

"General, the T'Kari have finished collecting their wounded and are falling back to the Rift."

"Good."

General Daniels seemed satisfied at the news and took it as a signal to move to the next phase of the action.

Now we get out of this place.

Their escape wasn't going to be that easy though. The ship's sensors flashed bright once more, as the powerful energy weapons on the station targeted ANS Serenity. The defensive turrets poured fire in the direction of the attack, but it was futile. The heavy beam struck the starboard of the Crusader class ship, exploding a section almost fifteen meters long. As they watched the destruction, a detail of three junior officers, one with a bandage on his head, ran into the CIC and took up their stations. The youngest, a short Asian man fitted on his headset before speaking. He looked around, trying to find General Daniels.

"General, a message from Serenity. Their main engines are offline. They estimate two hours, assuming no more damage."

He nodded in reply.

So, this is it. We evacuate our ship and run with our tail between our legs...or we stay, and fight.

Whereas the Admiral was calm, collected, and dispassionate, General Daniels was a marine at heart. Giving up ground after paying a high blood price rankled him. He gave the first choice a moment's decision and made up his mind.

"We are ending this, right now! All Alliance ships, you are clear to fire. Bring your ships into a dispersed assault pattern on three axes. Protect the fighters and ready your primary weapons!"

Admiral Anderson tried to stand, lifting his right hand as if to plead for him to stop. General Daniels couldn't afford to waste time, so he concentrated on the few officers remaining. With the helm and tactical stations remaining functional, the ship was still in the fight, albeit with reduced capability. He dreaded to think how many losses they'd sustained in the continuous bombardment from the station. The sound of the fighters' crew crackled near the desk of the CAG. He listened to one excited voice.

"It's a hit, her air defenses are down!" called one of the fighter commanders.

General Daniels skimmed through the icons moving on the tactical map and found the point on the station where the gun system had been weakened. It was slightly to the right of the upper levels. A quick glance told him where he suspected he could do the most damage.

"There!" he swore under his breath. The computer had already analyzed the station and pinpointed likely areas for power generation and ammunition supply. All the weapon systems, including the main gun that was proving so devastating, were drawing power from this section. He tapped each of his ships on the display and connected to their commanders.

"All ships, on my order, concentrate your fire on this location."

Each returned an acknowledgement. He swallowed as

he realized his voice sounded distorted. The mainscreen showed the other Crusader class warships were moving around him in a wide crescent formation, each presenting their bows to the enemy. The previous ship designs had been equipped with their main weapons on the flanks. These new designs could only be used from the bow or stern, as the systems ran most of the length of the ship. As the heavy warships edged closer and closer, they moved apart so that they could strike from six directions. This had the effect of putting hundreds of kilometres between each of them.

"General, we're in position," said Lieutenant Scookins, the ship's helmsman.

General Daniels nodded. It was his first major command, but commanding a battle fleet was something he'd never expected to have to do. With The Admiral out of action, and the Captain killed, he could either take charge or rely upon one of the other ships' captains. In the Alliance, the Marine Corps and Navy were closely entwined, and it was assumed that senior officers would exchange roles if required in combat.

Is this what the Admiral would do? he thought, a moment of doubt entering his mind. He looked back at the CIC and spotted two marines carrying out the XO. He was quickly reminded of how many losses they'd sustained.

"Lieutenant, how is the XO?"

The officer shook his head and continued towards the

door.

"Not good, General, he took an impact in the throat. He's gone, Sir."

That was all he needed to hear. The Alliance ships had taken a pounding, and still the enemy refused to stop the attack.

Maybe this will make you think twice.

He shouted down the intercom in a tone that was much louder and angrier sounding than he intended.

"All ships, open fire!"

All six Crusader class warships opened fire with their powerful particle beam weapons. In an instant, a series of flashes and blasts appeared across the outer sections of the station. The high-energy pulsed beam of subatomic particles from the capital ships triggered a single massive explosion that tore a large section from the station. It was a powerful attack, and General Daniels pondered on how many Helions would have been killed by its ferocity.

"Admiral, an emergency signal from the civilian fleet on the other side of the Rift. They are under attack! A dormant vessel is heading for the Rift."

Anderson looked back at the video feed of the stable Rift. It was still operational, though he doubted it was safe to use this close to the Helion station, except under the direst of circumstances. T'Kron had already reminded him twice that all of the eight races had the technology to destabilize the Rifts.

"General, something is coming through!" Lieutenant Powalk called out with a nervous groan.

Daniels looked back to the mainscreen that had now shifted focus behind the fleet and toward the Rift they'd entered from. The small group of T'Kari ships was already slinking back through the Rift. He cringed at their approached and tried to move the thought aside of what would happen if the Rift was destabilized when the vast bulk of a ship crashed through. One of the scout ships was instantly disintegrated before they could change course to avoid its massive size.

"What the hell is that?"

"Unknown, Sir, checking the computer now," said Commander D'Vani.

"General, the guns, they've stopped firing," said Lieutenant Powalk, looking intently at the second display. "No, wait, they are turning their flak weapons onto the new ship!"

General Daniels looked at the mainscreen so intently that he didn't even noticed the form of Admiral Anderson at his side. The battered and slightly unsteady officer reached out to rest his hand on the General's shoulder. He spun around to spot the blood-soaked man.

"General, what the hell is going on?"

"Admiral?"

Anderson moved two steps forward and held onto the outer rim of the unit supporting the tactical display. He spotted the massive ship exchanging gunfire with two of his Crusader ships that had already turned on it.

"That is a Guardian ship, the class used as a heavy warship by the enemy that attacked us in T'Karan," he explained, pointing at the newly arrived ship.

Lines of gunfire from the heavily damaged station ripped into the monstrous vessel, yet little damage seemed to be caused.

"Look!" said Commander D'Vani.

A stream of energy shot out from the Helion station below and directly into the mouth of the Rift. The effect was slow to start as the shape started to shake and distort. Then with a bright flash the entrance to the Rift turned into a raging storm of energy. Admiral Anderson opened his mouth to speak and then stumbled. General Daniels caught him and moved him to one of the chairs. A marine rushed over to assist, but he waved the man off.

"No, I will not leave until this battle is decided. The T'Kari, where are they?"

"All gone but T'Kron, Admiral," explained General Daniels. "His ship stayed back and is in position well inside our defensive line."

"And the Helions? They have turned their fire on the Guardian ship?"

He nodded in reply.

"Yes, but we've already destroyed their primary weapons. I doubt their last point defense systems will do anything but scratch its surface. At least nothing else will be coming through."

Admiral Anderson sighed, more out of frustration at their situation than toward any decision that had been taken.

True, but now we cannot get back.

"Very well, this is our one chance. We need to let them know we are with them, not against them. A few volleys of fire should do the trick."

The wounded Admiral beckoned for General Daniels to approach. He did so with haste; now starting to worry the massive ship that was already increasing in speed would strike them.

"What is their course?" called out the Admiral to the crew still standing in the CIC.

"Best estimate is the asteroid belt at approximately twenty-seven astronomical units away. They have fixed their course, and their main engines are powering up," replied one of the junior officers that had arrived with the replacements.

Admiral Anderson didn't recognize the tall man, but he had neither the time nor inclination to find out more. He looked at the plotted location and spun around to face General Daniels.

"The Rift!" said both of the senior commanders at the same time."

"T'Kron has an urgent message," announced

Commander D'Vani, who now operated a science station as well as communications.

Admiral Anderson nodded, and the image of T'Kron appeared.

"Admiral, they must be stopped!"

Anderson wiped some of the blood from his face and replied.

"Really, and why is that?"

T'Kron paused as though what he was about to say was some great secret. The enemy vessel must have encouraged him because his voice turned to a high-pitched squeal as he spoke. It took even longer than normal for the translators in his suit to convert the sounds.

"The ship, we have detected captured T'Kari technology deep inside it."

"So what?" said General Daniels abruptly, "Where can they go? The Helions will finish them off in this system. Or maybe they'll escape. So?"

He looked at the face of the T'Kari, looking for a hint or sign of what the alien was thinking.

"You don't understand. The ship could open up the Black Rift. They have obtained copies of our coding equipment for their Rift."

Anderson sighed and shook his head knowingly.

"The what?"

"The Black Rift, it is the entrance to the outer domains of the Enemy. The Rift was sealed during our war with them. Only one of the remaining races can open it using our technology. If the wrong codes are used, the Rift destabilizes. Like that one."

He pointed behind him, and Anderson could only assume the Rift lay in that position. He took a deep breath, as if only just realizing he hadn't been breathing.

"If they can reach the Black Rift with this ship and our technology, it could allow their forces to enter the Helion system. Only my people and the Helions have the technology to open, close, and destabilize these Rifts, and it is our most guarded technology. Only the elders of our societies have access to it."

"Great, and from here they can spread through this Network and hit our worlds, right?" asked General Daniels.

Before T'Kron could answer, Admiral Anderson lifted his hand.

"Why now? Why not fifty years ago?"

T'Kron waved his hands in an agitated fashion.

"They followed us through our own Rift, one that we have hidden all this time. They must have tracked out expedition to this point. You must trust us, Admiral. If they reach the Black Rift, every one of our worlds will be turned to ash."

Admiral Anderson wiped his face once more, this time removing sweat rather than blood. The information wasn't a complete surprise to him. The attacks from the Raiders already told him they wanted something, either information or technology.

He turned to General Daniels.

"These Guardian ships cannot be easily stopped. We hit the last one for a long time and still it got away. It was only the T'Kari and their technology that destroyed it by collapsing the Rift around it. Now we only have five fully functioning warships. We need something more permanent. Stop that ship, and the Helions will listen to us."

"Uh, Admiral. The ship is powering down and changing course."

"What? Where are they going?"

The officer seemed stunned by what was happening, much to the fury of the Admiral.

"Answer me, dammit!"

"The ship is coming back this way, and their weapons are powering up."

Anderson swallowed, his mouth now feeling like ash at the news. The warship was easily five times the size of the Crusader ships, perhaps even bigger. He remembered what had happened the last time Alliance ships had engaged one, and at that point the ships had all been undamaged and fully functional.

"He's right, the ship is setting a course between the Rift back home and our ships," Lieutenant Powalk added.

"They mean to stop us pursuing them before they continue on to the Black Rift. Is there no way the Helions can intercept them?"

Helmsmen Scookins shook her head.

"The nearest major ships are days away. There is a group of frigate-sized vessels heading this way, but it will take them at least an hour. They will never be able to reach them. The only chance the Helions have is if they have something major protecting the Black Rift itself."

General Daniels nodded at this part, "and if they don't, the ship could travel through."

Admiral Anderson looked disappointed at the news. He considered the options available to him, but there were few, and none particularly appealed to him.

"Very well, General, what do you suggest?"

General Daniels did his best to smile before providing a response.

"The only way to decide this will be here and now. I can hit the vessel with an assault force. The 17th, under Gun and Morato, are directly in the path of the ship. They can have marines on her in minutes."

The weapon systems of ANS Victory were now firing at full capacity. Both the particle beam weapons and the myriad of turrets pounded the Guardian ship. Even as the commanders discussed strategy, they could see the flashes across its massive structure. Large pieces of metal were blasted off or even melted to slag, and yet still it continued onward.

Admiral Anderson nodded, "A captured Guardian ship,

now that would be a prize."

The ship shuddered as a double burst of gunfire from the port gun batteries of the Guardian ship raked the ship's hull. The armor stopped the worst of it, yet nearly two-dozen hardened rounds breached the layered armor and exploded inside.

"Damage to the starboard particle assembly, just the port gun remaining," explained Lieutenant Powalk.

Admiral Anderson looked disheartened at the news. The weapons systems on the ship were powerful, but there were only four emitters, two on the stern and two on the bow. Once they were gone, they had nothing but the turrets and the fighter cover remaining.

"We have no choice. You command the assault operation, General. I will return to my position in the fleet and keep our ships operational as long as possible."

General Daniels held the Admiral's shoulder, noting how unsteady the man still was on his feet. A junior officer, one he hadn't seen before, helped to move him closer to the tactical unit. Admiral Anderson held on to it and took three long breaths.

"General, you're needed for this operation. I'll make sure our ships and fighters operate effectively as a screen. Don't take too long though; these ships are only so strong. We fight here, either we win or we lose. I'm not leaving Serenity on her own to die."

Without even waiting for General Daniel's reply, he

moved to the rest of the CIC crew and proceeded to give out orders to each of his ships. General Daniels seemed almost excited at the news. With the Admiral back in command of the taskforce, he could concentrate on what he'd trained for, major combat operations. He moved a short distance back and grabbed the intercom. With just two taps, he connected to his battalion commanders.

"This is the General, prepare for contested ship boarding."

He paused for just a moment and connected directly to ANS Savage.

There's only one battalion that has conducted more than one mock boarding action.

"Commander Gun, Major Morato. It is time. I have a job for you, and it's the most dangerous job out here."

* * *

Teresa was uncomfortable inside the cramped interior of the Hammerhead fighter, one of the many new craft being used by the Marine Corps. It was her first trip on the aircraft, and her first impression was not particularly favorable. It was a good deal larger than the Cobra shuttles she'd used in the past for special operations use, yet it could still only carry a dozen warriors. Seated near her were the eleven members of 1st Squad, including Sergeant Arina Nova. All of them were dressed in their almost midnight black APS armor, with only one subtle difference between theirs and the other marines. Rather than the dark grey tiger stripes used by the other squads, this personal protection unit had crimson stripes. Teresa had made the decision, and she was now starting to wonder if she should have chosen something a little darker.

"Major," said Gun's voice from the center of the craft.

"Commander, we're three hundred meters from the target."

"Good, the 17th made it out first. You'll hit them sixty seconds before the marines from Crusader and Victory."

Teresa nodded at the image of her commanding officer and leader of the 17th Battalion. Technically, he wasn't a commander, but the name had stuck in the War, and it had become more of an honorific title specific to Gun. Teresa looked at the command display and checked the position of the rest of the Battalion. Over four hundred marines were en route from ANS Savage already, with another eight companies on their way from the other two ships. Not all of the marines were coming though. There were, after all, only enough transports for a fraction of the marines at a time.

The mighty Guardian ship was already pulling away from its previous course and heading for the Rift. Scores of gun turrets sent projectiles out to the Alliance ships, as well as the Helion station. In reply, the ships and station struck it with a variety of ineffectual weapons. Its engines glowed a bright blue as it moved into position. Luckily for the Alliance forces, the ship was massive and took time to move into an advantageous position, and all the while the Alliance ships were scattering to attack from multiple angles.

We won't have long before they start to cause serious damage to our ships.

Teresa looked at the counter running on the inside of her visor. It counted down the number of seconds at which point they would reach the warship. They had to be inside the vessel before the counter ran down.

"Hold on!" called the pilot.

The lead vessels of the formation were the three Hammerhead heavy fighters. They moved past the stern of the huge ship, continuing about a third the way along its spine before dropping down and settling on a flat area. They came in fast, perhaps too fast, as the impact came as a massive jolt. Teresa felt shudders through the floor as the grav-clamps secured them to the hull.

"Hammerhead One is down. We're moving in."

They would normally disembark from the side doors, but this was different. One of the most useful design changes with the marine craft was the ability to board ships once attached. A low vibration was all it took for the thermite breaching charges fitted beneath the gunship to burn a hole two meters wide into the hull of the ship, immediately below the Hammerhead. The center section slid open like a narrow bomb bay and led inside. A gush of air rushed into the craft, but amazingly, the Hammerhead was able to maintain a secure seal, and the pressure quickly stabilized.

"Go, go, go!" Teresa shouted.

Sergeant Arina Nova moved into the hole first, using her magboots to attach and detach from the metal structure and inside the ship. The rest of the squad followed, including Major Morato; each fully encased in the best armor the Alliance could supply.

* * *

Gun stood in front of his tactical display like an ancient general poring over the details of some battle map. The room was only a short distance from the marines' quarters, and he was acutely aware of how close he was to the many shuttles and gunships that were loading up to take more marines into the fray.

"You have to manage the battle from the ship," he remembered Teresa saying as she was leaving for the battle.

It pained him to stay behind, but he was becoming used to the fact that the further up he went, the less opportunities there were for direct involvement in the battle. It was starting to annoy him greatly. He turned his attention back to the display. It showed the numbers of small craft as they mobilized around the rear of the

Guardian ship. A small number of the gun turrets on the station below had turned their attention to it, but they were having little effect. He thought for a few seconds and hit the connect button.

"Commander, what is it?" responded General Daniels with the minimum of patience.

"General, the 17th is currently boarding the Guardian ship. Now what about this station?"

"What about it?"

"I can take that station with a company of marines. They are prepping now."

General Daniels raised an eyebrow at the suggestion.

"No, our scans still show nearly three hundred Helions on board, plus who knows what kind of defensive systems. You could lose the entire unit. Anyway, they are not shooting at our ships anymore."

Gun was surprised at these words. He looked back to his map of the battle as it was unfolding. The display was zoomed in around the Guardian ship, and he hadn't noticed the changing positions of the other ships. He'd been too busy directing each of the platoons into position at key points over the ship.

You idiot, you have one job, that damned ship!

"Gun, the situation has changed."

"How so?"

The Guardian ship has released fighters. Most of them are busy with our own fighters, but there are also a dozen lighter craft that are hunting down craft launched from our ships. Two shuttles have been hit already."

Gun scowled at the news but said nothing.

"We're holding our own, but we cannot risk sending in any more marine units from our ships. Your ship is the closest. It's only a sixty-second journey from your hull to theirs. I can give you enough fighter cover for one more run, any more, and they'll shoot down your landing craft."

General Daniels knew what he was asking, and he also knew that there was no better man to lead the assault than the experienced war leader and Biomech veteran, Commander Gun.

"You need to launch every thing you have left in one big attack. Do you have any operational Vanguards on your ship?" asked Daniels.

Gun grinned at his words. The armor was the massive mechanical suit first used in combat by Spartan back in the Uprising. They'd been using them for training in the 17th, but only a small number of the strongest and those best suited to close quarter combat would be able to use them effectively.

"Yeah, I have twenty or so of them, all fully functional. Why?"

"Take out her fighter bays. They've been launching a new fighter every sixty seconds. If you can stop them sending anymore, it will allow us to send you more marines."

Gun couldn't have looked happier.

"General, give me five minutes, then send in your fighters."

The General saluted to the new commander of the 17th."

"Good luck, Commander."

* * *

Teresa climbed through the melted bulkhead structure and into the cylindrical passageway. The walkway was much larger than on any Alliance ship. She was reminded of a cave, based on its overall size and shape. Like the latest Crusader class warships, this vessel was using a form of artificial gravity. Even so, it was still less than she was used to, and it slowed their progress.

"Major, sensors are detecting no life signs within a hundred meters," said Sergeant Arina Nova in a hushed voice.

Teresa nodded, "Affirmative, keep moving."

As the first unit on the ship, the single squad had pushed deep inside the aft. More marines had managed to make it, but nowhere near as many as had been planned.

"Major," said Commander Gun, his voice seeming to be so far away on their ship, "The last wave has been turned back. It's just your three platoons of 1st Company and a single platoon from 3rd Company."

"What the hell! Where are the rest?"

"The Guardian ship has launched fighters, but don't worry, I'm working on that. See if you can do something about her engines or weapons. The tech teams here have this for you."

On the left of her visor a schematic appeared. It was a rough plan of the ship, based on sensor scans of the exterior plus the data sent by from the sensor feeds on the armor worn by the marines.

"This is one big ship," she said, forgetting that Gun could hear her.

"Yeah, about the size of a tanker, maybe bigger."

She skimmed over the details and spotted the locations of the main weapons fitted toward the rear of the ship. It was the closest primary system that she could find. Dark green spots indicated the positions of her marines at various points in the aft.

"Gun, I'm splitting my forces. One platoon will strike the engines, the rest will move inside the ship and target any primary systems we find."

"Good, I am preparing a final wave to assist you. When the fighters are thinned out, I'll lead them in."

Teresa looked ahead, ever vigilant and expecting trouble. She was sure she saw something moving, yet the scanner on her armor showed nothing. Simply by moving her retinas, she selected each of her units and sent command directives to all the platoons. It was quicker than using audio commands through the intercom. Something caught her eye, and she glanced back to see the marines from 1st Company making their way inside. She nodded and then looked back in the direction her own unit was heading.

"Marines, check your visuals. I don't like this."

She lifted her coilgun up to her shoulder at the exact same moment that the great machine burst out from the darkness. It actually dropped down from the ceiling, roughly thirty meters away. It was squat in shape and protected by smooth, ceramic looking plates from head to toe. It moved like it was alive, but she couldn't see a single hint of living matter anywhere on it. Sergeant Nova opened fire first and was followed by the rest of the marines at the front. The crimson striped marines put down a withering hail of fire that sent sparks and flashes off around its armor. It must have changed its mind, as the machine moved to its right and behind the covered provided by the thickly ribbed tunnel.

"Gun, we've got hostiles down here."

She checked the schematics as they continued to expand with details from the marines.

Okay, so the passageway reaches an intersection after this thing, then it splits up. It must be trying to stop us reaching the junction.

The machine leaned out from the cover and aimed its right arm at the marines. Yellow flames flashed and dozens of projectiles, each the size of a man's finger, ripped through the marines. Their armor deflected most of the fire, yet two of the guards took impacts in the faces and were slammed onto their backs, now nothing more than lifeless corpses.

"Gun?" called out Teresa again on the intercom.

"Understood. I will be there when I can. You know what to do."

Teresa smiled grimly to herself; it was exactly the kind of thing she would expect him to say. She took a step forward, her weapon raised and ready.

"Marines, maximum power, forward!"

The surviving guards of Sergeant Nova's squad moved closely around their leader, ensuring they could shoot while doing their best to present themselves as human shields against potential fire from the tunnel. The machine tried to return fire, but the coilgun of the marines utilized their high-power mode to tear chunks off it. By the time Teresa reached it, the marines had torn it apart and were moving on to secure the intersection. She stopped, examining it for a moment.

This must be another one of their warriors.

A symbol on its thigh caught her eye. She leaned in for a closer look and saw the coiled serpent of Echidna. It was similar to the iconography used by the Zealots and their allies back in the Uprising. A scream made her spine tingle, and she turned around, trying to identify the source. Instead, she identified man-sized Biomechs, but with the shape and muscle tone of the Jötnar, and carrying firearms. They appeared from hidden points throughout the passageway and fell upon her marines.

"Close quarter drill!" shouted Arina, remembering their training.

Unlike any other battalion in this part of space, the 17th had spent as much time practicing hand-to-hand combat as they did their shooting. It was unusual, but both Teresa and Gun had demanded it. All it took was a tap on the side of the coilgun to release the retracted bayonet. In seconds, each in the passageway had both coilgun and a razor sharp spear. The bayonets extended over thirty centimeters and ran into a hardened tip that was perfectly suited for stabbing into armor. Teresa would have been impressed if two of the Biomechs hadn't leapt at her.

"Major!" cried out Arina, but it was too late.

The Biomech brought its rifle down on her shoulder, striking the armor with a blow that almost crushed her collar. She dropped to one knee, using all her strength to stay upright. A quick jabbing motion from her right saw her coilgun thrust upward in a savage move that punched the spike bayonet into the thing's armpit. It pushed through the thick skin with ease and up into the base of the skull. The creature screamed and flailed before dropping to the ground, still shaking from the killing move. A corporal stopped next to her, firing a burst at another Biomech, and then helped her to stand upright.

"I'm okay, Corporal."

She placed her left armored boot on the Biomech's

stationary head and yanked the spiked rifle from it skull. Thick blood oozed from the wound, and she noted with satisfaction how it died. It was almost enough to dull the throbbing in her collar and shoulder. It didn't feel broken, but it was certainly badly bruised. She tried to lift her arm, but the pain was too much when she lifted the rifle to her shoulder. She spotted the Corporal looking at her.

"Keep moving. We need the engines and guns taken care of."

CHAPTER FIFTEEN

As the Alliance made its first tentative steps into the Helios System, a group of fledgling colonies struggled to expand back in the so recently discovered T'Karan System. The T'Kari had welcomed the Alliance with open arms, and the Jötnar had been amongst the first to set up colonies. The most prominent of these was on Luthien, the small iron silicate world that most considered inhospitable. In the past, it had been the homeworld of the T'Kari, a place of learning and advanced technology. The war against the biomechanical enemy reduced the cities to dust and polluted the atmosphere for hundreds of years. To the Jötnar, it became a second home after the jungle world of Hyperion.

The New Colonies

Another explosion ripped through the bow of ANS Victory, sending any unfortunate crewmembers still in the forward sections out into the void of space. The outer plating was torn apart as though a great iron fist had smashed through and pulled back the exposed segments. Massive bulkhead sections melted into slag from the incredible heat produced by the thermite missiles. Very few of them made it past the fighter screen, and even fewer penetrated the point-defense turrets. The ship rocked from the fearsome impact, and the officers in the CIC were forced to grasp the emergency grab rails dotted throughout the ship.

"Brace, brace, brace!" came a random voice toward the front.

Admiral Anderson watched in horror at the scenes of carnage when three more thermite missiles struck different sections of the ship. None detonated until they had embedded themselves deep inside the plating before releasing their superheated warheads. With each explosion, came a thump through his body like a burst of adrenalin. He had an even greater concern, and it came in the shape of a small group of Helion ships that was heading toward the space battle at great speed. They'd been tracking them now for over an hour, and he had no idea as to their plans.

"Get me T'Kron on the horn!" he snapped, his patience starting to wear thin.

Commander D'Vani moved his hands around the display and soon brought up the video feed of the T'Kari exile.

"Admiral!"

Anderson turned and looked directly into his face.

"T'Kron, I need something on those ships. What can you do?"

T'Kron twisted his head and spoke with one of his crew before looking back.

"Admiral, we've sent them information on why we are here. They are receiving us but are refusing to communicate directly back with us."

Anderson's face started to redden, and it took all of his self-control to keep calm.

"Send them a new message, T'Kron. We are here in peace, and we're enemies of this biomechanical enemy of yours. Either they help us stop this ship, or God help me, I'll bring a thousand more ships and burn Helios to ash."

T'Kron looked at him but said nothing. His expression was cold and static as though he was a mere sculpture. Finally, he replied.

"You would do that?"

"Just tell him!"

Anderson turned back to his own officers, doing his best to hide his look of exasperation from them. General Daniels seemed far too busy commanding the combat mission onboard the Guardian ship to even notice what he had been saying. His tactical display looked like a giant war-game, with blocks of marines at certain points on the enemy ship. Two of his officers stood alongside him to help with the communications. Admiral Anderson spotted him for a second and noted his grim expression. The General saw his stare.

"Admiral, the Guardian ship has sustained major damage to its hull and armor. I have one platoon from the 3rd Company moving up a pair of passageways and destroying anything they find. So far, they've managed to destroy seven weapon control units and a large number of Biomech warriors."

"What about the rest?"

The General moved the map slightly to show the positions of the three platoons under the command of Major Morato.

"The entire 1st Company under Major Morato has split up and is moving toward the bow."

"Why?" Anderson asked.

General Daniels pointed at a pulsing location about ninety meters from the bow of the ship. They are moving in on this location."

Commander D'Vani brought up a detailed schematic of the area covered by the marines so far. At one point, it showed a chamber the size of a training hall. Multiple passageways led to it, as well as pulsing rods that extended to all the main areas of the ship.

"My scans indicate this is where a massive amount of power is being generated."

"For what?"

The Chief Engineer shrugged.

"I couldn't say with any great certainty. It's the most significant location in the entire ship though. More importantly, the machines onboard are defending it at all costs."

Anderson nodded, looking back at the main display in the front of the CIC. The streaks of heavy gunfire ran out into Guardian ship, sending patterns of yellow flashes along the hull. He witnessed massive heat blooms and explosions, as yet more blasts from the Alliance warships' particle beams exploded layer upon layer of its armor.

"This is going to take a while, but I think we're getting there," he said calmly.

But something unsettled him. He tapped at the ship on the display.

"Why are they still attacking us? Surely they could just turn and run. If they stay here, they risk sustaining internal damage from our marines or being vaporized by our ships."

"Admiral, I suspect they do not think they can outrun us. Serenity and Savage are both unable to pursue. Once they've slowed our last four ships, they'll power up and head for the Rift. We are all taking damage in this fight, but their ship is designed for taking punishment, not giving it out. In a drawn out fight, the advantage goes to them."

Anderson looked unimpressed at the news.

"If they can disable us, what if we do the same to them? It doesn't make sense. They are risking an awful lot on this gamble."

The three-dimensional model of the ship rotated on the tactical display of Lieutenant Powalk. He moved his hand along one side of the ship where areas were now lighting up in red.

"I'm detecting breaches in over fifty locations, and she is venting ionized plasma on her starboard side where our marine units are in action.

"Starboard? We've been hitting her from every other direction."

Teresa, he remembered. *Her units must have breached the weapon capacitors on that side.*

"Based on this damage, I'd say the ship is sustaining damage at a similar level to us. Their guns are down fifty percent, and our units on board are causing more damage every minute. We've sustained fifteen percent casualties and rising. It could still be a close run thing."

Anderson nodded at the news. The ships were doing well, even if the casualties suggested otherwise. Without the marines, the Guardian ship would be making short work of his ships. General Daniels strode into the middle of the discussion and gave a shout as he pointed to Lieutenant Powalk's display.

"Admiral, I've got news from Major Morato. They've reached the central power point, and they've hit a problem."

"What kind of problem?"

"They're pinned down, and she's running out of

marines."

Anderson breathed slowly.

"Can she take out the power systems?"

Daniels shook his head.

"At this rate, she'll be dead in fifteen minutes. I'm sending in Gun."

Lieutenant Powalk cried out, "But, Sir, their flank guns are still operational. We have fighter cover, but only just. He'll be lucky to get within a hundred meters of the ship."

Anderson watched the discussion intently and agreed with both of them, but that wouldn't help resolve the situation. It wasn't just the hundred and fifty or so marines on the ship they risked losing, no, it was that if they lost the marines, they lost the chance of winning this encounter.

"Very well, General. I will bring everything I have to bear on that ship, even our point defense turrets. We'll saturate her with so much fire they won't even detect your approach.

"Admiral, if we turn all our firepower on her, we'll leave ourselves defenseless against their missiles," Lieutenant Powalk argued.

Anderson looked to him.

"I'm well aware of that," he then turned back to the General.

"Gun will have a narrow window. He'd better be ready."

* * *

Two metallic rounds struck Teresa in the chest, and she fell back a meter, hitting the wall. The secondary passageway was now slick with the blood of marines and Biomechs alike, as both sides fought a savage close ranged action just twenty meters from the entrance to the objective.

Sergeant Nova helped her up and both raised their coilguns to shoot. Every piece of cover from fallen warriors to shattered bulkheads was now used on both sides to shield them from the withering fire that glanced back and forth.

This is useless. We have to do something.

Teresa looked over her shoulder and could just make out the recently arrived 3rd Platoon from 1st Company. They'd been forced to regroup with those marines here after being pushed back by Biomechs. A blood spattered Captain made his way toward her while keeping as close to the passageway wall as possible.

"Major, we're pinned down by two machines. 2nd Platoon got hit on the way though, their wasted!"

Teresa could see the fear through the young man's visor. It was a feeling she could remember back from her early days in the Corps. But he had retained a degree of calmness and continued to direct his men. Teresa looked to the front of her unit and watched as the crimson tiger stripes of her personal guard moved to her position.

Corporal Smith, the oldest of the unit beckoned to the paneling on the passageway.

"Sir, there a vent system on the right. I think we can use it as a crawlspace to bypass their defenses. It isn't big, but a few of us should be able to get through."

Teresa didn't even hesitate, "Do it, we'll cover you from here."

The Corporal and three other marines rushed across the killing ground and to the spot he'd indicated. One pulled out an oxyacetylene torch and started cutting into the thick metal frame.

"Marines, covering fire!" called out Captain Sheehan, the command of 2nd Platoon.

He moved out from cover and took the full blast of the enemy fire. He staggered back and to the floor in a bloody mess. Incredibly, his armor absorbed almost all the impact, and he was still moving. A private pulled him to safety, and the rest fired for all their worth. Teresa took aim, fired a burst, and watched the three marines vanish into the crawlspace to the right.

Good luck, marines.

A quick look on her retina control unit connected her with Gun.

"Gun, what the hell is going on?"

The gruff sound from Gun was both surprising and reassuring at once.

"Teresa, hold your position. I'm coming, and we've

brought friends!"

* * *

Gun watched in disbelief from inside the heavily armored landing craft at the sight of the new arrivals. Through the maelstrom of gunfire, shrapnel, and missiles came the form of three Helion frigates. Each was beautifully shaped into a fusion of machine and sleek reptilian animal. The bows were intricately modeled to look like a water-going ship, and the four massive engines straddled its hull on both sides like stumpy legs. As they came closer, it was clear the shape was one purely of aesthetics, as the vents, engines, and communications arrays marked them out as ships of war. Gun watched with surprise as they moved closer and closer.

"Uh, I thought T'Kron said they were on an intercept course?" he asked himself.

Around the armored Jötnar stood dozens of marines. These were not the normal marines with their PDS armor. Gun had utilized every single set of Vanguard armor onboard his ship, and this landing craft now contained twenty-six of the heavily armored marines. The armor was thick and enhanced with powerful motors and electronics. Fitted into their arms were pairs of L48 rifles, each linked together to give a massive amount of firepower with little or no recoil. Gun looked at them and visions flashed back of the battles nearly two decades earlier. Battles where he and Spartan had stood side by side, surrounded by the blood of their enemies.

Good days, he thought with a smile.

"Commander, they're not stopping!" said the pilot.

Gun looked to the front of the craft where the large wall mounted screen showed what was happening outside. Behind his landing craft followed another five, each packed with heavily armed marines, as well as two squads of autonomous mules. These four-legged robotic machines were fitted with plating and a slaved gun on a rotating turret mount in the center of their bodies.

What the hell are they doing?

The three craft moved closer together, yet their engines were still burning hot and sending them toward the Guardian ship. Defensive fire from the many turrets on the ship turned away from the Alliance ships and even the landing craft. Instead, the firepower turned on the three Helion ships. Gun didn't understand what was happening, but he did know it was just what he needed.

A distraction!

Gun selected the formation's open channel.

"Move in and secure the target!"

With a flash of engines, the group of six landing craft accelerated the short distance between the protection of ANS Victory's guns and out toward the enemy vessel. Twice as many Lightning and Hammerhead fighters formed up around them to provide escort all the way to the target. As soon as they started to move, a number of flank batteries turned back to them. Two fighters vanished in a terrible orange explosion, sending chunks of debris flying from their shattered hulls.

"Commander Gun!" said General Daniels. His voice appeared by surprise inside Gun's helmet, "Your status?"

"We're going in."

"Change of plan, follow the Helions in."

"What?"

Gun didn't understand and looked back at the mainscreen. The three ships were now taking over half of the defensive fire, and their bows were shattered from the hundreds of impacts. Gun's landing craft shuddered as a burst of gunfire tore chunks of plating from their starboard armor. That was when Gun realized what they were doing. A grim smile formed on his face.

The crazy fools, they are going to ram the ship right in its face!

"Understood, changing course for the bow. We'll land directly into the inferno."

"Good hunting, Commander."

Gun nodded and connected to the pilot.

"Bring us around and into the bow of the ship."

* * *

Life pods ejected from the Helion ships like volleys of

missiles. The attack must have been carefully orchestrated, as the last of the pods left with just a kilometer left on the attack vector. The cloud of small craft rushed away and toward the heavily damaged station protecting the T'Karan Rift.

"There they go," Anderson whispered quietly.

Admiral Anderson and General Daniels watched with a mixture of horror and awe as the three Helion ships rammed into the bow of the Guardian ship. There was no sound, no vibration, nothing of note other than the smashing of metal and a hundred multicolored flashes as the four ships became one. Half of the lights across the exterior of the enemy ship were instantly extinguished, and a large number of its guns fell silent.

From the right of the terrible conflagration came the cloud of landing craft. They were tiny compared to the size of the ship around them, yet they flickered in the mixed lighting of the battle. Around them moved many more Alliance fighters, doing their best to screen them from missiles and gunfire. All of them made it until they reached the front of the ship. Even now, with the mass of wreckage, a number of turrets still functioned. One Hammerhead was hit in the engine and exploded, sending shards of metal into the last landing craft in the party. Its orientation thrusters must have been damaged, and it spun away and into space. The remaining landing craft approached the inferno, vanishing inside one of the larger tears in the bow of the ship.

Anderson tapped each of the Alliance warships and connected to the communications officers onboard each of them.

"This is Admiral Anderson, all ships are to withdraw to protect the Helion lifepods. Defensive fire only, we have friendlies moving in to finish the job."

He looked at the tactical display and the face of General Daniels. A face he'd seen before on many other Marine Corps commanders.

"Is he in?"

Daniels nodded.

"They're landing right now."

* * *

The landing inside the Guardian ship was more of a crash than a landing. Gun's craft crashed through the twisted metal and was forced to use its automatic turrets to clear a path into what remained of the forward landing area. They slammed into position and finally stopped when caught up in the wreckage of two fighters.

"Now!" Gun roared.

The doors on three sides slid open, but there was no need for ramps. With the ship so heavily damaged, there was little lighting and no artificial gravity. It didn't stop Gun, and he lurched forward, locking down the heavy magnetic seals on his armor as he moved. All marine armor was designed to do this either inside or on the exterior of ships. As soon as he stepped into the wrecked landing bay, he could see how effective the Helion attack had been. Scores of Biomech bodies floated about, and streaks of steam gushed from a dozen ruptures.

"Gun, where are you?" came the desperate sound of Teresa.

He checked his display in his armored helmet, finding the position of Teresa and the other marines. It estimated eighty-six meters.

"Follow me!" he growled.

Gun moved off toward a large and heavily damaged doorway. Behind him followed the entire group of Vanguards, each moving forward like large metal bugs. They made use of both the floor and the walls to walk along, with the lack of gravity making all surfaces suitable for movement. Once through the doorway, they emerged into a wrecked passageway with gantries collapsed from two directions. A massive gash in the wall revealed the cavernous interior of the ship that appeared to be filled with movement. The first Vanguard to move closer to the gash was struck by gunfire. The marine staggered back and lost his footing. He tumbled around in the vacuum before striking the wall.

"Bring them down!" called out the Sergeant.

The firepower of the Vanguards was a sight to behold,

and even Gun was impressed at the violence and ferocity of the unit. The L48 rifles were large caliber weapons with multi-role explosive ammunition, and easily capable of blowing a hole the size of a man's head out of metal or masonry; four Biomech creatures were shattered by the powerful volley.

"Keeping moving!" the Sergeant shouted.

The man's encouragement wasn't required. On the upper level a gash had been torn open and, the small number of surviving Biomechs took cover and blasted the Vanguards, doing their best to hold back the armored tide.

Let's finish this!

Gun ignored them and simply lifted his right arm. Fitted to his armor was the same multi-barreled gun he'd been forced to use back on Prometheus when he'd been a slave to these machines. The barrels spun, and a great gout of flame announced the launch of hundreds of projectiles. The other Vanguards moved past him and up toward the massive gash. He only stopped firing as the first of his comrades stepped inside.

"Watch out!" cried a female marine. She had lost her footing and spun about wildly.

Another was grabbed and tossed into a cavernous space by a clawed arm. The others pushed on, firing at anything moving. Gun lurched after them, closely followed by the last squad and into the open space. The first thing he saw was the form of a dozen massive Biomech warriors. They were much larger than any he had seen since the fight at Hyperion. The Vanguards were already firing when a final, much larger Biomech moved out from the blackness. This one was massive, at least five meters, perhaps taller and completely black. Its feet left indentations in the floor and walls as it moved to the Vanguards, their gunfire putting small holes in its thick armor. Its head was sunk down low behind a thickened collar of dull armor so that only the eyes of its helm peeked out over the ridge.

"Gun here, we're inside and have run into Biomechs, big ones!"

He pushed hard with his legs muscles, lurching ahead and toward the machines. The small group of Vanguards burst out, some on the walls, two on the ceiling, and the rest along the floor. Meeting them were scores of Biomechs, each dwarfed by the great hulk of their blackened master.

* * *

Teresa noticed the change in the fight immediately. Instead of dozens of creatures holding them back, the bulk of them had vanished. Only a dozen or so remained, and she could only assume they had moved off to deal with the arrival of Gun. At least, that was what she hoped.

We need to finish this quickly.

Movement caught her eye, and she noticed a small group of the Biomechs turning their attention to the wall on the right. A flash ensnared the group as a chunk of metal blew out a large part of the wall, and from the wreckage emerged her three comrades, directly into the middle of the Biomechs. Four of the creatures were cut down, and the rest scattered into the interior of the ship.

We're clear, about time!

"Marines, forward!" she cried.

The crimson stripes of her depleted guards unit pushed out through the passageway, closely followed by the survivors of the other squads. One marine took a blast to the chest before the entire length was finally secured. Teresa checked the schematics in her visor while ducking back to avoid a burst from a hidden warrior. A shaft ran up from their current position. It appeared to reach the corner of the power source they were looking for.

"Follow the shaft."

With a single hard push, she forced herself up with her boots while disconnecting the maglock. She drifted in the zero gravity as though she were freefalling in reverse. The other marines tried to emulate her swift movement but none, not even Sergeant Nova could match her speed and grace. Teresa had already reached the ceiling and was walking upside down and into the objective area before the others were even halfway up. She moved forward cautiously, her L52 Mark II carbine held up to her shoulder and ready for trouble. Sergeant Nova arrived next, followed by the other guards. Teresa indicated with her left hand for them to move carefully. As they entered the massive structure, they could see great blue coils pulsing with energy. They were five times the height of a marine and embedded into the ground and ceiling. Cables and pipes ran in great clumps along the walls. At the far end of the cavernous open space stood a great black machine, like a monstrous demon. It was upside down, and all around it were dozens of smaller Biomechs engaged in a terrible battle with another group. Teresa instantly knew who it was.

Gun!

"2nd Platoon, place the charges. Everybody else, destroy the beasts!"

The pitifully small band of marines ran, jumped, and hopped through the section of the ship, firing as they moved to try and pick off the Biomechs. Few fell before their arrival was spotted. The massive machine turned from the battle and looked at Teresa. It extended one arm, and a massive burst of blue energy rushed out toward her.

"Major!" Sergeant Nova screamed as she pushed Teresa aside.

Teresa spun out of control, drifting off to the left-hand wall. She was safe, but there wasn't time for Arina. The ball of energy struck the Sergeant full on in the chest, and she exploded in a flash of blood, armor, and fused metal. The remains of her body covered the marines as well as the floor and walls around them. Teresa regained her footing, and she stood on what was now the sidewall, with the energy coils directly in her path. The vast black Biomech had turned away. It was busy smashing away at Gun and the Vanguards as they continued to fight a lopsided battle. She saw two Vanguards crushed like flies by the machine's terrible arms.

"Get close and use your charges!" she snapped, continuing her rush to the machine. Dozens of marines fanned out and followed their Major into the battle. The Biomechs now split up, with some fighting the Vanguards, the rest moving off to attack Teresa. Even as she took aim, it was clear they were behaving in a particular way. She loosed off a powerful blast from all three barrels at the machine only for a Biomech to jump out, taking the strike to its leg. The impact tore off the limb, but it continued on and hit the other side. Ignoring the pain, the thing turned around and lurched at an approaching marine.

They are protecting the machine.

As quickly as Teresa had arrived, the Biomechs attacked her. At this close distance, she found herself slower than the Biomechs. A deft tap on her carbine and it altered to the lower powered rapid-fire mode that utilized one barrel at a time. Three quick bursts cleared a path and she was at the machine's leg. Teresa reached down for one of the thermite charges on her leg as the machine saw her. It kicked out and struck her in the stomach. The impact was like being hit by a truck, and she was smashed to the floor. Lights flashed and sparks rippled through the visor as multiple systems failed.

"Gun! We need this thing dead!" she snapped.

Oxygen was venting from her system, yet she refused to stop. The rest of her marines were now around her and running about in a bloody battle with the Biomechs. Simultaneously, two squads had taken up position a short distance away behind one of the shattered coils and fired aimed shots at the Biomechs, bringing them down one at a time. Teresa saw Gun push up from the ground and then land on the machine's chest. He stabbed at it with his blades and tore chunks out of its armor with his arm-mounted weapon. The machine swatted him aside with a single strike, yet Gun refused to let go and kept his left hand firmly attached to its torso. He reached up and brought his oddly curved blade down onto the machine's helm. There was a blue flash, and the weapon seemed to explode into a hundred shards. A pair of Biomechs ripped him from its armor, dragging him away where they surrounded him, each striking with an array of weapons.

"Gun!" screamed Teresa.

Using all the energy she had left, Teresa took a dozen steps until she was at the left of the black machine. Bodies floated about it as Biomech and marine fought in hand-to-hand combat. One Biomech got in her way, only to be knocked back by a Vanguard that continued after it. She moved even closer until she could touch the machine's flank. She reached down once more to her leg and grabbed her last thermite charge. It was the size of her fist, and with a firm pull, it released from its pouch. Two button presses activated the device that she then tossed up to the torso. It spun lazily and fixed itself to what would have been the abdomen of the machine.

"Marines, fall back!" shouted Teresa, but rather than follow her own orders, she moved toward where Gun had fallen. Over a dozen Biomechs blocked her path, and they continued to flail at what must have been her fallen friend. She made to lift her carbine, realizing she'd lost it in the fight. Without waiting, Teresa pulled her side arm and lurched forward, firing as she went. She made it half way when three of the creatures staggered back. A blood-covered metal figure lifted up, his armour cracked, burned, and damaged on almost every section. Teresa threw herself at him as the thermite charge detonated. Most of the power burst inward, but the heat fused anything within two meters in any direction. She felt pain in her leg as it damaged her armor when she crashed into Gun. The two drifted along, crashing into a heap of shattered Biomechs and Vanguard marines.

"Thanks," muttered Gun with as much humor as he could muster.

Teresa shook her head, the pain now wringing through her body. She looked back at the stationary shape of the great metal beast. It stood upright, its feet still clamped firmly down, and a great hole the size of a man burned through its torso. Gunfire continued to ripple through the open space, but the last few Biomechs were trying to escape, and not one stood its ground to fight. Teresa climbed to her feet and steadied herself on her mag sealed feet. The sensor package on her suit was still picking up trace elements from the machine. She reached down but could find no weapon.

"Wait," said Gun as she watched the great machine.

"It is still alive," he said with amusement.

Teresa allowed herself a grim smile and connected to ANS Victory.

"General, the ship is secure. It is ours."

"Good work, Major, I will have medical teams over in thirty minutes. This is a great victory."

"Thank you, Sir, there is something else."

There was a pause as if Daniels expected something terrible.

"Their leader, the machine that defended this ship. It lives. We have one of their leaders as our prisoner."

The voice changed to that of Admiral Anderson.

"Outstanding work, Major, outstanding. The 17th should be proud. Emissaries from the Helions are already en route to meet us after this little episode. Interesting that they suddenly want to meet us. Get back here for your debriefing. I suspect we are going to be very busy."

Teresa looked to Gun, and though he was in pain, she could see through the small visor on his armor that the old warrior couldn't have been happier.

"So, what do you think of the Corps?"

Gun beamed.

"It's just like old times! All we need to do now is fine where the hell Spartan got to."

Teresa expression changed in an instant as thoughts of him returned. She looked to Gun, doing her best to stay focused.

"Yes, we have their leader and we are at the heart of all of this now. Let's hope Helios has the answers, like we were promised."

* * *

Spartan shook his head for what felt like the hundredth time in one day. His body ached, yet he was unable to move his torso. He looked to his right where the red machine looked at him with cold, artificial eyes. Around him moved two similar companions, each a marvel of engineering and the size of a Biomech. The red machine moved closer and looked down at his face.

"Spartan, human...warrior."

He swallowed, his mouth dry and aching, and then spat out whatever fluid still remained in his choked throat.

"You bastards, what do you want?"

The machine moved closer still, ignoring the spittle on its armored head. It looked at Spartan with unusual interest. The other machines continued moving around him and connecting up a series of tubes and equipment. Spartan tried to get up, but none of his muscles above the shoulders responded. For a second he feared he'd been permanently paralyzed, but he remembered the needles in his arms and the straps holding him down. The machine was now just a meter away, and the plates around its head and chest started to move. The sound of servos, motors, and gears whined as the plates pulled apart to reveal the pilot inside. Spartan expected to see some great beast, but it was humanoid, no bigger than him though withered and weather. The form was contained in a flexible suit almost like a soft eggshell that lay suspended in a gyroscopic assembly. The face looked ancient, not much different to what he would expect to see as a corpse. It looked at him with its empty eye sockets and a toothless mouth.

"Your extinction."

The metal plating closed up around its fragile cargo until it was fully sealed. The metal monster stood upright and looked to its comrades. The doors hissed open and in walked another of the red machines, this one with even more battered looking metal armor. It looked to the other machine as if speaking, yet there was no sound. It eventually stopped and looked to Spartan.

"Spartan, the Rift..." A voice whispered in his mind.

He looked over to the newly arrived machine, but it remained stationary, like a statue, nothing more. The shape of a great, coiled demon, the very essence of Echidna herself appeared behind his eyes, and he cried out at the sight of the thing. In the background, moved legions of ships, none of which he recognized. All of them moved like a single shoal of fish toward a large black disc floating in space.

"The Rift," he whispered to himself and to the machines.

The image changed to one more familiar. It showed Terra Nova, capital of the Alliance and the most vibrant and cosmopolitan planet he'd ever seen. Great columns of black smoke arose from its shattered cities. Hundreds of ships tore down from the skies and discharged great creatures from hell itself onto the surface.

"Save your world."

The image changed to one final place, a world he'd never seen before, and one that moved around an alien sun. The black shape of the Rift appeared as if just a few million miles away.

"Helios...or annihilation!"

Spartan opened his eyes and found he was staring into the bloody face of Khan. His old friend was still in his chains and looked even worse for wear. He grinned with obvious pain at Spartan.

"So, you live."

"Just about. I know what they want."

Khan raised an eyebrow.

"Well?"

"Helios. They want to control Helios and something else, something they kept repeating, over and over."

"What do they want?"

"A rift, they call it the Black Rift."

THE END